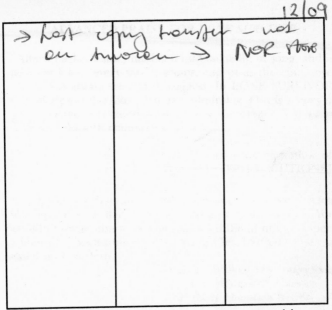

This book should be returned/renewed by
the latest date shown above. Overdue items
incur charges which prevent self-service
renewals. Please contact the library.

Wandsworth Libraries
24 hour Renewal Hotline
01159 293388
www.wandsworth.gov.uk Wandsworth

forget."

CAVE
E

LONE SURVIVOR

Ken Hodgson

PINNACLE BOOKS
Kensington Publishing Corp.

http://www.pinnaclebooks.com

501 472 806

PINNACLE BOOKS are published by

Kensington Publishing Corp.
850 Third Avenue
New York, NY 10022

All Kensington Titles, Imprints, and Distributed Lines are available at special quantity discounts for bulk purchases for sales promotions, premiums, fund-raising, and educational or institutional use. Special book excerpts or customized printings can also be created to fit specific needs. For details, write or phone the office of the Kensington special sales manager: Kensington Publishing Corp., 850 Third Avenue, New York, NY 10022, attn: Special Sales Department, Phone: 1-800-221-2647.

Pinnacle and the P logo Reg. U.S. Pat. & TM Off.

First Printing: February 2001
10 9 8 7 6 5 4 3 2 1

Printed in the United States of America

This book is for my editor, Karen V. Haas,
and Preston Darby, M.D.

Carpe Diem

ACKNOWLEDGMENTS

I wish to thank the following persons and organizations for their invaluable help and assistance: Fred and Dorothy Campbell; Felton Cochran; Byron Nelson; Joel Sharp; Richard Sklenarik; Dennis Sumrack; Pat Kant and the Colorado Territorial Prison Museum in Cañon City, Colorado; and the Saguache Museum in Saguache, Colorado.

As with any story that has become legend, the truth seems to have many versions. Any discrepancies or inaccuracies are totally mine.

Six miners went into the mountains
    to hunt for precious gold;
It was the middle of winter,
    the weather was dreadful cold,
Six miners went into the mountains,
    they had no food nor shack—
Six miners went into the mountains,
    but only one came back.

Traditional Colorado Mining Town Ballad

The more experience and insight I obtain into human
nature, the more convinced do I become that the
greater portion of a man is purely animal.

—Henry M. Stanley

Introduction

Nightmares of the past do not always slumber peacefully beneath cold granite tombstones and remain silent as the dust inside the coffins of those who lived them.

Sometimes the dead *do* speak.

And what they have to tell us can often be far different from what has been recorded in the impersonal pages of history books. I should know, for only recently did I come into possession of documents that shed a new light on one of the grisliest and most horrifying events to ever occur during the turbulent settling of the American West.

The narrative to which I refer was penned in the year 1907 by Alferd Giles Packer, a name that still evokes icy pinpricks of fear and revulsion to trickle down the spine of those who know of him and his dark deeds.

Packer was the only man in the United States of America to ever have been convicted in a court of law for a crime related to cannibalism.

He was incarcerated for fifteen years, from 1886 until paroled in 1901, for the crime of killing, then eating the flesh of, his five companions in the winter of 1874.

During our visit to Cañon City, Colorado, which lies at the foothills of the majestic Rocky Mountains, my wife Rita and I attended a weekly auction sale run by Allen Koehn, an old friend of mine.

Allen had just finished setting out a trailer load of antique furniture and dusty boxes. Rita's attention turned to a very old, scarred, and battered steamer trunk. Thick layers of corrosion on the clasp lock revealed it had been years since anyone had peered inside.

"Why don't you come to the sale tonight and buy it," Allen said to my wife with a grin. "Then it'll be yours along with whatever is inside, even if it is a dead body."

The trunk had come from the basement of the house of a reclusive spinster named Isabella Noon who had lived in Cañon City for over a hundred years.

I remembered that when I was in high school I had delivered newspapers to her at her small frame cottage, which stood in the shadows of the state prison.

Suffice to say, late that evening we skidded the pitiful trunk into the pickup bed, said our good-byes, and headed home to Texas.

I held hopes the trunk could be restored, so I took a long while to carefully work open its corroded brass lock. Inside were old and mildewed clothes.

At the very bottom lay a manuscript. Though it was wrapped with oilcloth, moisture had seeped in at some time and several pages were destroyed beyond any hope of recovery.

The manuscript was titled, "The Memoirs of Alferd Packer," and purportedly written by his own hand. The existence of such an account would be an amazing discovery. I spent weeks poring over the faded words.

Carefully and meticulously I compared the loops and swirls of Packer's known handwriting against the manuscript. To my eyes they matched perfectly. I sent copies to Dr. Franklin Douglas, a noted handwriting expert who is a well-known police consultant. His reply stated his belief that the hand of Alferd Packer wrote the manuscript.

An interesting detail was the presence of editorial corrections. These were written with a fine pen by a person who was skilled in the proper use of English. It was quite apparent that this manuscript was being prepared for publication.

I now take my leave, gentle reader, and leave the telling of this harrowing tale to those who lived it.

It is time to allow the dead to speak.

One

From the memoirs of Alferd Packer

Yes, I admit to having eaten human flesh. That is the sole reason I was forced to languish in a steel cage for fifteen years in that hellhole of a state penitentiary in Cañon City, Colorado. This was also why I was very nearly lynched by a drunken mob and later sentenced to death by an unforgiving judge and prejudiced jury.

Every step of my blighted existence since that unfortunate incident on Slumgullion Pass in the winter of Seventy-Four has been plagued by a biased press and dogged by a man whose uncalled-for hatred toward me knows no bounds.

By all rights and reasons I should not be sitting here in this warm and peaceful home on the outskirts of Denver, Colorado, penning my memoirs, for I have twice barely escaped the hangman.

Atop one stack of documents on the far side of my writing table I see a printed invitation to my own execution. It was issued to a Mister Louis Chapman and the date set for my death was the Nineteenth day of May in the year of our Lord Eighteen Eighty-Three.

As I begin my writings the year is Nineteen-Seven, in the outset of a new century. One of the most modern of conveniences, an Edison incandescent lightbulb, dangling from a black electric cord, illuminates my work. This marvelous device requires no fuel or fire and can be turned on and off by the mere moving of a small switch. Many things wonderful have been issued in with this new age.

I take no small satisfaction in the knowledge that Louis Chapman has been buried beneath cold black earth at the Lake City, Colorado, Cemetery for well over twenty years. I also wonder if perhaps he came to be interred in the same plot intended for me. It would be the sweetest of irony should that be the case.

Dear friend, I pray you not take offense at what you may perceive to be a jaded viewpoint, but as you shall quickly come to understand, I have suffered many injustices at the hands of my fellowman.

And all for simply doing what I had to do to stay alive. Can anyone who reads these words say with honesty that they would not defend their own hold on this mortal coil with any means available to them?

Spare me an answer, gentle friend. I have visited the blackness that lurks in the human heart and soul and know it well. Think of me what you will, but given the same situations which I have faced, you *would* act as I did. When the icy breath of the Grim Reaper blows down the nape of your neck, there is only one response possible: survival at any cost.

Now, after all these many years of suffering and anguish, Dame Fortune has finally smiled upon my countenance. Redemption is finally at hand due to a kindly man by the name of Leyton Laird of Slayton Publishing Company of New York City.

As Benjamin Disraeli so eloquently said, "Time is precious, but truth is more precious than time." These memoirs which I now pen will not only set forth the truth of my statements and actions, but provide me with satisfactory monetary rewards to enable me to enjoy the remaining years of my life to the fullest.

Mister Frederick Bonfils and H.H. Tammen, owners of *The Denver Post* newspaper and the Sells-Floto Circus, still want me to tour the country and speak on my trials and tribulations. They wished to do this earlier, but due to an arrogant and vicious Governor Thomas, who restricted me to the Denver area for six years and nine months as a condition of my parole, this was impossible. The resulting problem created a considerable disagreement between the owners of the *Post* and a lawyer they had hired by the name of "Plug Hat" Anderson to look after my interests. This culminated in the unfortunate shooting of Bonfils and Tammen by Anderson. Fortunately both survived and bear me no ill will from the incident and the actions of another.

Should more people be blessed with their forgiveness and understanding, this would be a far better world.

It is time for me to begin my story. I shall give but the briefest of backgrounds on my life before the year Eighteen Seventy-Four. That being the year I was to become so maligned and persecuted for eating my five traveling companions.

Two

The town of Franklin Park in Allegheny County, Pennsylvania, which lies a few miles northwest of Pittsburgh, was the place of my birth. I arrived on an icy cold morning the Twenty-First day of January in the year Eighteen Hundred and Forty-Eight.

To my father's chagrin my mother, whose name was Lily, had previously presented him with eight squealing daughters to raise. Expecting the appearance of another girl, he had gone to his job as a foreman in a large coal mine that was within walking distance of the house and left the affair to be handled by a midwife he had engaged for the previous arrivals.

The Packer family were good practicing Catholics, so I suppose the yearly advent of offspring had become somewhat mundane.

When Father returned home to discover he finally had a son, he was ecstatic. I was quickly christened with my grandfather's name of Alferd, a gentleman who had passed away some dozen years earlier. I often wish that I had been given my father's first name of Giles instead of it being relegated to the middle. To this day most people spell my name incorrectly as Alfred. I imagine this spelling will appear on my tombstone unless I take measures to assure otherwise.

My parents should not have been startled by the arrival of a son, for the year Eighteen Forty-Eight was destined to usher in many wonders. Just three days after my birth a man by the name of James Marshall discovered gold in the millrace of a sawmill at Sutter's Mill in what was then Mexican California.

On the Second day of February the treaty of Guadalupe Hidalgo was signed which ended the war with Mexico. For the payment of fifteen million dollars the Mexican Government ceded to the United States all lands lying to the north of the Rio Grande River, opening California to a grand rush for gold.

By all accounts only my mother's tears kept Father from risking everything and joining in that exciting exodus to El Dorado.

During my formative years chasing after gold was all he talked about. So at a very early age I became infected with an incessant urge to pursue the yellow metal.

Some ten years after my birth, a second gold rush—this one to the Colorado Rocky Mountains, then called Kansas Territory—solidified dreams of riches into my young soul. Four years later a raging war between the States over the issue of slavery was, in a roundabout manner, to provide me with the opportunity.

At the tender age of fourteen I decided I was a man and having received a basic education from the public school system, left home to join the Union Army.

All ten of my sisters, including the two new ones, were still under one roof, which added impetus to my resolve to leave. They were all so ornery no man could stand to marry one of them. Anything Robert E. Lee and the Confederate Army could threaten me with paled against living with those bossy females.

I planned ahead for my exodus by spending several months working for an obnoxious German farmer named Hapsburg. I chopped wood, built and repaired fences, or milked cows from the first light of morning until darkness brought a halt to his yelling.

The old tyrant delighted in docking my meager pay for any infraction he could devise, but by April I had made enough money to take my leave.

I knew my father would attempt to track me down and, as I had mentioned a desire to join in the war, he would immediately journey to any nearby Army facilities. All he would need do was to tell them my real age and they would send me back home with him to my total disgrace. It seemed wise to travel some distance from home where I could represent myself as being sixteen, which was the required age for military service at the time.

I could think of no better place than Washington, D.C. There was likely enough government available there to provide cover for a fourteen-year-old boy, even if his distraught father should pursue him that far.

My first order of business was to purchase transportation. Old Man Hapsburg offered me a horse in lieu of money he owed me. In retrospect I should have taken him up on his offer, but had become so affronted by the German I drew my pay and bought a mule from an Englishman.

A person can, on occasion, make a sour deal. To be taken advantage of by a fellow countryman is especially upsetting. The mule was a young animal with a sleek brown coat, bright eyes, and an agreeable disposition; I was so proud of that mule I named him Rocket before the truth became apparent.

It turned out Rocket suffered from some disorder that caused him to go to sleep at the most inopportune times. I would be riding him down the road and he'd simply doze off and stay that way until I either whacked him awake with a whip or he ran into something. This meant I had to be on the alert at all times with a quirt in my hand to avert disaster.

In spite of having ignominious transportation, on a blustery April morning I loaded all of my worldly belongings onto that mule. I placed under my belt a Cooper six-barrel pepperbox pistol that I paid only three dollars for because the former owner said when he shot the thing all six barrels fired at the same time. I felt this wouldn't be a major shortcoming for I had very little training in the use of firearms and figured it wouldn't take a marksman to shoot someone with a gun that sent out six slugs in their direction.

As I rode away from home that cold, gray morning, the only sorrow I felt was for my parents. All those sisters I had suffered with would undoubtedly be glad to have me gone.

I made the two-hundred-and-fifty-mile journey to Washington, D.C., in nine days without incident. Rocket dozed off once and sidled into a freight wagon, but only got a scratch out of it. Thankfully, I managed to get my leg out of the way and wasn't injured. I did hear some language from the teamster that was new to me, but I guess he'd never had a mule run into him before.

I had no difficulty enlisting in the Union Army. About that time the Confederacy was making a grand showing and they wanted all the bodies in uniform they could get.

After receiving a physical from a drunken doctor that consisted of assuring himself that I had two arms, two legs, and a pulse, I became a bona fide private in Abraham Lincoln's Army.

During the next two weeks I endured what was termed "basic military training" under a Sergeant William Bruckner, another obnoxious German. My stint

working for Old Man Hapsburg had served me well. I
did what I was told without complaint, and drifted off
to sleep at night devising novel ways for Sergeant Bruckner to meet with a terrible accident.

I never got the chance to thank him properly, for the
troop of infantry I was assigned to was called out the
day after I was considered a soldier.

I had been issued two uniforms and a thick felt coat
along with a musket and pistol. If ever a soldier felt ready
to do battle with the enemy, it was me. Then I was to discover just how stupid a bureaucracy can operate.

Instead of being sent South to fight the Graycoats,
our troop was ordered north to Winona, Minnesota, a
dreary town on the shores of the Mississippi River. The
reasoning was to guard the steamship port from sabo-
tage. During my months there the only thing gray I ever
saw was the sky. If the sun had come out I'm certain
the locals would have panicked from raw fear.

Sergeant Bruckner, who accompanied us, insisted on
maintaining military discipline. Since he was a true Prus-
sian, I'm certain it was a tendency he couldn't control.
Early every Friday morning he would order the troop to
mount up in full uniform and practice firing at targets.

When the sergeant had found out back in Washington
that I had a good mule to ride, he made me keep it,
saying that horses were more valuable down South than
soldiers. Needless to say, simply keeping Rocket awake
was the biggest task I faced aside from learning how to
shoot.

It was on a usual gray and cold Friday in December
that it happened. Bruckner was teaching us to rapid-fire
those single-shot muskets, which was always a risky thing
to do. I had fired twice, then tore open a packet of
powder with my teeth and emptied it down the maw of
that musket, when the damn thing exploded, sending
me into unconsciousness.

I awoke in a tent hospital being attended by a young doctor who at least appeared to be sober. "You have had two fingers blown off your left hand," he said as if describing the weather. "A piece of shrapnel stuck in your skull above your right eye, but I extracted it and do not believe it will cause any permanent damage."

"I'm sorry about your mule," Sergeant Bruckner said from the other side of the cot I was lying on. My head hurt like an ax had been imbedded in it and my eyes had a hard time focusing on him.

"What do you mean?" I managed to ask.

"The explosion drove the barrel of that musket right through that mule and killed him on the spot. Sure am glad you weren't ridin' a good horse. General Grant can't spare to lose any of those."

About then I would have used my good hand to shoot that German, only the doctor had taken my guns from me while I was unconscious. Here I was stuck in god-forsaken Minnesota, crippled for life, and now I didn't even have a worthless mule to ride home.

"I'm putting you in for an honorable discharge, due to disability, boy," the doc said in his matter-of-fact tone. "The Army will not only replace your mule, but likely pay you a lifelong pension of twenty-five dollars a month."

Once that fact sunk in, I decided to forgo plugging the German. I would likely regain at least some good use of my left hand once it healed. Rocket's demise was certainly no great loss. Any mule that replaced him would be an improvement. Twenty-five dollars a month was plenty of money to allow me to go do what I had desired to do all along. I never really wanted to become a war hero anyway.

I could now head West and become rich mining gold.

Three

"What are you doin' riding around on an Army mule, boy? You go an' steal it?"

This had become a standard greeting from most sheriffs I'd run into since leaving Minnesota. I reckon I shouldn't have expected Denver to be a big change.

"No, sir," I answered, feigning respect and holding up my still-bandaged hand. "I got shot in the war and they mustered me out on disability."

"You got papers showin' you own that mule?"

One thing I was fast learning about lawmen; once they get set on a train of thought, they're tenacious as a snapping turtle.

I used my good hand to extract my discharge papers and bill of sale for the red mule from my coat pocket and handed them to the beady-eyed deputy.

I hadn't gotten around to giving this mule a name. She wasn't much to desire anyway; the animal was old and had been in the Army so long it only knew two speeds, slow and stop. The problem was the big U.S. brand on her haunch attracted more attention than a fifty-dollar gold piece.

The burly officer glared at the papers, then at me. "They're givin' you a twenty-five-dollar-a-month pension for just gettin' nicked. Hell, boy, I don't make much more than that an' I have to work for what I get."

I could tell I wasn't making a new friend here, so I used just the center finger of my injured hand to raise my hat to show off the angry red scar over my eye. The man was too dense to notice my gesture.

"Reckon you did get banged up a tad," he said, handing me back my papers. Then he spat a huge wad of tobacco toward his boots and looked me over again. "I'm just doin' my job. There's a lot of deserters from the war come out West. The reward for turning them in to be shot is well worth my effort."

"Sorry I ain't worth nothing," I said testily, and prepared to flick the reins and put my mule back into its slow pace west.

"Hold on a moment. I don't want you to think folks hereabout aren't friendly. Why, Denver's a great place to live or find a job. Now I just happen to know old Cal Farley who owns the Oasis Saloon is looking for a trustworthy man to go to California an' fetch back a wagon load of whiskey. He'll pay a hundred dollars and expenses for the trip."

I cocked my head. "I was planning on doing some prospecting. There's supposedly been some good strikes made lately up in the high country at a place called Oro City."

"There's more prospectors up there than fleas on a jackrabbit. Besides that, if you take the job from Farley you'll get paid to see the gold country both comin' and goin'."

For a lawman he was actually making good sense, or so I thought at the time. Then I really stepped in it. "I think I might just be interested. Where is this Oasis Saloon at anyway?"

"Why, just down the street a couple of blocks," he said, pointing toward the only two-story building in sight. Then he actually smiled. "Tell ole Cal that Charlie

Faber said to treat you right, you bein' a wounded Yankee veteran and all."

I never did forget that deputy's name, and for many years planned on returning to Denver and repaying his favor. A gunfighter by the name of Clay Allison beat me to this public service by shooting him where his heart should have been over in Las Anaimas, Colorado, in Eighteen Seventy-Six.

Cal Farley was as big around as a pickle barrel and twice as ugly. The Oasis Saloon did have its attractions, however. A pair of soiled doves leaning over the upstairs bannister showing off more of God's bounty than was proper provided a real distraction to my usual common sense.

Two days later I found myself on a bouncing stagecoach headed for California. Farley had offered to look after my mule, and I'd made arrangements with a bank to receive my pension payments. Even though I was not to reach my fifteenth birthday for three days, I felt like a man of the world. A feisty little brunette by the name of Sadie had provided me with more education than could ever be found between the covers of any book.

I should have been a lot smarter in other ways, however, and not nearly so trusting. Just why anyone would pay a hundred dollars to have a wagon load of whiskey driven back to Colorado was a question that never crossed my mind.

It was answered only when I got to San Francisco and went down to the waterfront and met John Wickwire for instructions.

This lovely gentleman was kind enough to give me a cool glass of sarsaparilla to wash the dust out of my throat.

Then the room began spinning like a top and I remember falling to the dirty plank floor of Wickwire's office.

When I awoke, the cubbyhole of a room in which I found myself locked kept rocking about. It slowly dawned in my aching head what a fool I had been. I realized I had been shanghaied and was aboard a ship bound for God knew where.

That pair of hooligans in Denver had a wonderful scheme in place and I had fallen for it without suspecting a thing. There was no way I could have known at the time how many years would pass before I would ever set foot in the States again.

Four

The only good thing I could say at the time about my situation was the fact that I hadn't gotten seasick. I berated myself for being so naive and trusting, especially when it came to that star-wearing-piece-of-dog-crap deputy back in Denver. I knew now there was more than one way to collect a reward.

Bounties were often paid by either shipping lines or captains for men shanghaied to work. The gold rushes had left them plenty shorthanded. A lot of crews jumped ship when they docked in San Francisco. Prospecting for gold always has been a great lure.

That was what I had planned to do myself until I played the fool and wound up serving on a brigantine named the *Amazon.*

Turtle John, the first mate, informed me of my fate when he unlocked the door to my cabin and offered me a drink of water. My head was still spinning from whatever drug I'd been given and my throat felt like sandpaper.

I eventually staggered out and walked up on deck supported by one of Turtle John's massive arms. He was quite a bit older than me; I figured him to be maybe thirty and built like a safe.

Turtle John, I was to find, received his name from numerous tattoos of turtles that were scatted over his bulk. If he had a hair on his body, I never saw it. Healed scars from what were most likely knife wounds, gunshot holes, and teeth marks he wore in abundance. To keep a person off center he always sported a broad smile. Not a nice pleasant smile, mind you, but the cold reptilian sneer of a snake ready to strike its prey.

The clean salt spray cleared my head, and I quickly sized up the situation and realized we were well out to sea. Wherever this ship was headed, I was going along. I had never learned how to swim, but since I couldn't even see land I guess it wouldn't have mattered anyway.

I was then introduced to the captain, a slender, well-dressed, and pleasant fellow by the name of Alton Meigs. He surprised me with a friendly greeting and told me I would be paid apprentice seaman's wages. Then he noticed my bandaged hand and missing fingers.

"How did you become wounded, son?" he asked.

I had already found that telling folks I was wounded in the war got a better response than the truth, which was a defective gun blowing up in my hands while target shooting. It worked wonderfully this time, too.

The captain listened to my tale, then turned to Turtle John. "This young man is a veteran of our country's Army. I expect him to be given light duty until his wounds have healed properly, and he is to be treated with respect."

"Yes, sir," Turtle John said with that cold smile of his fixed on me.

As the days passed I became quite amazed at what life aboard a ship was actually like. I was assigned to work with a likable old salt named Fritz Kenyon. Fritz had been aboard ships for over forty years and knew everything there was to know about sailing vessels. He had been an able seaman until a fall from the mast shattered one of his legs, relegating him to the job of ship's cook.

I washed pans and dishes, set the mess table, peeled tons of potatoes, and listened to Fritz tell stories while he hobbled around on one crutch.

It was from Fritz that I found we were bound for the Sandwich Islands, then on to China, India, and the Persian Gulf.

"You're going to see some wonderful sights, boy," Fritz told me with a faraway look in his eye. "Wait until we make port in the Sandwiches. Why, those bronze-skinned little ladies there will come swimmin' out to meet us naked as the day they were born."

I confess to becoming somewhat more interested in life at sea. After I worked my time in the galley, I had free run of the ship except for the captain's quarters, which I was informed was the only place barred to the crew.

Fritz seemed to enjoy taking me around the *Amazon* and acquainting me with her operation. The vessel was one hundred and three feet long and had two large masts that supported a plethora of billowy white square sails.

"She weighs over two hundred and fifty tons," he said, pointing with his crutch to the hold. "We can carry another two hundred tons of cargo. A ship like this one can be mighty profitable to operate."

The entire crew consisted of a total of eight men and the captain. Five of them spoke but broken English and mostly stayed to themselves. They were of Dutch origin and seemed incapable of smiling. Surprisingly, Turtle John turned out to not be such a bad sort. He even began occasionally complimenting me on my cooking and willingness to learn.

And learn I did. When my hand finally healed and the stumps where my two fingers had been blown away calloused over, I took to working furling and unfurling the sails. A month later, when we finally made port in the Sandwich Islands, I had salt water in my veins. Prospecting for gold in Colorado was something I would put off for many years.

I spent nearly the next ten years sailing with that ship. Slicing through deep blue water while under full sail became a wonderful way of life. Turtle John and Fritz became the closest of friends. We visited exotic ports of call and shared many exciting adventures together.

Here I must hurry my story, dear reader, for it is of my misfortunes and terrible circumstances that occurred in those cold, forbidding mountains of Colorado that you wish to know.

Suffice me to say, the ship on which I served on all those years became christened with another name. And a cursed one at that. For my last voyage upon her was a most shattering experience, and I alone survived with knowledge of what occurred that fateful day.

Upon reaching land and making my way back to civilization, it was the year of Eighteen Seventy-Two. I was a man now, albeit a tortured man over the experience that so horribly took the lives of everyone else aboard that ship. I have kept the vow I took then never to return to the sea.

Only I was to find that nightmares can also occur on land as well as the sea.

The ship of which I speak, I am certain you know well the new name she was given; it was the *Mary Celeste*.

But that is another story for another time.

Five

Having lost all of my money and personal possessions except for the pepperbox pistol when I was forced to so quickly flee the *Mary Celeste,* I found myself ashore in Florida with nearly only the tattered clothes on my back.

I sold the ship's sextant for ten dollars. It was a wonderful instrument by which I had managed to navigate the well-appointed lifeboat to safety. Then I visited a saloon where I managed, however briefly, to forget my recent terrors before heading inland by way of shank's mare.

At the time my desire was to get back to Colorado and as far away from the ocean as possible. I knew the Denver bank account had grown to contain nearly three thousand dollars from my military pension. The problem was getting there. Traveling took money, and of that commodity I had but a pittance.

Briefly, I entertained heading north to Pennsylvania, but quickly dismissed the idea. After such a prolonged absence a son should return home wealthy enough to help out his family, not as a penniless prodigal who would only add to their financial difficulties. There was no choice but for me to earn a fair sum of money as quickly as possible.

The employment I came to find was that of an alligator hunter and skinner in the steaming swamps of the Everglades. This occupation had a rather high mortality rate, so there were always plenty of jobs available. The amount of pay appeared to be, however, quite agreeable.

Sam Broward, a fat slob of a man, hired me on the spot. He owned a ramshackle trading post on the edge of some deep murky water near the town of Weston. I had not eaten for two days, and mentioned this fact.

Broward shot me a sickly smile. "I've got a pot of gator stew an' some bread on the stove. You can help yourself for a quarter."

I fished through my pockets and came up with a dime and two nickels.

"Grab a bowl of stew," Sam said, scooping up my coins with his paw, then grumbled, "but you can't have no bread to go with it."

I was too famished to complain. His dour disposition did serve to give me direction as to how to handle our future relationship.

After wolfing down three helpings of greasy alligator gruel, I retired to the shade of the porch, where I spent the night swatting away flies and hordes of mosquitoes. The stench from hundreds of rotting alligator carcasses not only attracted the flies, but also added to the dismal atmosphere of the place.

At first light the man who was to be my partner arrived in a wooden flat-bottom boat that he propelled by pushing it along with a long pole. Sam introduced him as a Mister Lehman Rufin or Rudin—I can't recall his name with any degree of certainty.

My new partner looked me over with bloodshot, suspicious eyes. "You wanna learn the gator-killin' business, huh? Well, get in an' I'll teach ya, only you'll make thirty percent until ya get the hang of it."

Mister Rudin or Rufin turned out to be an excellent teacher, and I was to learn quite quickly from him. He showed me how to push along the boat with that long pole while he stood on the bow sipping from a bottle of rotgut whiskey.

After a short time we spotted a huge alligator sunning itself on the muddy bank. He took a battered rifle and shot it in the head, right behind and between its dark eyes. That gator just quivered. Then he ordered me to pole the boat ashore behind it. My lessons in alligator hunting were about to begin in earnest.

Then my partner staggered to the gator, rolled it over, and plunged a long knife into the beast's soft underside. The second that knife struck, the huge gator proved it wasn't dead at all. The monster hissed, spun, and with a lightning-quick flash of razor-sharp teeth, removed my mentor's head from his shoulders in the blink of an eye.

I grabbed up the rifle and used enough ammunition to assure myself the alligator was actually deceased. I then rolled the heavy carcass onto the boat with my late teacher's head still firmly clenched in its jaws. I dragged on the headless corpse, and poled my way back to the trading post.

I yelled for Sam as I tied the boat up to the dock. After a few minutes he came waddling out on the deck blowing on a steaming cup of coffee. He looked down and surveyed the bloody scene with cold dispassion.

"That man ain't no kin of mine," Broward said with a shrug. "It's custom hereabouts for a man to bury his own partner." He motioned with a head wag to a shovel leaning against the wall. "Put it back where you found it when you're done. By the way, I pay three dollars for a skin that size. You gotta do the job, though. I got too damn much good sense to go skinnin' gators."

My years as a seaman had sharpened my senses to the keenness of a razor and hardened my muscles to steel. Turtle John had also taken me under his wing and given me many useful pointers on how to handle difficult people.

Just two days after I buried my partner, Sam Broward performed a public service by getting himself roaring drunk and falling from the porch of his trading post into the murky swamp, where he drowned. I would venture the only decent act of his miserable existence was leaving me his business.

One misguided fellow showed up later on claiming to be Sam Broward's brother, but he was simply a liar. Once I convinced him of his error, he wandered off to become lost in the swamp and caused me no further difficulties.

I had not planned on staying in that sweltering hellhole and live among the illustrious citizens who inhabit the Everglades any longer than was absolutely necessary. My hope was to sell off Broward's property for enough money to pay my way to Colorado Territory.

But the gods of fate sometimes play with our lives and actions as a child manipulates a string marionette. I was destined to remain there long enough to become damned by making the acquaintance of Gidd Trevor.

There are only two kinds of weather in the Florida swamps; hot or steaming hot. It was on a steaming-hot afternoon in the month of June, Eighteen Seventy-Three, that Trevor tied his horse to the railing in front of what was now named the Packer Trading Company and came inside.

"Barkeep," he said, shaking me from a peaceful nap, for only fools moved about in the stifling afternoon heat. "I wish to order a mint julep."

The pleasant sound of a gold double eagle ringing on the rude plank bar kept me from throwing him out the open door. Fools with money are *always* a useful commodity.

I rose from the cane-backed rocking chair and

blinked sleep from my eyes as I surveyed the man. He was tall and rather stocky with a spray of gray along his temples. He sported a neatly trimmed black beard and had piercing blue eyes. What I noticed most of all were his spiffy, clean clothes and infectious smile. This fellow was certainly just passing through. None of the local idiots ever dressed to the nines.

"Whiskey or coffee's all I can offer you, friend," I said pleasantly. "Ice is scarce as a pretty woman in these parts and only a dolt drinks the water hereabouts."

He grinned broadly. "I've been told that before. A whiskey will do. I sincerely hope that you can provide a decent bottle. Some of the stuff they pass off for spirits in these parts is simply dreadful."

"I can't agree more," I said, extracting the single bottle of Monongahela that I'd stashed away for customers with money to spend. Seeing the name of a river in Pennsylvania printed on that bottle brought back fond memories of home and strengthened my resolve to return there a rich man.

I took down two of my cleanest glasses, pulled the cork out of the bottle, and filled them to the brim. "You're obviously a man of refinement who has good taste. I've been hoping for someone like you to drop by. What, may I ask, caused you to wind up here in Hell?"

He chuckled, sipped some whiskey, and extended his hand over the bar. "Gidd Trevor's the name and I 'spect you're correct about where we are. I take it you don't call Florida home?"

After introducing myself, I said with a smile, "No, sir, I'm originally from Pennsylvania but hope to return to Denver, Colorado, shortly, where I have some—interests. A rather sad set of circumstances placed me here in Florida and caused me to come to own this business."

Gidd took another drink of whiskey. "I know what

you mean. My parents were killed when a carriage they had engaged for an outing overturned. I was forced to abandon a gold strike I had made in Colorado and come to Fort Lauderdale to settle the estate."

"I'm sorry," I said, surveying him over my raised glass. "I do hope for your sake the estate was a substantial one."

He became glum. "No, not at all. Their demise was unexpected and my father had many debts. I was able to glean only enough to cover my expenses and enable me to return to the mountains."

I refilled our glasses, leaving the double eagle untouched. "But you *do* have a rich gold mine there?"

"I've also got plenty of problems to go along with it," he sighed. "Pete Fellows—he was my partner before he cut his finger whackin' off a chew of tobacco and died of lockjaw—well, sir, we sure did make a strike. Now Pete was from Georgia and knew a lot about gold from his experiences mining in that state. We became acquainted in the summer of Sixty-Eight when I was prospectin' the Gunnison country.

"Ole Pete had a placer mine on the Taylor River. I dropped by his camp to bum a cup of coffee and wound up bein' his partner. We made a fair wage until the pay streak run out. Then we loaded up our burros and went prospectin' further south."

Gidd Trevor now had my full attention. "I can understand why you're mighty anxious to get back there and dig some more ore," I said. "Mining gold in Colorado's been my dream for many years."

"*Where* we made our strike's the problem." He fished a fist-sized rock from his pocket and laid it on the bar. The streaks of yellow metal in white quartz fairly glistened. "This came from an outcrop in the San Juan Mountains. Those blasted Ute Injuns and that Chief

Ouray claim the whole dad-blasted country. A bunch of braves run us off with rifles an' filled in our diggin's."

"But you know where it is and can find it again?"

Trevor snorted, "Why, sure, I ain't no greenhorn. Pete an' I weren't fools either; we stashed what gold we dug out in canvas sacks and buried them near our camp ever darn night. I reckon there's nigh onto a thousand dollars in that cache. All a body's got to do to get rich is get past those blasted Indians. And, you know, that might not be a problem much longer. When I left the territory the government was negotiatin' with Chief Ouray to buy that land, which'll make it open for claim."

"I always thought gunpowder gave good title."

"Ouray's no fool an' I reckon he understands that. I'm bettin' he'll give up the San Juans and head south to keep from losin' more braves. For an Indian he's got better sense than most."

I ventured, "Waiting for the government to do something can take a spell. What are your plans when you get back there?"

Trevor shrugged. "I reckon I'll go to Denver and find work until the matter's settled. I don't know what else to do. If those Indians come across me in the San Juans again, my goose is cooked. They made it plenty plain before, an' I don't plan on upsettin' them anytime soon. All the gold in the Rockies ain't worth nothing if you're pushin' up daisies."

I emptied the last of that wonderful bottle of Monongahela into our glasses. "How about if we put together a large party of men armed with those new repeating rifles Winchester's come out with? That oughtta send those savages packin'."

Gidd Trevor appeared interested, then shook his head sadly. "It might work, but an army that size would take a lot of money to hire an' outfit. I reckon the best I can do is wait out the situation."

That gold specimen glistened like jewels in a king's crown. "I've got about three thousand dollars in a Denver bank. Do you suppose that'd be enough?"

Trevor cocked his head. "Well, now, Al Packer, are you offering to become my partner in this venture?"

I nodded. "Fifty-fifty and I'll throw in ever dime I've got. We *will* go dig that gold you're got located, Indian treaty or not."

"I like your attitude." Trevor looked about. "But what of your business here? It will likely take a long while to sell it."

"You have enough money to get us both to Denver?"

He nodded. "A couple of hundred dollars is all, but if we watch ourselves that'll do it."

"Pick up your money," I said, nodding to the double eagle as I pocketed the few dollars that were in a tin box under the bar. I went and tossed a change of clothes into a pair of saddlebags, stuck the pepperbox pistol under my belt, then carried the saddlebags and Broward's old Volcanic rifle outside and set them alongside a spreading cypress tree.

"When I saddle that sorry mule in the corral out yonder we'll be on our way," I said. "There's something I need to do first."

I strode back inside the trading post and splashed about a few gallons of coal oil. I pulled a long nine cigar from my pocket and lit it with a Lucifer match. Then with a feeling of satisfaction, I tossed the burning match onto the wet coal oil and made a hasty exit.

As we rode away in the sweltering Florida heat, only Gidd Trevor bothered to turn and watch the black tower of smoke wavering against a cloudless blue sky.

Six

Except for my having to kill a man in Texas, our journey to Denver was uneventful. At the time we were following the Goodnight-Loving cattle trail where it made its swing to the north some distance west of the Pecos River. Several thousand cattle being herded together in a row leaves a path that is as easy to follow as a telegraph line.

God never cared much for Texas, and the results are painfully obvious to anyone who has ever had the misfortune to visit the place.

Everything that grows there has thorns, and all of the critters have the disposition of a rattlesnake with boils. I reckon this description also fits most of the people who, for some reason, call that dry and dusty country home.

It was nigh onto the middle of July, for Gidd and I were making decent progress of twenty to thirty miles a day. Sam Broward may not have been smart enough to put his boots on the right feet, but he surely had owned a good mule. The young jenny I rode was well dispositioned and in her prime.

A blessing in the form of a rare thundershower allowed us to make camp early that day. After spending a day in the saddle under a blazing Texas sun, the cooling rain came as a wonderful respite from the grueling heat.

As had become our custom, Gidd started gathering wood for a fire while I began to prepare to cook our evening meal. Trevor and I were getting along quite well despite the fact he was a native of South Carolina and a ranting secessionist. I had early on told him my age, and mentioned the loss of my two fingers due to a farming accident had kept me from becoming involved with the war. My worthy determination to become rich so I could help out my struggling family allowed me to endure stoically his verbal slings and arrows against the noble Northern cause.

Our meager rations consisted only of some stringy hardtack, salt, and flour, hardly the ingredients of a meal to celebrate a rain in Texas. I grabbed up my rifle.

"Gidd," I said, "I think I'll do a little hunting. Likely enough I can shoot us a rabbit or two."

He dropped an armload of small sticks and nodded his approval. "I'll have us a fire goin' when you get back. That rain didn't even dampen the wood under the cedar trees. I wish you luck. My belly has been rubbin' a sore spot on my backbone all afternoon."

I climbed back on the brown mule I had left saddled, and rode toward a low rise to the west where a lowering sun was peeking through a covering of black clouds. There was a canyon on the other side that had a wide strip of mesquite and cedars running along its depth.

Carefully, I sidled the mule down the craggy slope, knowing there was undoubtedly plenty of wild game to be found in such a treed area. In short order I spied what was certainly a more tempting meal than a rabbit. Grazing contentedly away on stunted grass was a young longhorn heifer.

I surveyed the area for smoke rising from a chimney or any signs of habitation and found none. This animal had obviously strayed away from one of the large herds of a drive and become a maverick open for the taking. The heifer was unmarked by any brand on its flank. A single shot behind its ear dropped it like a rock.

The liver being a choice morsel, I removed this first and had just finished slicing a generous supply of long, lean strips of meat from a hindquarter when suddenly a gravely voice boomed from a nearby cluster of junipers.

"Hold it right there, mister! If you make a grab for that rifle I'll plug a hole through you where you stand. I'm gonna see that you hang anyway, so it's all the same to me. That's what we do with cattle rustlers in these parts."

Slowly, I wiped the blood from my bowie knife onto my pants, dropped it on the carcass, and turned to face this arrogant Texan who held a gun pointed square at my middle.

"This was a maverick," I said calmly. "My partner and I are starving and it had no brand."

"You're on my spread, mister. Any cattle hereabouts are mine unless I decide to sell 'em to you."

I quickly saw through his game. Making my voice quaver, I stammered, "I am sorry for any misunderstanding, sir. Perhaps we could make restitution and put this sad matter aside."

The man stepped from his cover and approached. As are most Texans, he was lanky, and he kept his beady black eyes focused on me. I did notice the barrel of his rifle now pointed toward the ground. This fellow had no more claim to that beef than I did. He was simply a thief out to rob me.

"That was a ten-dollar cow you just killed," he said.

I smiled. "My friend, I shall be happy to pay you everything you have coming to you."

Before the idiot could blink, I yanked the pepperbox

pistol from my belt and shot him in the chest. As usual, all six barrels fired at the same time, sending the lout flying backwards to land in a huge patch of cactus.

It is an unfortunate fact of life that some people only understand one form of reasoning. At least this ruffian would never again accost an honest person with the intention of doing them bodily harm or robbing them of their goods.

I found over fifty dollars in his pockets. And here this vile, greedy man had tried to rob me of more. Sadly, I shook my head, then finished butchering the beef and returned to camp.

Gidd Trevor was ecstatic over my success at finding a stray.

"We're gonna have a feast tonight," he said happily. Then he cocked his head in thought. "I heard two shots. Did something happen?"

"It was just a snake," I said, adding strips of beef to those sizzling in the skillet. "I just shot a snake was all."

Denver had grown immensely during my years of absence. When I was last there the town had only recently changed its name to Denver from Auraria. Larimer Street had been but a broad dirt pathway lined by numerous, mainly wooden business buildings of various sorts.

Now it was a city with proud towering brick structures that attested to the richness and permanence of the earlier gold strikes. Where before were only rows of simple shacks, stood stately homes and cottages.

Plank board sidewalks lined numerous streets that held many prosperous-looking business buildings, many of which had large colorful awnings to keep the hot sun from annoying their customers.

The problem of locating the bank with which I had

entrusted my funds became woefully apparent to me. I could not recognize a single landmark. I knew approximately where the Oasis Saloon had stood. Cal Farley of that establishment was also a man I wished to meet again so I could adequately repay him for his past favors.

There were a few saloons in evidence, but nothing named the Oasis. I scoured the street desperately searching for the Chalmers and Hollingsworth Bank. It was to no avail; so much had changed during my seafaring years as to make the task impossible.

"You look plenty confused," Gidd said, commenting on my obvious puzzlement. "I would hope nothing is too wrong, for we need to reach the mine soon. Winter comes mighty early in the high country. That vein will be snowed in by October for sure. Then it'll be May or June before we can get up there again."

"The bank has just moved to another location is all," I grumbled. We had been over this before and I was becoming somewhat annoyed at my friend's whining.

Gidd pointed toward a two-story brick building across the street. "There's the C.A. Cook and Company Bank. Likely enough someone there will know where your Chalmers and Hollingsworth has moved to."

"I reckon you're right. Let's go over and ask the cashier."

This bank had white marble floors with numerous sparkling-clean brass cuspidors set alongside each teller's cage that had black steel bars to keep one at a respectable distance from the money.

The place wasn't busy, so I ambled up to the nearest teller.

"May I help you, sir?" the silver-haired man asked fawningly.

"Yes, perhaps you may. I am looking for the Chalmers

and Hollingsworth Bank. They seem to have moved since I was last here."

"They moved, all right," the man said with a sneering grin. "You must've been gone for a spell because that place got washed away when the big Cherry Creek flood struck way back in Sixty-Four. There hasn't been an establishment here by that name since."

"What of the deposits there?" I spat. "Man, I had money in that bank, lots of it."

The bespectacled weasel simply said, "You should have entrusted your funds to a more secure and reliable bank such as this one, my good man. The firm of Chalmers and Hollingsworth was declared insolvent and went through bankruptcy years ago. I'm sorry to tell you any money placed with them has long since fled to parts unknown along with Frank Chalmers. The law has been unable to locate his whereabouts."

"Where's Hollingsworth then? I'll get my three thousand dollars out of his worthless hide."

"When the flood struck and his partner absconded with whatever funds he could get his hands on, Mister Hollingsworth took a rather large dose of laudanum. I believe you will find him residing in the local cemetery. Good day to you, sir."

I thought about reaching through those black steel bars and wrapping my hands around his scrawny neck when I felt a heavy hand on my shoulder.

"Let's go get a drink, Al," Gidd Trevor said. "I reckon we both could use one. There's nothing more we can do here."

I remember little until a few shots of Taos Lightning lifted the red fog of anger in which I had become enveloped. I have never been one to take abuse lightly. With each fiery sip my senses began crystalizing to their usual keenness and a plan began formulating in my mind.

Gidd cocked his head and gave an idiotic grin. "Well, on the good side, this turn of events might have saved us from one of those Injun haircuts."

"Those crooks stole my money."

"Don't fret it, pard. I know you meant well. We're still in this together and I'm stickin' with our deal. It just looks like we'll need to find work and lay in for the winter. Denver's not a bad place to wait. Shucks, by next summer the treaty might be signed. Then we can just ride up there and claim that mine."

"Unless others beat us to it," I added solemnly. "If you found it, so could someone else."

Gidd's grin faded. "I hadn't considered that."

"You said there was a thousand dollars worth of gold you and your old partner cached up there."

"Yep, at least that much. We must've buried a good hundred pounds of high-grade. It oughtta mill out for more money than that if we find an honest ore buyer."

It was my turn to grin. "Well, let's sneak up there and grab that gold. If we leave our mounts some distance away and walk in, we'll have that ore and be gone before those Utes know we're in the area. We can use that money to hire some guns and go back next year if there's no damn treaty."

Gidd said, "You may be onto a plan. I dread goin' back up there, but if we just went for the cache and headed right out, I'm bettin' we can make it. Pete and I mined there for a month before the Indians noticed us. We can also put up a claim notice with all our names on it. If some prospectors show up next summer before we do, they'll be outta luck because the mine will already be ours legally."

I thought on the matter for a moment, mainly to get rein on my emotions, which were already stressed. "Well, my friend, I suppose summertime is burning. We should leave at daybreak. By this time next year we'll be smoking good cigars and drinking the best whiskey. By the way, just who all's names are we fixing to put on the claim papers?"

Gidd finished his drink. "Why, only ours an' ole Pete's. He has family in Kansas City. Him being the one who found it, I'm sure you'll agree he should be in for a third. His widow an' kids could likely use it."

I fished a silver dollar I'd taken from that cowboy who had tried to rob me in Texas and tossed it on the bar. It rolled around giving out a peal like a fine church bell.

"Give us another round," I said to the portly bartender, who moved as if he were wading in molasses. "My partner and I are thirsty."

Gidd Trevor sighed. "I am glad we don't have any problems with Pete's share."

"Drink up, Gidd, old friend," I said happily. "Tomorrow we'll be on our way to getting rich. From what you have told me there's plenty of gold up there to go around."

My thoughts flashed back to Florida when I agreed to stake every dollar I had for a fifty-fifty split with this man. Now that I knew what type of individual I was dealing with, I could handle the matter appropriately when the time was advantageous.

As I mentioned earlier, I have never been one to tolerate abuse lightly.

And Gidd Trevor *was* a damn Confederate.

Seven

Gidd Trevor and I departed the city of Denver on a shining blue August morning. The weather was absolutely delightful, cloudless, with just a slight nip in the air that would soon give way to wonderful warmth. After spending a few weeks traveling through the steaming hell of Louisiana and Texas, this was a taste of heaven. All considered, it was one of those days when a person is happy to be alive.

In short order I could tell my partner was anxious to return to his gold strike. Gidd kept a beaming smile pasted on his face while gazing longingly at the distant peaks, some of which still retained vestiges of snow.

The fact that Trevor was being so cooperative gladdened my heart for I, too, was looking forward to setting eyes on that rich vein. He had only spoken in generalities as to the mine's actual location. And I took care not to push him on the matter or even pretend to make note of any landmarks. There would be plenty of time for this later.

Our journey was not one of rapid pace. Traversing the rugged high country slows one's progress considerably. The air becomes rarified with every mile of advance toward those towering peaks. Both men and animals suffer a distinct lack of stamina until they adjust to the altitude. Jagged mountains and craggy cliffs must be bypassed by following valleys and stream courses. Good, clear water, however, was plentiful, and so was wild game such as deer, rabbits, and grouse.

Around noon on our third day out of Denver we rode into what appeared to be a near ghost town. Gidd surveyed the numerous boarded-up cabins and stores and clucked his tongue. "This place is called Tarryall. The last time I was through here the joint was boomin' something grand."

I observed only one business that had an open door and smoke coming from its chimney. This was a low, one-story log saloon that faced looking across what passed for a main street onto a creek that had been fairly well dug up by gold mining efforts.

"From the looks of things the boom here has gone bust," I commented.

"That's the way it is with this business. Once the gold peters out, there generally ain't much reason for folks to hang around."

When we rode past the saloon I nodded toward two old men working gold pans down in the creek. "Doesn't look like everybody has given up."

Gidd shook his head and said softly, "Oh, that's just Whiskey Hole. The miners left a little pay dirt there so the old and crippled could pan out enough to pay for a bowl of beans or a shot of whiskey. I'd reckon even Whiskey Hole has 'bout done its due."

I noticed one of the white-whiskered men kneeling in the icy waters had lost an arm and was having a difficult time working his gold pan. I reached into my pocket and fished out a couple of silver dollars, which I tossed down to the old fellows.

"God bless ya, sir," they said in unison as we rode away.

After a few moments Gidd said, "Al Packer, you surprised me with your generosity. That was a plumb decent thing you done back there."

I felt it wise not to mention that since the money had come from a thieving Texan I thought it appropriate to be rather free in spending it.

I said, "A man should always care for his less fortunate brethren."

Gidd Trevor smiled. "Amen. This would be a far better world with more people like you in it."

"I only strive to do what is right."

Then I spurred the mule into a faster gait toward the south.

The sun was lowering behind jutting peaks and a chill was building in the thin air when we came to South Park City. Unlike Tarryall, this town was bustling with activity. Only a scant year later it would have its name changed to Fairplay, as it is known to this day.

Gidd and I stabled out our mounts, then checked into the Silver Heels Hotel, a rather impressive three-story structure with room rates to match its stateliness. I visited a barber there, who charged me the exorbitant price of fifty cents for a haircut and shave. Since I was preparing to become a man of means, I felt it appropriate to look fitting for the occasion. I instructed the corpulent tonsorial artist to shave me leaving only a goatee and my mustache. When I inspected his handiwork in a mirror, I was most impressed with my countenance and decided to keep this style for many years.

Later we enjoyed drinks in the bar, then retreated to the dining room, where I greatly relished having a dinner prepared by hands other than my own.

After a wonderful hot bath in a deep copper tub, I laid myself into the embrace of a soft feather bed. I was quickly swept away in the arms of Morpheus, where I dreamt sweet dreams of glistening veins of rich gold.

"Keep your eyes peeled," Gidd Trevor said gravely. "This is Salida Valley we're coming into. The Ute Indians are rather fond of the place."

I glanced at the sparkling-clear waters of the Arkansas River, then studied the green, tree-covered gentle valley that was surrounded by snowcapped mountains.

"Mighty pretty country," I said. "Reckon they do like it here. Maybe the government will wise up and run them off. Those savages should be put someplace where they aren't a bother to opening up the country to people who will do something with the land."

"It's been tried." Gidd sliced off a fresh chew of tobacco and stuffed it in his mouth. "Back in Fifty-Five, a Colonel Fauntleroy with a troop of calvary attacked a Ute village on that flat yonder. He killed three or four dozen of 'em and took the rest as prisoners. The lesson didn't take 'cause there's still lots of savages about. They're just more cautious these days and prefer to pick on folks like us that they stand an easier chance of killin'."

On that glad note we rode out of the trees and forded the frigid waters of the Arkansas. The river was low and our crossing shallow, but the rushing water still brushed against my mule's belly.

We quickly went back into cover and angled up from our crossing in case we had been observed by hostile eyes.

Suddenly, nature grew silent as the inside of a tomb. Birds ceased their twittering and the only sounds to be heard were the clumping of shod hooves on soft soil. The short hairs on the nape of my neck stood out like porcupine quills. I could hear the beating of my own heart.

I held up my hand as a signal to Gidd and reined the mule to a stop. The animal began quivering as if it had caught a chill.

Trevor stopped and began scanning the area with wide eyes while sliding his Spencer .56-50 caliber rifle from its scabbard. Likewise, I pulled out the Volcanic thirty-shot carbine that had belonged to the late Sam Broward and cocked it. Any Indians who attacked us would pay dearly for their indiscretion. The problem was, neither of us could see anything that needed shooting.

I feared a flurry of silent and deadly arrows could be in the offing, when a terrible growl and crashing sound came from a heavy patch of larch to our flank. A monstrous grizzly bear came charging with a lowered head and open maw that displayed rows of long, razor-sharp teeth. The beast's roar and thunderous approach that uprooted small trees made it seem unstoppable as a steam locomotive.

Our mounts reared and wheeled in blind panic, throwing off our aim as we began raining hot lead at the oncoming brute. The bear seemed to not notice our hail of bullets, and did not slow its charge in the least until it was upon us.

Luck was with me. I fired my next-to-last shell from only a few feet away into the monster's eye, which must have exploded its brain, for the beast dropped like a stone at the very feet of my panic-stricken mule.

Then I noticed Gidd Trevor's left leg was bleeding profusely. In its blind primal rage that grizzly had somehow managed to rip a horrible gash in him with one of its six-inch-long claws. I had been so busy concentrating on aiming my rifle from atop the spooked and spin-

ning mule I had not seen this happen. Fortunately
Gidd's horse appeared uninjured.

I dismounted and attempted to calm our mounts, but
was unsuccessful until I had led them some distance
upwind from the dead bear. After I had securely tied
their reins to a sturdy tree, I gently helped Gidd down
from his saddle.

"My God, Al," he gasped. "I'm glad you got that
beast. I thought we were both goners for sure."

"I just hope to Pete there aren't any Indians about
for five miles or so in any direction or they'll be here
right shortly to find out what the ruckus was. If that
happens, you can keep right on worrying."

Gidd stared down at his wounded leg. "That bleedin'
has to be stopped before I leak out." He wagged his
head toward his horse. "There's a needle and thread in
my—"

He swooned into my arms. I caught him and carried
him to a large patch of green grass, where I carefully
laid him down. I took out my bowie knife and cut the
leg off his Levi's. He had an extra pair with him anyway.

The gash was on the outside of his upper thigh, well
over a foot long, and likely went to the bone. I took
heart for I knew if I could successfully stem the flow of
blood, Gidd would live to show me that mine.

I wrapped my belt around his leg, then cinched it
tight. I had brought along a flask of whiskey, a good
deal of which I used to clean the wound. This must
have shocked his system because he let out a yowl and
came awake.

Quickly, I found a stick and crammed it crossways in
his mouth. We had already made enough noise to wake
the dead. "Bite down on that, Gidd, for what I'm fixing
to do will hurt like hell, but it'll save your hide."

I eventually found the needle and thread in his saddlebags. The thing was big enough to mend a harness

with, but at least it was already threaded with a long thin strip of rawhide. When I started stitching, Gidd moaned into the stick and spittle trickled down his cheeks. Finally he passed out again, which allowed me to work without his thrashing about. I put a total of eighteen stitches in his leg and tied each of them tightly. Then I removed my belt to allow the blood flow to resume. I was gratified to find my efforts had been fruitful. Only a few small trickles of crimson were in evidence. I wrapped the wound with the pants leg I had cut off and tied it firm with some rope. All there was to do now was wait for Gidd to regain consciousness and his strength.

Indians had not made an appearance, so I decided to build a fire and make a comfortable camp. I sliced several large steaks from the rump of that bear, and was roasting them on a stick when Gidd came around. I gave him the rest of my whiskey to drink, which roused him enough to eat a few bites of meat. Afterward he dozed off again, and slept fitfully the rest of the night while I kept watch over him.

We spent three days in that camp before Gidd was able to continue on. I must say he had a strong constitution and recovered admirably. By the second day he was able to hobble about using a makeshift crutch I had whittled from the branch of a willow tree.

To while away the time I smoked a generous quantity of bear meat into jerky. Using two rocks, I pounded some of this into powder and mixed it with rendered fat along with wild raspberries, which grew here in abundance. This gave us a supply of delicious-tasting pemmican to sustain us on the long journey we faced.

Eight

It was on a rainy and cold morning that we rode south into the mountains. Gidd sat tall in the saddle, giving me great hopes for his complete recovery from his ordeal.

We followed the San Luis River that meandered through an opening between the high peaks that is called Poncha Pass. A few miles hence the trees and mountains gave way to a grand open valley.

Gidd said, "We oughtta make the town of Saguache by tomorrow. The place ain't much, it's mainly just saloons and whorehouses to provide for the needs of the Los Pinos Indian Agency. They might have a doctor there to see to my leg, though I doubt it."

I felt a pang of concern. Avoiding any contact with any folks who were connected with Indians seemed in order.

"I don't know about that, Gidd. Wouldn't a couple of prospectors riding in there attract the wrong kind of attention? I'd say we've been plenty lucky so far. It would be a shame to push our good fortune and get followed when we leave for that mine of yours."

Gidd sighed. "Dang, you might be on to something, Al. I guess I hadn't thought the matter through. Thanks to your good stitchin', my leg's healing up fine. Likely there ain't no doctor there anyhow."

"So you reckon we oughtta pass by the place?"

"There ain't much to miss. We can skirt it to the north and no one will notice. If we stay north we'll bypass the Los Pinos Agency, too."

"You're sure we shouldn't go see if they've got a doctor? We can always go winter somewhere and try again next spring."

"Nah." He shrugged. "We've come this far, I can't let a little bear scratch stop us. Besides, that mine ain't but three or four more days' ride from where we sit jawin'."

"If you're feeling up to it, let's go," I said as I reined that mule into the broad expanse of open grassland.

"It beats all that we ain't seen even one blasted Injun or even any sign of 'em," Gidd commented as we rode side by side along the rushing waters of the Lake Fork of the Gunnison River.

"The Good Lord looks out for fools and drunks," I said jauntily. "And our whiskey has been gone for days."

Trevor's chin dropped to his chest. He said nothing. He just kept heading onward toward some landmark that only he knew. Five days had passed since we made our decision to push on to the mine. He seemed to tire more easily as we progressed, and we were forced to stop early for him to rest. All of our camps had been cold ones; to build a fire would be to invite certain trouble.

I said, "When we stop this evening I want to check out that leg of yours."

"It doesn't hurt at all. I reckon I'm just tuckered out from losin' all of that blood. We'll be at the most beautiful lake you've ever set eyes on in a couple of hours or so. From there it's only two or three miles to the gold vein."

"I still intend on looking after that leg of yours. I may need to yank out those stitches."

Gidd smiled thinly. "It might not be a bad idea. It would be a shame to catch a blood poison just when I'm about to become a rich man."

"Don't worry none, pard. I won't let anything like that happen to a friend of mine."

Trevor had been correct in his description of what is now known as Lake San Cristobal. When we were there this was still unexplored country. The domain of savages who could not appreciate the stark beauty of this magnificent area.

When God takes a mind to show off the splendidness of his handiwork, the results may best be seen here. Lofty peaks lift up their snowcapped crests into the domain of angels. A breeze rustling through aspen trees and tall pines sing sweet lullabies to any soul who takes time to listen to music played by the Almighty.

It was on the bank of this idyllic lake that I came to realize Gidd Trevor was dying. When I removed the bandage from his leg, the putrid stench of rotting meat that signifies gangrene was nearly overpowering. I felt devastated that I had not insisted on going to the town of Saguache and search for a doctor.

"Looks like I'm done for," Gidd said after surveying his ruined flesh. "It's a shame for a rich man to have to die way out here."

"I'm not gonna let you go shake hands with Saint Peter. The worst of the matter will be you having to hobble around on a wooden leg once I slice off that bad one."

Gidd forced a chuckle. "You're not worth a hoot in hell as a liar. I know I'm gonna cash in my chips in a day or two. Before I do I want to show you that gold vein. The least I can do is leave something for my family and my old pard. I know you're an honest man, Al Packer, and I wish to leave my legacy in your capable hands."

"I still believe I can take that leg off and you'll make it."

"Nope," Gidd said firmly. "Not today anyway. That mine's only a couple of miles or so from here. Tomorrow I'll show it to you and we'll dig up that cache of ore. Then I'll let you do your cuttin'. I owe others too much to quit now."

I sighed sadly and with a heavy heart washed the wound with cool water and rebandaged it. Gidd managed to eat a few mouthfuls of pemmican before he dozed off as the sun set golden behind the blue mountains.

Early the next morning, after I helped Gidd into his saddle, we rode into the trees to the west. As I have said, he was a man of strength. Within an hour he had pointed out to me the depression in a low rise where the Utes had filled in the rich gold strike. Following his directions I quickly unearthed six canvas bags filled with high-grade ore.

"Make note of those two sharp-pointed peaks to the west, Al," he told me. "In the summer the sun sets directly between them. Take your knife and blaze some trees as we go back to the lake. I want to make certain you can find this place again."

I took out my bowie knife and sliced arrows into two large aspen trees. The heads of the arrows I pointed straight at the covered-up mine.

"That should do the trick," Gidd said. "Load up those sacks of ore into our saddlebags and let's head back to the lake. I'm feelin' poorly."

I followed Gidd's wishes, and hesitated on our way

down only long enough to slice bark from a few trees to blaze a return trail.

From the position of the sun I figured it to be around the middle of the afternoon when we returned to make camp beside that serene blue lake.

Then I brought up the inevitable. "Trevor, I'm going to chance a fire. I have to cauterize the stump once I take your leg off or you'll bleed to death."

Gidd nodded weakly. "First we need to take care of a matter." He pulled a paper from his coat with a shaky hand. "This claim paper has to be filled out. While I'm healin' up you go build a mound of rocks right in front of that mine and put this in it. There's no other way to make a claim legal. Especially if the Indian treaty gets signed and throws this country open."

I obliged him and said nothing, even when he scribbled the name of Pete Fellows as one of the owners.

"I'll take care of everything," I reassured him. "Now let's take that bandage off and let me get to work."

The awful stench of rotting flesh nearly gagged me, but I kept a poker face when I studied where the poison had spread to envelop his hip. Realization that I could only end his terrible suffering stabbed at my heart.

It would have been cruel of me to postpone what I had to do. To ease my poor partner into the next world, I made a pretense of moving a large rock to make him more comfortable. Then, to put him out of his misery, I mercifully bashed in his head with it before I cut his throat.

There were still several hours of daylight left, so I put them to good use by thoroughly examining Trevor's personal effects. I failed to find any address or means by which I could ever trace down any of his—or Pete Fellows'—family members. I knew his parents had been killed. This being the case, to save muddying the legal waters of ownership to the mine, I carefully tore off their names from the claim paper, leaving only my own.

This is a cold and cruel world in which we live. All one can do is the best they can at the time. As I watched a lone eagle gliding lazily above on a cushion of air, I vowed to make right what I could with Trevor's wishes in the future.

For this to happen I had to survive myself.

I knew Trevor's body would likely be found. It would be far better if the blame fell on a band of savage Ute Indians. This could help stir the government to action.

While Gidd Trevor's corpse was still warm, I forced myself to remove his scalp before I rode back to stake my claim to that rich vein of gold.

Nine

When I awoke the next morning in those Indian-infested mountains there was a distinct chill in the air. My breath blew out as a white fog. I wished I could have built a fire to warm myself, but that act would have been a foolhardy one. As the late Gidd Trevor had advised, winter can come quite early to the high country of Colorado.

I had slept poorly. Much of the past night I had lain awake beneath my felt blanket and stared at the twinkling stars while contemplating my somewhat awkward situation. I decided it would be an unwise move to return to the city of Denver.

Reappearing there minus a partner many people saw me leave with, leading his horse with sacks of rich gold ore in its saddlebags, could set tongues to wagging. And lawmen have curiosity that would put a cat to shame.

Although I had done absolutely nothing wrong, I felt it would be in my best interests to head west into the Utah Territory. It is an unfortunate fact of life that truth is often lost in words. I did not feel it wise to expose myself to any needless, uncalled-for questions from anyone, let alone some lout with a badge.

The mining claim was now legally mine, or at least it would be if Chief Ouray made the right decision and gave up this country. I did not, however, feel it prudent to rely on the government to look after my welfare. There was adequate inducement in those sparkling rocks laced with gold to recruit some help. If I returned here with enough armed men, treaty or not, I could become quite well-to-do and that would enable me to help out my struggling family in Pennsylvania.

My course of action had been plotted. I staked out Gidd's horse to graze on a nice patch of grass and made one final trip to the mine before leaving. I had brought along a leather-covered notebook and a compass for just such an occasion.

From the mine site I took detailed compass bearings on all of the visible peaks and recorded them in my book along with every landmark. I took the added precaution of carefully blazing several more trees. I wanted no difficulty in finding this spot again.

Thankfully, not a single savage had made an appearance since our entry into this country. I hoped my luck would hold. I saddled the horse and loaded the rather heavy bags of ore into the saddlebags. Curiosity did get the better of me and I opened one of the sacks. The rocks inside were at least a third pure gold. I stuck a couple of the richest chunks in my pocket to admire, then finished with my packing.

I removed my hat and held it over my heart when I rode past Gidd Trevor's lifeless body. The poor fellow had showed me to a very rich gold mine and I owed the man my deepest respects.

On my fourth day out disaster struck as I was following the treacherous Black Canyon of the Gunnison River along its southern edge. My misfortune did not come from hostile Indians, but was caused by a worthless rodent known as the prairie dog. My stupid packhorse stepped into one of their numerous holes and broke one of its forelegs.

This created a terrible circumstance, for I was unable to transport the heavy sacks of ore on my mule. Trevor's purse had only held thirteen dollars, and my funds totaled a mere two dollars plus some change. I had hoped to sell this ore at my first opportunity to avoid the necessity of finding employment until I could open the mine. Now that could not be.

I dispatched the squealing horse with my bowie knife to avoid the sound of a shot being fired and the waste of a bullet. Then I studied on my predicament. It quickly became apparent that I would have to cache the ore and return for it at a later date.

About a hundred yards to the east stood three jagged rocks that could easily be found again. They stood straight out of the ground like telegraph poles.

Having no shovel, I dug a hole using a tree branch I had found. Then I buried my treasure ten paces in front of the middle rock and brushed the site clean. I was gratified to notice none of my activity was visible from the trail I had been following.

My food supply was perilously low, so I sliced several lean steaks from the dead horse's flank. I desperately wished there was some way I could cook it, but that would have been inviting even more trouble. Raw horsemeat isn't so bad, once one gets used to eating it.

Suffice for me to say that my journey to Utah took nearly a month. The country I was forced to traverse was mostly unsettled in those days and decent roads were a rarity. On two occasions I did see some hostiles in the distance, but I must have escaped their notice for they gave me no trouble.

It was the Twenty-Sixth day of September when I rode

the red mule into Salt Lake City. I learned this from a calendar on the wall of a restaurant where I had stopped to eat, for I was totally famished.

The country thereabouts is stupendously beautiful with fertile, well-watered valleys embraced by lofty green mountains. I might have wintered there, but the place was infested with Mormon Zealots who charged an arm and a leg for meals and lodging. They also refused to hire anyone who wasn't as crazy as they were.

If the government would send in some troops and rout all of the Mormons out of Utah like they were a tribe of savage Indians, the place would become a tolerable one to live in.

Luckily, I struck up a conversation with a gentleman in the restaurant who was a fellow Gentile. He informed me there was employment available just twenty miles to the southwest in a boom town of the east slope of the Oquirrh Mountains called Bingham City. A railroad had just this year been opened to the place so the lead and silver mines could now ship out their ore to be smeltered at a much cheaper rate than before, resulting in a tremendous amount of growth.

When this fellow quietly whispered in my ear that there were few Mormons there and saloons and recreation houses in abundance, I made my decision quite quickly. I paid the unbelievably expensive bill of one dollar for the steak and eggs I had consumed and headed forthwith for Bingham City.

While the descriptive name of "boom town" dredges up images of grandeur, this was not the case at all with Bingham City. Even the Indians had no good use for that country and never raised a ruckus when mining started there back in Eighteen Sixty-Three. I could also understand why the Mormons left it be.

The Oquirrh Mountains made a jagged outline against a blue sky that reminded me of a row of broken teeth. Strung along the bottom of a deep gulch with sheer cliffs for sides lies the town of Bingham City. The houses and businesses were built stepped one above the other until the cliff became too steep to continue.

Every building seemed to have been constructed from the same gray plank lumber, giving the town a dismal appearance. Being smack dab in the bottom of a canyon, the sun only hit the streets for a few hours every day. This location also gave the added benefit of holding in all of the smoke from every chimney, mine boiler, and smelter furnace in the vicinity. This formed a thick blanket of yellow fog that burned eyes red and seared lungs raw.

Only my dire financial straits caused me to place my mule in the care of a livery stable and check into a hotel. I paid six dollars in advance for a room with board for a week. I then enjoyed my first bath in two months while I sent my clothes out for a much-needed laundering.

Feeling very much refreshed, I visited a few saloons that evening. I was pleased to find many men with money in evidence. Gold coins rang on the wooden bars with abandon. I knew now that once I showed those rich gold specimens I had carried all this great distance to the right people, I would soon have the backing I needed. My mine in Colorado would certainly be opened when the snows melted.

Later that night I discovered I had been remiss in my earlier assessment of Bingham City. A voluptuous little lady named Jennie, who had deep blue eyes, ruby lips, and a most infectious giggle, proved to me beyond any doubt that not *everything* about the place was bad.

Ten

My pitiful financial condition forced me to take employment as a common laborer with the West Jordan Mining Company. This firm was primarily owned by General Patrick E. Connor, who was one of the pioneers of the district. He had become wealthy enough to influence the railroad being built to here from Salt Lake City.

My first plan was to approach this man and hopefully induce him to finance my own mining venture. Unfortunately, this hope became dashed when I found the illustrious gentleman had removed himself from the region to reside in New York City.

Anyone who has ever had occasion to visit Bingham City could not fault the general's reasoning, but I must confess to wondering what turn my fate may have taken should I have been able to make contact with this man.

I hired on with the West Jordan Company as a mucker. Now this is the lowest job of any in an underground mine. My function was to shovel mine cars full of broken rock, then push them outside and dump the contents either into a wooden ore bin or over the side of the mountain, depending on whether or not it was ore or waste. These sturdy iron carts run on steel rails, much like a railroad car, and hold on the average a ton of "muck," which is miners' slang for any rock that had been blasted into smithereens.

Every hellhole such as Bingham City is deserving of its own personal devil. The one they had went by the name of Orman Ten Eyck, who turned out to be the foreman for the Jordan Company and also my boss. He was a most arrogant person with deep-seated, piglike eyes that glared at the world from a square head that was connected to his burly body without any evidence of a neck.

Orman's sole method of communicating with people, including myself, was by screaming and threatening. The hulk was so devoid of the milk of human kindness and decency I am certain he had to hire someone to fetch his dog for him. This shouting devil demanded that I shovel and move eight tons of rock before dinner break, and eight more before quitting time or be fired.

Luckily, I was in prime physical condition and easily performed my appointed tasks, much to the foreman's stormy astonishment. He relished discharging men with a barrage of curses without any inquiry into their problems or difficulties such as faulty equipment or dangerous conditions.

"Rock in the box is all that matters," were the words Orman Ten Eyck lived by and repeated over and over again with all the fever of a chanting monk.

I received four dollars for a ten-hour shift, so I tolerated Mister Ten Eyck's rantings and ravings for nearly two weeks. Then somehow, in the stygian blackness deep inside of that mine, the poor fellow made a misstep and plunged down an air shaft to his death.

I can safely recount that this event failed to cause even a twinge of sorrow to anyone who ever knew him. A priest and the undertaker were the only ones present at his funeral, or so I was later informed.

Israel Swan was the man chosen to replace the recently departed mine foreman. This fellow had been cut from softer cloth than Orman Ten Eyck and was of a kindly, happy disposition. By this I do not mean that he did not demand everyone do their utmost to perform their appointed tasks. Swan preferred talking calmly and genuinely tried to understand his charges' problems rather than simply firing a man because he had the power to do so.

I immediately took a liking to this stalwart individual. I also made some discreet inquiries into his background. It would have been rash of me to disclose the existence of my rich mine to an untrustworthy person.

If you want to find out anything about another man, ask a woman. I can't recall who first said that, but I would venture that it was long before Noah got his boat ride. Some truths are simple and plain as the nose on your face.

I asked Jennie O'Leary to ask around about him. Ever since I had shown the cute little brunette a few pieces of rich gold ore from my mine, she had become *so* sweet and caring toward me. A few well-chosen words on my part regarding our future together gave her great joy. They also saved me a dollar, sometimes two, every night, for in those days my sap rose quite often.

"Al, dearie," Jennie cooed into my ear the next evening while rubbing my tired shoulders. "This Mister Swan checks out as a decent chappie. None of the other girls knows a bad thing about 'im. Sarah, who works down at Beulah's joint, has a regular by the name of Wilson Bell who has known 'im for years. She says he's a straight arrow."

"Who is this Bell character and what does he do hereabouts?"

"Him and Frank Miller, they own the meat market over on Canyon Street. Sarah says Miller's an old fellow whose poker has lost its temper, but that partner of his has done a good job of takin' up the slack."

I rolled over on the small bed and faced her. "Jennie, darling, this is very important to our future. That mine will make us rich if we play our cards right. We're going to need some good men to back us on this, people who are honest. Does this Sarah know much about Bell and Miller outside of doing her business with them?"

Jennie drew her lips into a cute pout. "Israel Swan an' them came out here from California nearly two years ago. They all share a cabin with a bartender at the Gold Coin Saloon, James Humphreys, along with a kid they took in after his pa died. The boy works as a swamper an' runs errands for some of the girls on occasion. He's a nice kid, but sure hates to be called one. His name's Noon, George Noon."

"Five men," I said idly, "or four men and a boy. I don't know, Jen, if there would be enough of us to put up much of a fight if those damn Ute Indians raise a fuss."

Her cute pout vanished to be replaced by a practiced smile. "Hon, we can't go chopping up ownership in that mine you worked so hard and bravely to locate. Maybe we could offer them a small interest, like a third. Then I can put out word that you all are heading off to a new gold area. A lot of men will follow along in hopes of making their own strike."

I thought on her logic for a few moments and found no fault with it, save one.

"Jennie," I said, "I know full well that it will take a fairly large, well-armed party of men to keep the Indians at bay if the treaty isn't signed before we get there. The problem is, this is only October. The high country up there in Colorado will likely be snowed in until April or May."

She slid velvet hands alongside my cheeks, drew me

close, and gave me a steamy kiss. "Oh, but Al, dearie, it could take you two months to reach there, possibly a lot longer. If you and your brave friends were camped out there when the snow melts, wouldn't it give you an edge on protecting *our* interests? You are *such* a good prospector you might even find another rich mine before any of the others do."

Every woman has the power to cause a man to do most any fool thing. This has nothing to do with witchcraft or voodooism like they used to burn them at the stake for. It simply consists of keeping a man's thinking below his belt line. And Jennie O'Leary had a *lot* of skill and experience in that area.

"Okay," I said. "I'll drop by their cabin after work tomorrow, show them the gold specimens, and see what they think. Then I'll come over and let you know what they have to say on the matter."

"You're such a dearie," she purred while stripping off her lacy nightgown. "Just don't go out there and forget about li'l ole me."

"I won't," I answered. And I never have forgotten her to this very day.

The date was the Eighth of October. Just two years earlier, a woman in Chicago by the name of O'Leary had burned down the whole dad-blasted city when she caused her cow to kick over a lantern. Three hundred people had been incinerated because of that woman.

I didn't know then how darn unlucky it was to be around anyone named O'Leary. I was sure going to find out quickly enough, however.

Eleven

Israel Swan studied those hunks of rich ore like a preacher does a Bible. He rolled one around with his fingers under the yellow flickering light of a coal-oil lamp.

After a long while he said, "This is mighty rich ore, Al Packer. Yep, you've hit on a rich one for sure."

With a flash of greed he fixed his green eyes on me from across the rude table we all sat at. Israel Swan had a reddish crop of long hair with a bushy beard to match. "How wide's the vein an' how far were you able to trace it on the ground?"

Those were excellent questions, and now I sincerely wished that I had posed them to Gidd Trevor while he was still amongst the living. I felt this matter was of small potatoes taking into consideration how rich the ore was. Swan had been around gold mining all of his life and knew more about the technicalities than were comfortable. I thought on my answer while studying the faces of my future partners through pale light.

Jennie had been correct in her description of Frank Miller. He was older than God's dog. The man shook all of the time as if he had the ague. I really wondered if the white-haired elderly German butcher with rheumy, dark eyes was up to such a grueling trip that faced us. I did not ask his age, but he appeared near seventy.

Wilson Bell, Miller's partner, sat by his side, greedily eyeing the gold specimens. Bell, it turned out, was nearly two years my junior. He would be twenty-two next March. I turned twenty-four on January Twenty-First. I wondered why the old butcher had taken in such a young partner, then answered my own question; someone had to do all of the hard work. I did not care for Bell. He had a high-pitched screechy voice that came across like a stepped-on cat. He was skinny as a poorhouse snake with blond, shoulder-length hair, no whiskers, and darting blue eyes. I figured him to be the type of man to turn coward very quickly. Yet, I felt that for Miller to help finance the expedition, my silence on his partner's character would be prudent.

James Humphreys, on the other hand, was a man of sterling disposition. Of muscular build for a bartender, he had a twinkle in his gray eyes and his black beard curved upwards at the edges of his mouth giving him a perpetual smile. He was a hardy thirty-five years of age and I liked him right away.

At one end of the table sat "the kid" as everyone referred to him, causing obvious discomfort. George Noon, while only sixteen years of age, seemed far more mature and trustworthy to me than the butcher's partner. Noon was making a futile attempt to grow a set of chin whiskers, which made him look ridiculous. Young men, as Army generals know, have the wonderful quality of doing what they are told with no fear of bodily injury to themselves. I knew George Noon would likely be of valuable service to me.

"Well, Packer," Swan said rather harshly. "We're waitin' for you to tell us about this here vein you found."

"That *is* why we're all gathered here, isn't it," I answered somewhat gruffly.

Since I was the man who was going to make all of

them wealthy, I didn't feel I needed to be subjected to any abuse.

"He's just anxious to hear about it is all, Al," Humphreys interjected apologetically, confirming my earlier favorable impression of him. "We all are."

I paused long enough to take a shot from the bottle of the excellent whiskey that sat in front of me. "Boys," I said, carefully measuring my words. "Before those damn Indians attacked without warning and killed my poor partner in cold blood, we had opened a veritable treasure house of riches.

"That quartz vein runs straight up the mountainside plain as a red light in a whorehouse window. The seam is wide as a fat woman's fanny and we had the thing traced out for a length of a city block. It beats all you could ever imagine. Why, that whole area is crisscrossed with other veins, too. Some of them might even turn out to be richer than the one I found. A body never knows. One thing is for certain; there's plenty of gold there to make *all* of us richer than Midas."

I scanned the faces of everyone at the table. With the sole exception of Swan, I knew they were spellbound by my tale. I could almost gaze into their eyes and see visions of stately mansions, fawning servants, and beautiful, luscious women. This presented no difficulty for I had the same divination myself.

Israel Swan glared at me through the wavering light of the coal-oil lamp. I noticed one of his eyebrows was cocked higher than the other. "Packer," Swan said, "are you telling us *all* of that vein is rich as the chunks you're showin' us?"

I could tell by his skeptical tone of voice that I might have overdone my description of the mine a tad. The truth of the matter, as you well know, was that I had never set eyes on the quartz seam. It had already been covered over by the Indians. But I knew those beautiful specimens had come from it, and I felt deep in my heart that I must have given a truthful and accurate account of what the situation was really like. To squash any questions on his part, and considering the fact that Swan was the only man present with any mining experience, I felt it prudent to replay my hand.

"Of course not," I said firmly. "I only brought out some of the richest pieces. The area of high-grade comes in pods along the ore zone. The pocket those samples came from was likely a good foot wide. Taken as a whole the vein should run several hundred dollars to the ton. If we just gopher the high-grade, I'd venture we will all get pretty well off. As you can see with your own eyes, some of that ore is powerful rich."

I was glad that I had paid attention as to how my fellow workers at the West Jordan Company described mineral occurrences. Gidd Trevor had been a simple prospector and had not known beans about actual mining. Fate, however, had brought me to Utah, where I learned the trade quite rapidly.

Israel Swan clucked his tongue while idly rolling a chunk of ore between his thumb and forefinger. "Boys, I've seen a lot of ore in my day an' not very damn much of it was anywhere near this rich. High-grade like Al Packer's shown us always tends to form in pockets just like he said this done. If we can cut us a deal, I'm for throwin' in with him and headin' for Colorado Territory come spring."

"We're all going to be rich!" Wilson Bell exclaimed with a squeal, confirming my suspicions that he was a biscuit short of a full breakfast.

"Settle down, my young friend," Miller said, holding up his hand. "First we must make an arrangement equitable to us all. I am not about to quit our lucrative business here without an adequate incentive to do so."

Germans have a way about them of raising picky business issues no matter what the situation. I figured I was in for a problem with the butcher when Humphreys spoke. "I've been in the saloon when many grubstake deals was hashed out," he said with authority. "The cut is pretty customary; half for the finder and half for the folks who put up the money or do the diggin'. To my way of thinkin', we're grubstakin' Al Packer on his mine."

I could tell from the expression on Wilson Bell's face that he was trying to slice up fifty percent five equal ways in his head and not making a success of it.

Israel Swan broke into a fit of coughing that seemed like it would never stop. He poured himself a shot of whiskey with jerking hands, spilling much of it. Then he slugged down the drink, which seemed to clear his throat. I had already noticed that after a man spends a few years working in an underground mine he begins dying by degrees. Swan was thirty-eight years old and proudly bragged that he had been mining since he was only fourteen, back in the big rush of Forty-Nine. He had to know by now that his working days were drawing to a close.

The saloons and restaurants had a goodly share of "experienced" miners who could barely hold a job swamping out the joint because of their lack of wind and coughing, and many of these were younger than Swan. I was correct in my assumption that Israel Swan would join us.

"All of us here needs a stake to get ahead in life," he said hoarsely. "If there's just a few tons of rich ore in Packer's mine, that'd be enough to set each of us up. Those Indians up in Colorado can't kill me any deader than a couple more years in the mines will. I'm for throwin' in on this deal with one exception."

"What might that be?" I asked, still thinking the matter over. Jennie had counseled me to only give away a third interest, but Humphreys' grubstake deal seemed eminently fair, considering the risks involved. I decided that since Jennie O'Leary wasn't the one risking an Indian haircut, I would make up my own mind.

"Just this," Swan said, his voice firm again. "Any new claims we file, whether or not they adjoin Packer's, will be shared equally amongst the six of us."

I glanced at Bell and suppressed a grin at the monkeyshines his face was making trying to slice that pie up. Frank Miller, being a skinflint, was the one I felt concern over. We would need a quantity of supplies; new guns of the repeating type with plenty of ammo, pack mules laden with grub and mining tools that we could also use to pack out our ore. I kept silent to await his response, for he alone had enough money to make this expedition feasible.

The butcher poured himself a shot, slugged it down, and refilled his glass. He squinted those rheumy eyes at me. "*Ja*, but since it is I and my young partner who must put up most of the money, I think we should have another ten percent."

I grabbed the bottle and poured Wilson Bell a shot. I was certain he was in need of it. All of this high finance had him shaking worse than Old Man Miller. Then I glanced at the one person who had remained silent; George Noon.

"How do you feel about all of this, Mister Noon?" I asked him.

My respect of not calling him "kid" had the desired effect.

George Noon beamed with delight, then sputtered. "Mister Humphreys said fifty-fifty was the custom. That sounds plenty fair to me."

"*Ja*," Miller growled, "it is easy for you to say. You only have your labor to give. I and my partner must sell our thriving business and put all of the money into the venture. We only vant what is fair to us."

"Maybe *this* will work," James Humphreys said. "If Frank Miller and Bell will keep track of their expenses, we can pay them back double out of our first ore sales."

I could tell by the gleam in the German's eyes that his greed had cut a deal. I kept a poker face and scanned around the table in silence.

"Boys," Israel Swan spoke, "I think we oughtta do that for Miller. It don't seem no more than fair." He glared at the German. "If he will go along with it, that is. If not, I have a few contacts with money I can approach. Rich gold like those chunks on the table seldom fails to garner a stake."

Frank Miller's eyes widened and his jaw nearly hit the top of the table when it dropped. "Oh, I think this is fair to us all. *Ja*, my young partner and I vill go in on this deal."

I noticed Miller never even glanced at Bell, who seemed to have overloaded his thinker and simply sat there staring at the glass of whiskey I had poured him with a dazed look pasted on his pockmarked face.

James Humphreys said, "I'd reckon there ain't no deal until Packer says there is." He looked at me with pleading eyes. "After all, he lost a partner an' damn near got himself killed over that mine. To my way of thinkin', the decision is his."

I poured another whiskey, then leaned back in my chair. "Let's drink to Colorado and getting rich."

With a flurry of sincere smiles and gripping handshakes all around our plans were settled, except for one detail.

"There's something I've been worrying over, fellows," I said gravely, getting everyone's attention quite quickly. "I think we should leave here and make for the mine right away. If that Ute Indian treaty gets signed, prospectors will be thicker than fleas on a Missouri hound up there. Even if it doesn't, we ought to be there when the snow melts so we can start work. If we pack in plenty of supplies, I figure we'll be plenty comfortable. I'd hate to see us lollygag around and lose out."

"Al Packer's got a good point," Humphreys said. "Opportunities like this one don't come around but once in a lifetime. It'll likely take us a couple of months just to get there. I can put up with a little snow and cold. Besides, I've seen what word of a gold strike does to people. If any of this leaks out, we'll be steppin' over folks once we get there."

I felt Jennie's idea of a few more guns along to be a good idea. This just didn't seem like a good time to tell them that. Then I thought on the matter further. "Boys, I hate to bring this up, but to raise a little money, I sold some of this ore to Jake Garnes at the assay office."

"Shitfire and ring Hells' bells," Swan spat. "You might as well have told a woman. Garnes is the biggest blabbermouth west of anywhere. Now we'll have to get movin' for sure. An' it's a natural fact we'll have plenty of company followin' us."

"We vill sell our butcher shop in a hurry," Miller said.

"I was lookin' for a job when I found this one," Swan said.

Humphreys laughed. "Nobody in their right mind expects a bartender to be dependable."

"Let's go to Colorado," George Noon said, excitement sparkling in his eyes. "I'm hankerin' to get rich."

Wilson Bell said nothing. If I had known all of the grief this man was to cause me later on, I would have pulled out my pepperbox pistol and put six bullets in his black heart then and there.

But hindsight is always perfect. At the time I had a prospecting trip to organize and a little lady I wanted to say a long and fond farewell to.

I bade everyone a good evening, stood, and left the small cabin. As I walked into the cold and starry night, the only sound to break the still quiet was Israel Swan suffering through another fit of coughing. There was a spring to my step. I felt for once, things were going my way.

Twelve

Jennie was sweet enough to take a couple of chunks of ore to the assay office and sell them for me. This covered my little white lie quite nicely. Considering her line of work, she had nothing much to do during the daytime hours anyway.

Everyone in the vicinity knew Jake Garnes was crooked as a rain barrel full of water moccasins. In spite of that fact, the assayer paid Jennie a ten-dollar gold eagle for those rocks. This attested to the richness of my mine quite nicely.

After work I dropped by the Gold Coin Saloon for a few drinks to wash the mine dust out of my parched throat. James Humphreys greeted me with a freshly uncorked bottle of whiskey and glared at me when he set it on the bar.

"This is compliments of those two gentlemen," he said with a nod toward a pair of burly characters sitting at a far table. Then he whispered as he slid a glass close, "It's out about the gold mine, Packer. That damn Garnes let it slip just like we knew he would. I sure wisht you'd of not gone and sold him any ore. We'll have lots of company now for certain."

"If those Ute Indians make an appearance," I answered quietly, "you'll likely be singing a different tune. Besides, you already have a cut of the mother lode."

I poured a shot, downed it, and turned to my bene-factors. "Thank you, gentlemen, your kindness is greatly appreciated."

Grady O'Donald and Alf Rankin turned out to be my new friends' names. They told me they were experi-enced prospectors and frontiersmen who had heard about my rich strike. Much to Humphreys' obvious dis-dain, I finished my bottle in their company. I even proudly displayed my sole remaining ore sample and smiled with satisfaction at their wide-eyed admiration of my success.

The fact of the matter was, my partners had no real sense of the dangers we would face in the wilds of Colo-rado. It was my duty to keep them safe at all costs, whether or not they agreed with my well-intentioned methods.

Jennie was in excellent spirits when I arrived at the rude log cabin of hers that we had been sharing of late. She quickly blew out the flame on her red-globed lan-tern to indicate her time was taken. Then she grabbed me and planted a toe-curling steamy kiss square on my lips.

"Oh, my darling Alferd," she squealed. "Soon you will be rich and can take me away from this terrible place. I hate doing what I must to survive here. You are my salvation and my only chance at true love and hap-piness."

I brushed away an unruly wisp of hair from her rouged cheek. "It's simply a matter of time, my love. I fear I may have some difficulties with some of the ruf-fians I have been forced to engage. It was no small task to get everyone to agree to leave and camp there until the snow melts, as you so wisely suggested. Selling those ore specimens appears to have done the trick."

I hesitated for a moment. "You convinced the assayer that he had bought those samples a few days ago?"

Jennie giggled evilly and flipped open the top of her frilly chemise. "I sure did, sugar. Any man can be persuaded if you present the right equipment."

"That's my sweet Jennie," I said.

She moaned softly as I finished removing her skimpy attire and gently guided her toward the rumpled single bed. Jennie was such an accomplished actress. Her role had been rehearsed so many times, I doubted if she could any longer tell reality from fantasy. I, however, had no such perplexing problems in understanding human nature.

Frank Miller and his shifty-eyed partner, Bell, whined and whimpered like spoiled brats after they sold their butcher shop. They bewailed the fact that my actions had forced them to sell at a loss. I had expected Miller to sputter and complain; it was simply his nature to behave in that manner. Wilson Bell, I chose to ignore.

In spite of the butcher's caterwauling, his money did outfit our party quite admirably. All of us already owned sturdy mounts, so we were not forced to listen to him bawl about that subject.

It was on the Third day of November that I purchased a string of twelve packhorses. They were all healthy and experienced animals. The price, if I remember correctly, was one hundred dollars each. But that included well-made packsaddles, all necessary tack, and new shoes from an excellent blacksmith.

As I knew Miller and Bell would never approve of anything I did in their behalf, earlier we had held a group meeting where a vote had been taken giving me full powers to handle the affairs of our partnership.

To have time to oversee the many details of our expedition, I was forced to quit my job with the West Jordan Mining Company. Jennie had even encouraged me to do this. My staying late in the saloon at night gave her time to work, so she was able to furnish us with a decent income and we were not unduly burdened by my being unemployed.

I spent many long and grueling days shopping around for choice goods at the best prices. Thankfully, the butchers had agreed to stay on with the new owners of their business for a while, which spared me their company.

For each of us I bought a new Winchester Model 73 repeating rifle of .44 caliber. I also included three boxes of fifty cartridges for every rifle. Should those pesky Redskins decide we were trespassing on what they mistakenly called "their" lands, I wished to give those damn savages no quarter.

Since everyone of our party owned pistols, I simply added a goodly supply of ammunition of the appropriate caliber. My bowie knife, which once belonged to Gidd Trevor, had unfortunately lost its ability to hold an edge after I used it to stir some cattail roots I was roasting in a campfire. I found one in Jenkin's Dry Goods Store that had an ivory handle I much admired. It had also been honed to the keenness of a fine razor. I felt the ten-dollar asking price to be quite reasonable.

New brogans and heavy felt frock coats were an absolute necessity considering the vicious climate we were to face. Water-repelling wagon canvas for tents, tins of Arbuckle's coffee, bags of Bull Durham smoking and chewing tobacco, boxes of long nine cigars, bottles of whiskey to induce restful sleep, and a small supply of laudanum rounded out the necessities that the individual members of our group did not have on their own.

Wild game, which was certainly in abundance, would easily furnish us with staple foods. I included only light metal frying pans, salt, lard, and flour with which to prepare our meat.

I must admit to enjoying my evenings in the many saloons of Bingham City. Word of my rich gold mine spread like a wildfire during a summer drought. No one would allow me to purchase a single drink or even a sumptuous steak supper in a fine restaurant such as the Bingham Hotel. I am certain that if President Ulysses S. Grant himself had made an appearance there, he would have been ignored in my favor.

The lure of soft yellow gold glinting in the horizons of a person's mind will beat out a windbag politician anytime.

"Al," Jennie cooed sweetly in my ear, "it's time to wake up, sweetie."

I groaned and forced open what I knew were bloodshot eyes. Keeping all of those fine fellows entertained with tales of my gold mine every night was taking a distinct toll.

I rolled over and looked at her. The way rays of flickering yellow lantern light from the nightstand played on Jennie's features, it made her look used and hard. It was as if the veneer of loveliness had been rubbed away, baring her true soul. I thought it strange how easily whiskey and the dark of night can conspire to create beauty.

"Yes, dear," I said, realizing my voice was raspy and the inside of my head throbbed like it was enduring a thunderstorm. "I know it's time to be going, but I think I might ought to have some coffee and breakfast first. We have a long and arduous journey to make."

"You're not to meet your party for another two hours," she reminded me. "I woke you up to give you something to remember little Jennie by and cause you to hurry back for some more, sugar."

Being the focus of everyone's attention was becoming quite tiring. I considered just how badly Jennie needed me and acquiesced to her desires. I felt somewhat sorry for the little lady, for she would likely never again have the joy of my companionship.

It would be gauche for a wealthy mining magnate to associate with a common whore.

Thirteen

The morning sun was building a fiery red orb on the eastern horizon when I left Jennie's pallid log cabin and walked to our appointed meeting place at the Acme Livery Stable. There was a distinct chill hanging in the still air. I noticed a few ragged gray clouds clinging to the tops of the sharp mountain peaks as if they had been floating by and gotten snagged. I lit a long nine cigar and took the cold in stride. I needed to get used to it. From what Gidd Trevor had told me, the weather in Colorado was likely to be somewhat worse.

From the greeting scowls etched on my partners' faces, I could tell right away they were upset with me. Aside from them and our twelve well-loaded packhorses, I counted twenty-five mounted men along with at least that many more mules and horses burdened with supplies. It was quite obvious we were going to have lots of company on our trip, invited or not.

I suppressed my happiness at having a total of thirty-one armed men to keep those bloodthirsty savages at bay while we opened that rich mine. It was painfully obvious my partners simply didn't understand the situation. They were fortunate to have me to look out for their interests.

Israel Swan rode out to meet me. Jennie's desires had caused me to be a mite late.

"We were all wonderin' when you was gonna show up, Packer," he grumbled. "There's trouble brewin' here."

I walked past him and went to where George Noon held the reins to my readied mule. With a sense of purpose I slipped a foot into the stirrup and swung myself up into the saddle. I had noticed Alf Rankin to be in the forefront of the other group that was faced off with my partners. Then I noticed Wilson Bell had his pistol drawn and cocked.

"Put that away, you blasted idiot," I hissed at him. "Can't you see we're outnumbered dang near four to one?"

I had forgotten how easily numbers confused him, but once the blank look passed from his face, he lowered the hammer on his gun and placed it back in the holster.

"Alf," I hollered, "why don't you and Grady come over here and let's talk this out."

The duo looked at us suspiciously, then rode slowly over. I kept my eyes fixed on Bell in case the fool got a wild hair up his hind end and decided to pull his gun again. If he did I planned to shoot him myself and save others the trouble, but he simply watched.

Not surprisingly his partner, Frank Miller, spoke first. "You men are not velcome to come with us. I haf paid for all of this." He swept an arm at our packhorses. "It is my life savings here and that mine is ours, not yours to take from us."

I kept a poker face and motioned to Alf. "Tell Miller and the rest of us just what your plans are."

This matter had already been gone over closer than a banker checking someone out for a loan by Alf's group and me. My partners had been reluctant to even discuss allowing others to come along and help us out.

Now that we were ready to leave for Colorado they finally had to face the facts.

"Boys," Alf said loudly enough for all to hear. "We're all honest prospectors here and we ain't out to jump anyone's claim. That mine of Packer's belongs to you an' all of us will give you our word on that." Alf turned and we watched as twenty-four men nodded in agreement. "A new gold strike always has room for everybody an' those mountains are plenty big. Packer says there's lots of rich veins there. So long as we work together and respect every man's claim, I can't see no reason for you all to get upset by us coming along."

"Besides that," Grady O'Donald added, "that's Indian country. If we show up in force they'll likely let us be. I never seen a gold mine that done a man any good once he's killed."

Israel Swan said, "He makes a good point, men. If they agree to leave our claim be, I'd reckon that's all we can ask."

"There's plenty of gold up there to go around," I added. "And we sure may need their help."

Frank Miller eyed our packhorses and snorted. "I buy those supplies. They are ours."

Alf said, "We all know it and will respect that. Nobody here is askin' for more than to come along on their own and have a chance at makin' a strike."

James Humphreys rode closer. His breath blew white when he turned to our group and spoke. "This is a free country and to my way of thinkin' those boys have every right to come along. I've seen what savages can do an' let me tell you, it ain't a purty sight to see a bunch of folks that have been shot full of arrows, then scalped and their bodies all chopped up. If they catch you alive, you'll spend a long time beggin' to die. For my part, I bid these boys welcome."

"Reckon I feel the same," Israel said.

George Noon looked at me. "What do you think, Mister Packer?"

"I say we all go as friends."

"Then, sir, I agree," Noon said.

The German butcher cast one more look at the packhorses, then grumbled, *"Ja,* ve vill go as agreed. And as friends."

Wilson Bell nodded his pockmarked face to indicate he would go along with his partner's decision.

"Then we leave here united as one," I announced loudly. To my delight, not a contrary word was spoken by anyone.

"Let's go to Colorado and get rich," some fellow from Rankin's group bellowed.

"Look out, Colorado, here we come," Wilson Bell squeaked.

I couldn't see where any more jawing was necessary. Since I was the leader of this expedition, I spurred my mule and headed east.

Thirty mounted men and thirty-four more well-provisioned pack animals began forming a snaky line behind me as I pointed the way to what, at the time, I felt would be fame and fortune for me.

As it turned out, I was only half right in my prognostication.

Fourteen

The high spirits everyone was floating along on came crashing down that first night. We were making camp alongside a clear running stream in a nice parklike area just south of the Mormon capital of Salt Lake City when some dunderhead went and shot himself in the gut.

It was an accident, of course, and there was no way I could have foreseen or prevented the incident.

Langhorn Bright was eighteen years old and should have known better than to leave a live round underneath the hammer of his revolver. Any person with enough common sense to pour sand out of their boots always keeps that cylinder unloaded. It seems he was in the process of unsaddling his horse when, for some reason, the jughead animal spooked. In the ensuing melee, Bright's pistol came to fall from its holster and land hammer down on the hard earth and discharge. The .44-caliber ball hit the hapless fellow square in the middle of his breadbasket.

While the young man had been laid low by his own foolish actions, I immediately took him under my personal care. I administered laudanum for the pain and did my very best to stop the terrible bleeding. Sadly, my efforts to save his life came to naught. Just as the lowering sun sank golden behind those jagged peaks to the west, Langhorn Bright slipped this mortal coil.

We had brought along plenty of shovels, so the grave digging progressed quite rapidly once we had chopped through the frozen upper crust of earth. I said a few appropriate words over the deceased. This being a prospecting expedition, there was not a single Bible to be found amongst us. I remembered back to when my dear mother used to take me to church on Sundays and drew on what words I could recall.

"Ashes to ashes, dust to dust," I intoned, standing at the head of the shallow grave that now held the deceased. "He may be gone from our presence, but he shall never be forgotten."

"I'll whittle his name on a marker," Alf Rankin said. "Reckon even someone that went an' shot himself deserves a marker." He thought for a moment, then added, "I think maybe I'll just carve L. Bright on it. Langhorn is one helluva long first name to deal with after dark."

A young man with a mustache came forward. Even by the wan light I could make out shiny lines where tears had trickled down his dusty cheeks. "My name's Billy Kincaid. I've knowed Langhorn Bright for over a year now. He was a good partner an' I'd reckon that's about the best thing you can say about a man once he's gone. When we come to a place that's got a post office I'll write his folks up in Cincinnati an' tell 'em Bright got hisself killed, but I reckon I'll not tell 'em more than I have to. He shudda knowed better."

"That's right nice of you, son," James Humphreys said. "Now let's fill in his hole an' build us a fire. It's gonna be colder than a whore's heart out tonight."

Humphreys was not only a decent bartender, he also made a pretty fair weather prophet, to boot.

After all of the excitement it took everyone a while to settle down. Frank Miller fried up a slab of bacon he'd brought along. We ate some of it, then placed the

rest into sliced open biscuits and poured a generous
portion of hot grease into each one. These would serve
us admirably for dinner the next day. When the weather
turns cold there is nothing like bacon grease to keep a
man's energy up.

A couple of bottles of whiskey were uncorked and
passed around in memory of our fallen companion.
When I finally turned in for the night, I slipped into
blissful sleep beneath a canopy of twinkling stars. Then,
sometime before dawn, a storm drifted down from the
north. I awoke to find nearly a foot of snow on the
ground, with more of that miserable white stuff drifting
to earth like feathers.

Israel Swan had a good fire going, and the wonderful
aroma of coffee blended with the scent of pine. I shook
the snow from the canvas under which I had been sleeping, got up, and poured my tin cup full of steaming
brew.

"Durn weather went an' snuck up on us," Swan said.

"Yep," I agreed, blowing a white cloud from my cup.
"Reckon it shouldn't come as any big surprise. It is the
Ninth day of November, you know."

Swan broke into one of his coughing fits, and was
forced to set his coffee cup down to keep from spilling
it. When he gained his wind back, he said, "I hear the
snow gets ass deep to a tall Indian up there in Colorado.
I don't know about this, Al. Maybe we oughtta have
waited until spring to go."

I shook my head and smiled. "We've been over that
ground before. It would be too risky for us. When we
get there and put up some decent shelters things will
look better, trust me."

Swan looked at me grimly. "That's why we're all here,
Al. It's because we *do* trust you."

"Then let's go get that gold."

James Humphreys and George Noon came over and

helped themselves to a cup. They had both overheard our conversation.

James Humphreys spoke first. "No one ever thought this would be easy, but when we come back rich it will all be worth it. Hell, I'm goin' for it even if I have to walk."

"And I'll be trampin' along with you," Noon said.

I chuckled. "Now that's the attitude to take. Let's get the rest of this lazy outfit woke up and headed out. Colorado ain't going to get any closer with us lollygagging around here drinking coffee."

Later, as we rode past the single pine post protruding from a mound of unblemished whiteness with the name of L. Bright carved into it, all of us removed our hats out of respect. I fervently hoped no more of my dear comrades would suffer in this quest.

The snow was letting up and my spirits were high as I reined my mule into the morning glow that pointed the way eastward.

The next nine days of our journey proved relatively uneventful. Game was plentiful, though much of our fare consisted of those large and stringy rabbits found on the sagebrush prairies called "jacks" or "antelope rabbits." While no restaurant that cared to stay in business would dare serve one for supper, the rabbits were abundant, nutritious, and easily killed for they are quite stupid animals. George Noon became quite adept at felling them with rocks, which saved our precious ammunition.

After the snowstorm of that second morning, the weather turned clear and much warmer. The ground was dry and the hooves of our mounts kicked up puffs of dust.

Israel Swan's bouts of coughing increased to the point

where he often had difficulty staying in the saddle. I decided the powder dust was aggravating his condition, and insisted that he ride up front by my side where the air was clean. This seemed to help, but I continued to worry over my partner's health.

It was on a splendidly blue and beautiful morning, the Eighteenth day of November, that we rode down into the canyon that contained the swollen and roily Green River.

During my earlier passage through here I had engaged a large raft constructed of many large logs tied together; this contraption was operated by large ropes and winches that were on each bank of the crossing. This enterprise was, of course, run by families of Mormons for a profit. As I had easily found the main trail days earlier, we came straight onto the only way to cross that flooded, churning, harsh expanse of water.

"That's one mean-lookin' river," Swan said.

"At least we have a way to cross it," I said. "From the looks of that river we'd be here until the Second Coming if we had to wait for it to go down on its own. I sure never thought I'd see a river ever get so wild this time of the year. Floods like this usually happen in the spring when the snows melt."

"That's likely what happened. This Indian summer probably caused a bunch of white fluffy stuff to turn back into water."

I raised my hand and motioned the group of men following us onward to the crossing. There were about a half-dozen cabins or so on each bank of the river that were built well above high water level.

One observation I made about the Mormons was that they were very adept at growing things. Yelling, snotty-nosed kids and barking dogs were in abundance. I held little doubt that the whole of Utah would soon be completely infested with Zealots, for they were hatching more of their own in prodigious numbers. I well understood why having several wives was a necessity for this plan to work; one woman simply wasn't enough for the task.

Each different settlement of Mormons has its own leader. They are called either a bishop or an elder, to the best of my knowledge on the subject. Anyway, the arrangement made it a simple matter to deal with them because the man in charge, whatever his title was, always showed up and made all of the decisions. I appreciated how everyone jumped to follow their leader's orders without complaint. I suppose being threatened with the fires of Hell if you didn't was adequate incentive.

When our party halted by the raft, a tall older man dressed in black who had deep-seated anthracite eyes and a flowing white beard that reached clear to his belly button came to meet us. He introduced himself as Benfro Redd. I didn't need to ask if he was the person in charge of the crossing. The man had such an overbearing presence about him it would have been a waste of good breath to inquire.

"Gentlemen," Redd said, looking straight at me, "I assume you wish to hire a crossing. As you can plainly see the river is at an unusually high flood for this time of year. In my opinion, it would be wise to wait a few days and see if it subsides. We have fresh meat and canned goods for purchase at reasonable prices."

"Ve haf plenty of food, thank you," Frank Miller said from behind me. I hadn't noticed his approach, but was not taken aback by his presence. Ever since he financed most of the trip, the German had increasingly become a pain to deal with.

"How much will you charge to winch us across?" I asked Redd.

The Mormon studied the raging waters and shook his

head. "I'd rather wait a few days. It would be safer, for sure."

"Ve vill not be robbed by you," Miller grumbled. "Mister Packer asked you a question and ve vish an answer."

I noticed a flash of anger in Benfro Redd's dark eyes. "Very well, gentlemen, but in view of the fact our ferry will be placed in danger, I am forced to ask one hundred dollars for each trip across."

Frank Miller grew so angry his voice shook worse than his body usually did. "This is robbery, *robbery!* I vill not pay such a price. It is an outrage."

"Then you'll stay on this side of the river," Redd said coldly.

"Now, Frank," I said calmly, "these folks are only trying to make a living out here in the middle of nowhere. Perhaps if we asked them again, this time in a real nice way, they might take us across for"—I looked at Benfro Redd—"say, fifty dollars just to help us on our way?"

"I vill not be robbed," Miller said again. When a German gets on a track, they stay there like a train.

"We always endeavor to help our fellowman," Redd said, then glared at Miller. "Sometimes it is a real pleasure to see folks get across this river. I will agree to accepting fifty dollars per trip."

I turned to Frank and said, "If we're ever going to see Colorado, you ought to pay the man."

"This money I vill add to my share."

Israel Swan said, "That *is* our agreement with you, Miller. Are we going across or what?"

"*Ja,* I do not see vhere we haf any choice."

The German dug into his coat pocket and came up with fifty dollars in gold coins, which he handed to me.

"This is only enough for one trip," I said sharply. "We have to make at least two."

"No," Miller said, shaking his head. "I haf no more money, ve must make do with vhat I haf given you."

Benfro Redd cast a skeptical eye at our group. "You men are going to take a mighty big risk loading that ferry heavy in this water. I count over fifty head of horses and mules."

"Sixty-four to be exact, sir," I said. "Perhaps you could find it in your heart to do two crossings for this fifty dollars."

Redd shot a fiery glance at Miller and snorted. "Not after being called a robber I'm not. Either give me the money and go across or get out of here. I am not going to be insulted further."

I rode over and handed the irate Mormon five gold eagles. "Thank you, sir, and allow me to apologize for our comrade."

Redd grabbed up the money, nodded at me, then began yelling orders to ready the huge swaying raft for us to load.

I, of course, was the last man to board. There was scant room for me and my mule inside the flimsy pole enclosure that wrapped around that overburdened ferry. Every man had been forced to stay mounted for all of us to fit.

The raft rode low in the roily river and water was running across the top of it ankle deep to our horses. Then a young boy closed the pole gate behind me, latched it, and signaled the winch operators to begin cranking.

Right away I deduced the current was much stronger than anyone had realized. By the time we reached the center of that raging torrent those huge ropes, which were our lifeline, began creaking ominously.

A horse on the upward side whinnied with fear and began bucking wildly. This had the effect of forcing the rest of those jugheads to the other side. The stress of the shifting weight was more than one of the ropes could take. It snapped like a rifle shot.

The ferry spun, then suddenly as a snake can strike, it edged sideways into the swift current and flipped, sending all of us plunging into the cold and deadly swirling waters of the Green River.

Fifteen

During my seafaring years I had become an excellent swimmer. This skill was severely tested as I desperately began making my way to the distant shore. The waters were terribly frigid and my coat and boots added greatly to my difficulties. I remember watching helplessly while squealing horses and one screaming man swirled past me to become lost in the strong current. The only thing I could do was strive for safety and save myself.

I finally managed to grab hold of a protruding branch and used it to drag myself onto the sandy shore. You can imagine my joy at finding George Noon and Israel Swan were on the bank only a short distance away. I shook as much of that cold water I could from my person and ran to see how my partners were faring.

"Damn it all, Packer," Swan said after a few coughs. "I shudda stayed in Bingham City."

I looked at him and Noon. Aside from being cold and shook, they were not in any immediate danger. "At least you have survived. I must go and save any lives I can."

At that time I noticed Wilson Bell and Alf Rankin bobbing close to shore, doing their best to keep Frank Miller afloat. I waded into the current while using a bush for safety and dragged them onto the bank. Miller was white as a ghost and shaking like an aspen leaf.

Aside from being drenched, the other two looked none the worse for the wear.

"Dang, but that sawed-off runt of a German's heavier than he looks," Rankin swore after catching his breath. "Rescuin' a cast-iron cookstove wouldda been easier."

Miller attempted to rise to a sitting position only to groan and fall back down. Wilson Bell and I went to help him up. When I grabbed onto his soaked felt coat I knew his problem. The miser had sewn hundreds of twenty-dollar gold pieces in the heavy lining. From the immense weight of both him and that coat, he undoubtedly had thousands of dollars on his person. And we had suffered a terrible disaster simply because he was too cheap to help his fellowman.

"Damn you, Frank Miller," I yelled. "You have caused us this ruin."

"Hey, Packer, glad to see you all are safe and sound." James Humphreys' voice boomed happily from high ground behind us. "From up here it looks like most of us made it. There's a good dozen or so on the bank upstream. The Mormons are comin' packin' ropes and dry coats. Can't see any of our horses or mules, though. Reckon those loaded packs an' saddles done went and sunk 'em all like they was bricks."

I glared at the shaking, pale man who had caused our misfortune. Frank Miller rolled his rheumy eyes and groaned pitifully.

"He's *your* partner," I growled to Bell. "Take care of him for I could care less if he dies." I then strode up the bank to join Humphreys.

Later that day, after warming myself by the stove in a Mormon's cabin and becoming revived by eating a bowl of delicious bean soup along with several thick slices of bread, I was able to begin tallying the depth of our losses.

My benefactor, Samuel Kent, turned out to be the bishop

in charge of the crossing. He was rightfully conscience-stricken that Mister Redd had not shown a true Christian spirit by failing to allow us to make two trips.

"The Lord has seen fit to be merciful this day," the Bishop Kent said, squeezing the Book of Mormon so tightly his knuckles turned white. "Two of your number washed up safely on yon shore." He beamed. "Two of our lines across are intact so we are not only able to send across messages, the ferry will be able to be rebuilt once some more logs are obtained."

"Praise the Lord," I said somewhat testily. "How many men got drowned?"

Samuel Kent pursed his lips. "It seems from what we know at this time, six souls went to their final reward."

"What of our horses and supplies?"

The Bishop shook his head sadly. "I'm sorry to say all were lost in the accident. Any animal burdened so heavily as all of yours were stood no chance in the swift current of the flooded river. You must be strong, my good man, and trust in the Good Lord to see you through these terrible times."

"Thank you for the food and allowing me to warm myself. Now, my good sir, I must see to my partners."

James Humphreys tossed another log into the fireplace of the cabin we had been given, then turned his back to warm himself. "Dang, I wisht those Mormons had some whiskey to drink or at least some coffee. After a day like this one a man is in need of somethin' to settle his nerves."

"All is gone," Frank Miller said, leaning against a wall, his body shaking and his eyes vacant. "All *ist* gone—my money *ist kaput*."

Israel Swan sipped on a steaming cup of sage tea. This seemed to be the only beverage the Mormons felt a person could consume and still get past Saint Peter. "Dang you, Miller, if you hadn't gone an' played poor we'd be ridin' to Colorado an' still have us some whiskey."

"Kaput," the butcher repeated. "All *ist kaput."*

None of us knew what he meant, or really cared. It was plain to everyone that he alone had caused our disaster. I just shook my head sadly when Wilson Bell brought over a heavy blanket he had warmed by the fire and draped it over Miller. The only thing that squeaky-voiced weasel really cared about was the old man's money. That much was plain as the nose on your face.

"We must forge bravely ahead, men," I said. "For that gold mine hasn't changed a single bit."

Frank Miller shivered like a wet dog. "I must haf a horse to ride."

"Well, the one you had got sunk," Humphreys said. "And the only ones the Mormons have to sell are on the other side of that blasted river. And that spells either a long wait or a long walk in my book."

"I *ist* not vell," Miller said.

Israel Swan glared at him. "If you hadn't been such a skinflint, all of us would be in better shape and six more would be alive. There ain't been anyone else come wandering up so I reckon they're drowned for sure."

"This bickering isn't going to get us to Colorado," I said calmly. "We have plenty of time to walk the distance before the snow melts up there anyway. I say we bargain with the Mormons for some guns and ammo to replace what we lost, add in some warm clothes and a few essentials we can carry, and head out."

Wilson Bell squeaked, "Mister Miller is the only one with any money to buy anything with, an' he's in no shape to walk all that ways."

I knew the only thing that would motivate that hard-headed German. "Then he can stay here and forfeit his share of the mine. Our agreement was to make the split *after* we got it opened up. If Miller can't make it, then he's out."

Swan broke into another coughing fit that gave the butcher time to consider my words before he spoke.

"We vill walk to Colorado," Frank announced weakly. "But if I spend more money to buy guns and stuff, we vill walk not so fast that I cannot keep up."

"That's the spirit," I said cheerfully. "Now why don't you slice out a few of those double eagles you've got sewed into that coat of yours and then I'll go see what the Mormons have for sale on this side of the river."

Israel Swan glared at the butcher as he handed him his pocket knife. "You don't need to say it. We'll add this money to what you're got coming from the first gold shipment."

At first light the next morning we left Green River Crossing to begin our long trek to Colorado. Aside from my five partners, Alf Rankin and fifteen of his original group accompanied us. Grady O'Donald had unfortunately been among those six poor souls who had been swept to their demise beneath the roily waters. The two men who had washed up on the other shore had sent a message across stating that they were returning to Bingham City. That decision would be their loss.

From the Mormons I had been able to obtain only a meager supply of guns and weapons. I did, however, purchase some nice warm coats, fur hats, and blankets at fair prices. I was gratified that my pepperbox pistol and wonderfully sharp bowie knife had not been lost. Surprisingly, I had even been able to obtain a full box of cartridges for it. I also carried a Sharps "big fifty" rifle along with a dozen shells for it rattling in my coat pocket. Any Indian within a half mile could be blown out of his saddle with this weapon.

All told, our entire troop packed six usable rifles along with an odd assortment of pistols and knives. Wilson Bell had bought an eight-gauge single-shot shotgun that he was quite proud of. I was looking forward to the first time he fired that cannon. I knew the recoil would lay the skinny idiot out like a rug.

The morning sun glowed cheery on the eastern horizon of the vast rolling plains that faced us. While we had suffered a minor setback due to a skinflint, we were once again progressing onward toward that beckoning rainbow's end of vast riches in Colorado. It would simply take us longer to get there than I had originally estimated.

I was very proud of myself for having had the excellent foresight to have blazed all of those trees from that lake to the mine site. My compass and book containing those meticulous bearings I had taken on the various mountain peaks from my treasure house were in the saddlebags of my mule. I supposed that stupid animal to be still rolling along the river bottom and well on its way to the Arizona Territory by now.

There was no need to worry anyone over trifles. I slowed my pace to allow a coughing Israel Swan and the stumbling, shaking butcher to catch up with me. I was grateful gold is something that never spoils.

Sixteen

"A three-legged turtle sufferin' from gout would get to Colorado afore we will," James Humphreys said to me about a month later. "That German butcher has to rest for an hour after he passes wind, an' Swan piles on the agony when we have to wait for him to get over one of his coughing fits."

"Patience is a virtue, my friend," I answered. "We must care for the weakest of our companions even though it may be trying."

I could not fault Humphreys for being somewhat upset with our progress, or lack of it. On a good day we traversed an entire five miles. We had very few "good" days.

I shall not weary you with all of my trials and tribulations during this part of our journey. Save to say my usual patient nature and kindhearted disposition became taxed quite severely.

Drinking water had become a problem early on. From the money Frank Miller had reluctantly parted with, I only had enough left to purchase two canteens, weapons to protect us from Indians being deemed more important. An occasional sinkhole filled with the foulest-tasting alkali water imaginable was all that saved us from dying of thirst.

Those large, ungainly, and stringy-to-eat rabbits of the

"jack" variety again become our primary source of food, though once in a while we were lucky enough to shoot a deer, which provided the entire group with a feast. I must say that Miller and his imbecile partner did know their stuff when it came to butchering meat. The German had a thin-bladed knife with a bone handle of a type I had never seen before. He kept it honed to a remarkably keen edge and by using this instrument he made thin strips of jerky, which were draped over a green stick and slow-roasted over a low fire. Venison prepared this way is delightfully tasty and yielded us with meals for days afterward, for meat made into jerky will last indefinitely.

When all of the venison had been eaten and rabbits scarce, everyone was forced to make do as best they could. This foraging for food led to the death of Billy Kincaid, the friend of that dunderhead Bright who had shot himself in the gut when we first started our journey. I suppose they had been partners for a mite too long and some of Bright's lack of common sense must have stuck on young Kincaid.

About six weeks out of Green River Crossing when our supplies were at a low ebb, Kincaid chanced upon a slow-moving prairie dog and killed it with a stick. He slung the dead animal over his shoulder and packed it around for a couple of days before he got around to cooking it. The first evening afterward we had shot a brace of rabbits, so he didn't bother with it. When he did get around to eating the thing, he immediately developed a case of the bloody flux and died after a day of writhing in pain.

"I tried to tell him that prairie dog was diseased," Alf Rankin said while we were delayed by the incident. "Those things generally move quicker than a whore reachin' for a fifty-dollar gold piece."

"Nah," Humphreys said, "he just shudda gutted the

thing. Even a coyote has better sense than to eat some critter that's been danglin' over someone's shoulder for two friggin' days. That prairie dog wouldn't have done him no harm if he'd cared for it proper."

When Billy Kincaid passed on we had no shovels to dig a grave with. Rocks being in abundance, we decided to cover him over with slabs of white sandstone.

"This is sort of like a grave," James Humphreys commented after surveying our handiwork. "The hole just extends up instead of down. I reckon Billy don't mind a whit. Leastwise the varmints will leave him be."

I recall no one said any words over him. After hauling in those rocks, all of us were plenty tuckered out. I did stand up a nice flat rock to suffice for a headstone, however. There was no way to carve anything on it, but at least the good intentions were present.

A few days later George Noon came to me as we were making camp for the night. I could tell from the stern expression on his young face that he was clearly worried.

"Mister Packer," he paused, his gaze fixed across that barren and vast land. "After Billy went an' died, I've been wonderin' if any of us'll make it to that mine of yours. There was thirty-one of us started this trip. Now I count just twenty-one of us are all that's left."

I placed a firm hand on the lad's shoulder. "Now, partner, if you think back on the matter, two of those there men are still fit as a fiddle. The other eight were just a tad unlucky, and for all we know some of them might have washed up safe and sound further down the river. Why, anyway, the worst is well behind us now. Keep focused on yon horizon, my friend, and trust me, for I shall soon lead you to share in gold the likes of which the riches of King Solomon would pale against."

I spoke loudly so my rousing speech was able to be

heard by everyone. This had a splendid effect on the
group, for that next day we made nearly six miles before
some idiot caused the sole of one of his boots to come
off, which forced us to make camp for the night.

Our Christmas gift that winter of Eighteen Seventy-
Three was finally striking upon the life-giving Grand or
Colorado River as it is now known. From here we merely
had to follow its course to where the clear running waters of the Gunnison entered. From there we could ad-
here to that mighty river until coming to the easily
recognizable Lake Fork, which flowed directly from that
sparkling lake in the rugged valley below my rich mine.

From here on our journey would be as simple as following a set of train tracks.

Good and pure drinking water no longer presented
a problem. Wild game along any river was always in
abundance. Even here at the roily Grand, ducks and
geese flew overhead in prodigious numbers. Deer were
plentiful as were wild turkeys. After the wastelands of
eastern Utah this was like coming onto paradise.

There was one small detail I had yet to bring up. We
were on the north side of this wide and rolling river
and we had to cross, somehow, to the south side. After
our unfortunate experience at Green River Crossing, I
decided to delay in this disclosure until after everyone
had gotten their bellies full.

Earlier this year I had forded further up. Even then
that red mule of mine had struggled against the swift
current. A few days of lollygagging along the north bank
and packing away food would make my suggestion of
building a raft easier for the men to take, that was for
certain.

I well remember dwelling on how we could use strips

of deer hides to bind logs together with when the task suddenly become moot.

Israel Swan, who had eyes like an eagle, began sputtering to gain wind while pointing wild-eyed and with a paling face toward a distant ridge behind us.

"Christ on a crutch, boys," Swan finally managed to yell. "There's Indians ever dad-blasted place I look. We're about to get ourselves massacred!"

Seventeen

Israel Swan's loud yelling coupled with the stress of the situation cost him all of his wind. He dropped to his knees, wheezing and coughing with a face so pale it looked as if he was fixing to deprive those savages of the fun of killing him.

It amazed me that an entire war party of Indians could have lined themselves up on a bluff a few hundred yards away and watched us for who knew how long before one man finally caught sight of them. I suppose taking several weeks to walk across a hundred miles of wasteland dragging along an old German butcher had taken its toll.

There were a passel of Indians, though, no matter how they came to sneak upon us. I counted at least two dozen of those Redskins. From the way they just kept watching us without attacking, I assumed there were many more moving about. Once all was in readiness, I held little doubt they would descend upon us like a plague.

Wilson Bell ran to my side holding out that eight-gauge shotgun he had yet to fire. "We'll at least take a bunch of them to Hell with us," he squeaked.

I sighed and called our small and woefully armed band together. "Boys," I said with more conviction than I felt. "We are outnumbered and at desperate odds. If we stand firm and make a good fight of it, we may be able to drive them off."

James Humphreys said grimly, "Save the last few bullets for your friends and the final one for yourself. Stick the barrel in your mouth or be looking into it when you pull the trigger. Either way you do it, it will be a lot easier death than what will happen if you're taken captive."

"You mean for us to kill ourselves?" some sprout sobbed.

"Sonny boy," Alf Rankin said, "everybody's that's been born is waitin' for a time and place to die. This way you won't have to keep on wonderin' about the when part."

On that cheery note George Noon bolted up and began pointing a shaking finger toward that bluff. "Oh, God!" he yelled. "Here they come."

Every man took up shelter behind trees, fallen logs, or boulders and began preparations for what we knew would be the most desperate fight of our lives.

As I was the leader of our group, I grabbed up my Sharps rifle and stood to meet those savages head-on. It is the lot of stalwart men to fall first in defense of their comrades.

I quickly deduced something peculiar was happening. Those Indians were casually loping along single file toward us. When they made their way closer to my position, I could not see a drawn gun among them. This was definitely *not* the way I had expected savages to behave.

"Don't shoot at them, boys," I turned and yelled to my men. "From the way they're acting I suspect they may not want to mess with us. Maybe I can go parley with them and work something out that will get us through this."

I heard murmurings of admiration for my braveness.

I leaned the Sharps against a leafless cottonwood, then turned and began walking toward those hostiles and my fate. In what seemed like a moment I stood to face their leader. Snaking along that trail down from the bluff behind him were dozens of braves. I remember how the bright sunlight bounced off patches of snow and flashed against the many silver beads and bracelets of the Indian chief. He held up his hand to halt the war party.

I was in a quandary as to how we would be able to communicate. What few Indians I had been around spoke with a series of grunts. Then I remembered they sometimes employed a primitive sign language. I made a step closer, forced a smile on my face, and displayed an open palm to indicate I held no weapon.

"How," I said. "White men come here in peace."

I thought I was dreaming when that Indian spoke with a mischievous glint in his eye. He not only addressed me in perfect English, I detected a distinct Yankee inflection in his voice. "That's nice. It always ruins my day when people start trying to kill each other. By the way, my name is not 'How.' I am Powder Face, subchief under Ouray, ruler of all of the Ute Tribes."

"We're not looking for any trouble," I said, dumbstruck.

"I would hope not," Powder Face answered. "From the looks of your group, I think perhaps a good meal would serve your needs far better than picking a fight with our peaceful hunting party."

A cold chill trickled down my spine when I heard an ominous metallic click from far behind me. I knew it had to be Wilson Bell cocking that shoulder cannon he was so proud of.

"I had better go tell my men things are all right here," I said quickly. "Some of them get kind of skittish when Indians come around."

"Please do that," Powder Face said. "We shall be most

glad to share our food with you. Then you must tell me how you came to be here and in such a terrible condition."

"I'll be happy to do that," I said, then spun and went back to join our group before that idiot Bell went and ruined everything by shooting a perfectly good Indian out of his saddle.

"Put your guns away, men," I said when I approached our position. "I've got things worked out with those Indians."

Humphreys kept his pistol aimed past me. "Savages can be mighty tricky, Packer. Don't trust 'em."

"Sounded to me like you two was talkin' in English," George Noon said.

That damn kid could hear a mouse fart. "Their leader is called Powder Face and he's better at speaking American than Ole Miller is. Remember that when he gets here."

"Don't be a fool, Packer." Humphreys was shaking worse than the butcher. It saddened me he had such a fear of Indians that it clouded his judgment. "They'll scalp us the moment we let our guard down."

"They're a hunting party from Chief Ouray's camp," I said. "If we don't go shoot at them, Powder Face told me they'll share their food with us."

It had been a long while since we had had enough to eat. I figured those last words of mine would calm everyone down. With the exception of Humphreys and Bell, I was correct.

"I ain't puttin' my gun away," Humphreys said. "They'll never take me alive."

Bell still had that shoulder cannon of his cocked and pointed toward the Indians. I stepped over and snatched it from his grasp. The blasted thing must have weighed twenty pounds. I lowered the hammer with my thumb, then opened it and slid the shell out.

"Give me the rest of 'em," I said, holding up that big brass cartridge. "*All* of them."

Bell blinked like he was staring into the sun. After a moment he reached into his coat and handed over five more shells. I closed the breech on the shotgun and returned it to him. "Now calm yourself down," I said, then turned my attention toward the wild-eyed bartender.

"James," I said, "if you'll put your piece away, I give you my solemn word that I'll blow your brains out with my gun if one of those Indians even so much as winks wrong. I just think should you be mistaken about things, it would be a terrible waste to go and kill ourselves before it becomes a necessity."

"They offer us food," Frank Miller said. "Ve are all hungry to the death. I tink ve should see if they speak the truth."

"I reckon we oughtta let Packer play his hand," Humphreys finally said. He glared at me as he holstered his Colt. "If you get me killed by those savages I ain't never gonna forgive you."

"That won't happen," I said. "Like I promised, I'll be proud to kill you myself long before any of those Indians can."

Humphreys cocked a querulous eye toward me and decided it might be healthier if he kept his trap shut.

Now that I had disarmed that flaming idiot Wilson Bell and calmed down a spooked bartender, I decided it was safe to invite the most educated and hospitable Indian I had ever met to join us. A rumble deep in my stomach put haste to my steps when I went back to visit with Powder Face.

"You attended *Harvard!*" James Humphreys was aghast at Powder Face. He shook his head and grabbed up another chuck of raspberry pemmican. "How in the world did that come about?"

Having his belly full had changed the bartender's opinion of Indians considerably. Everyone of our troop ate ravenously on the jerky and pemmican the Utes generously provided in great quantities. Even Wilson Bell had decided that filling his potato trap was better than shooting someone. I was gratified my diligence and levelheadedness had borne fruit.

Powder Face was not much older than me. I judged him to be in his middle twenties. He wore his long, black hair in braids that draped over his chest. All told, he looked very much like the other Utes who accompanied him. Although none of them spoke good English, they did manage to communicate with us. What set Powder Face apart was his shiny black leather boots.

"Moccasins will freeze your feet off in the wintertime," was his response when I questioned him about them. "All they're good for is sneaking up on someone. I don't do that. I believe it to be a lack of etiquette."

I lit up a cigar Powder Face had given me and listened with great interest to his answer to Humphreys' question.

Powder Face grinned. "I not only attended Harvard, I graduated third in my class. I also excelled in sports such as rowing. But to answer your question, some years ago, Chief Ouray, in his wisdom, foresaw that the Indian tribes would have to deal with the white man. It had become quite plain that the government in Washington could not be trusted to honor any agreements they made."

Alf Rankin chuckled. "It doesn't take a Harvard education to figure *that* out."

Powder Face did not grin any longer. "Our way of life was threatened with extinction. Too many times Chief Ouray had witnessed or learned of the government's lack of ability to keep its words, and nearly every time the Indians paid with their lives and their land.

"I was chosen to become educated by the white men, to learn the motivations behind their actions, and hopefully to guide our people into a lasting peace."

I spoke up. "We're all glad you have decided not to go around killing innocent prospectors."

Powder Face's expression turned sad. "I believe that I have learned too much. The white race is motivated by greed for possessions; things, land, and of course gold. The yellow metal that causes men to destroy the very land on which they live to get their hands on it. Any man who would do such a thing is insane and not responsible for his actions. The People do not kill those who are not sane. This would go against the teachings of any god you care to name."

"Are you sayin' we're all nuts?" Alf Rankin said sharply.

"I do not need to judge this," Powder Face said. "Look at yourselves. All of you are dressed in rags. The worst of the winter is yet to come and already you were starving. I know you did this to yourselves in a quest for gold. There is no other explanation possible."

"*Ja,* ve haf a gold mine," Frank Miller interjected.

"Then it will still be there next summer," Powder Face said, motioning toward the south with his hand. "Come, all of you, to Chief Ouray's encampment for the duration of winter. We will provide you with lodges and food. Then when the snows melt, if you have not recovered, you may go chase after your gold."

James Humphreys snorted, "Then you'll send braves out to kill us for mining in your mountains. There ain't no Indians gonna let us do that."

I noticed a wetness in Powder Face's eyes when he continued. "We no longer have any claim to the shining purple mountains. A man by the name of Felix Brunot and Chief Ouray have agreed to this. I told him there was no other choice. The once mighty Utes will now have but a fraction of the great lands on which we used to roam free. At least we will have *some* lands to call home. I only pray that for once, Washington will honor an agreement."

My heart leapt. *The treaty had been signed.*

Then it struck me like a bolt of lightning that all of my efforts to recruit a small army had been totally unnecessary. I simply could have ridden back to Colorado, filed my claim, and gotten rich. Now I was stuck with five idiots for partners and had given them half interest to my mine. Hell, those bloodthirsty Indians Gidd Trevor had ranted about were even offering me food and shelter until I could go about opening my treasure house.

For me to admit to being upset would be akin to Mrs. Lincoln saying that she hadn't really enjoyed her evening at Ford's Theater.

Eighteen

"How are we going to get across the river?" I asked Powder Face as we rode horseback along the north bank the next morning. The Utes had luckily brought along enough extra mounts to use as pack animals that we could all ride. After having walked for over a hundred miles, it was a delight to have decent transportation again. Even being forced to ride bareback gave no reason for complaint by anyone.

There had been no need to discuss Powder Face's offer to go to Chief Ouray's winter camp with him. When he said the Utes had given up the San Juan Mountains for mining, this had the effect of making everyone simply more anxious to head to the camp. Being offered horses to ride for just part of the distance made his invitation even more attractive.

"You may cross the river however you choose." Powder Face had his mischievous grin back. "Most of us will likely use the bridge. The water is uncomfortably cold this time of the year."

"Bridge!" I exclaimed. "When and how did a bridge get built across the Gunnison River?"

"It was completed this fall," Powder Face answered. "There are some benefits to negotiating an agreement with the government of the United States. They never seem to quibble over spending money on building things. This bridge was one of *my* little triumphs."

I thought back to Green River Crossing. "I wish those Mormons over in Utah would make a deal or two with Washington. They really need a few bridges built there mighty bad."

Powder Face laughed. "At the rate they're multiplying, I predict they'll likely control the government one day. The People do not frown on a man taking more than one wife, but in my opinion, Brigham Young's bunch is crazier than gold prospectors. Putting up with *one* woman is enough to drive most men batty."

Three days later we rode into Chief Ouray's winter encampment. Today this would be smack dab in the middle of the town of Montrose, Colorado. Smoke spired into the chill air from openings in the tops of what appeared to be literally hundreds of tepees. Scores of yapping mongrels and screaming kids ran to greet us.

It was hard to accept that just a short time hence, all of us believed only our scalps would ever make an entrance into an Indian village such as this one. Even James Humphreys, a man who was prepared to shoot himself in the eye rather than face a few Utes, had a look of serenity pasted on his bearded visage.

Powder Face produced a rock from one of his saddlebags and bounced it off the back of some mutt that tried to take a nip out of his horse's ankle. The cur yelped with pain and ran to hide behind a tepee.

"Darn dogs," Powder Face complained. "If they were not so good to eat I'd get rid of every last one of them."

"You eat dogs?" Alf Rankin asked from behind us.

"As do you, my friend," Powder Face said. "What kind of meat do you think was in the pemmican you've been eating with so much relish these past few days?"

I looked back and noticed Alf had turned a little green around the gills, but at least he had the good sense to keep quiet.

We tied our horses to a long rail in front of the largest and most decorated of the tepees. I figured this lodge must belong to Chief Ouray. I was quite surprised to see that hitching rail. It was becoming more and more apparent to me that I had a lot to learn about these so-called savages. The very fact they had wisely given up their claim to those mountains that held my rich mine proved beyond any doubt the Ute Indians packed around more good sense on their shoulders than a lot of white folks I could think of.

I was completely taken aback by the young lady who tossed back the flap of the giant tepee and glided outside. She wore a tight-fitting doeskin dress that fit her lithe form so well it was as if she had been melted down and poured into it. I had never before set eyes on such a beautiful woman. Jennie, back in Bingham City, was built like a spittoon in comparison to this raven-haired Indian maiden with high cheekbones and laughing eyes.

"This is Chipeta, wife of our Chief Ouray," Powder Face said, dashing my fantasies into smithereens. "Come with me into the lodge. I will introduce you to him. Ouray speaks the English language quite well, even though he has picked up an odd accent from Otto Mears, who is presently at the Los Pinos Agency."

I felt a tingling sensation on my skin and my sap was on the rise when I passed close by Chipeta as I followed Powder Face into the tepee.

Turtle John had maintained that all women were witches who could cast all sorts of spells over men. After setting eyes on this fair maiden, I knew he had been correct. A beckoning glance from Chipeta would cause a Baptist preacher to sin without a second thought on the matter.

"Alferd Packer, this is Ouray, Chief of all the People,"

Powder Face said with a sweeping motion of his arm toward me.

"How do you do, sir," I said politely, and offered my hand to the man sitting on a stack of elk skins smoking a corncob pipe. Since my training in Ute etiquette was somewhat limited, I hoped this was adequate.

My eyes adjusted to the dim light inside the lodge rather quickly and I was able to size up the chief while awaiting a reply. Ouray was, I figured, about forty years old. With both Indians and Celestials, age is difficult to determine. He wore his long black hair in braids that draped over a beaded vest. What surprised me most was his squatness. Even sitting he was as wide as he was tall. I remember thinking that he must have grown up with a rock tied on his head that caused him to develop sideways as well as straight up. Ouray also had some fuzz over his upper lip, which is about the closest thing to whiskers an Indian seems to be able to sprout.

"Sit down, Mister Packer," Ouray said pleasantly, motioning to another stack of skins. "We will smoke and visit."

I nodded and sat down, making sure to cross my legs like I noticed his were. "Thank you. I have heard of the custom of smoking the peace pipe."

Powder Face chuckled and plopped down beside me. "You've been reading too many dime novels, Al. Those things are written by men who have never been west of the Hudson River." He handed me a long nine cigar. "We have taken quite a liking to these. Ouray, however, does not care for cigars and prefers his own blend of pipe tobacco."

"The finest Kentucky burley aged for many months in rum," Ouray said. "I am supplied with it by General Adams, who introduced me to its pleasures." His gaze turned serious. "My braves tell me you and your people are crazy because of the sickness of the yellow rocks.

This is a sad thing. Smoke your cigar with me. I will have my medicine men do a dance later on and say many prayers. Maybe it will be enough to cure you all. Sometimes the Great Spirit is in a good mood."

"Thank you for your many kindnesses," I said.

Then I nearly bit the end off my cigar when Chipeta suddenly appeared, reached down, took a burning stick from the fire that blazed in the center of the lodge, and offered to light my long nine. Her approach had been silent as a cat and her presence unnerved me.

"Our women consider it an honor to care for the needs of men," Powder Face said. "She will be saddened if you do not allow her to light your cigar."

I nodded, leaned forward, and touched my cigar to the flame. The lovely lady smiled at me in a manner that caused my earlier maladies to return. She lit Powder Face's smoke, replaced the faggot in the fire, then floated silently as a cloud from the tepee, which allowed my head and mouth to function once again.

Ouray must have already had a fire built in his pipe. He inhaled deeply and regarded me through the cloud of smoke he puffed out. "You and your party must stay here until the sun warms the earth. We will offer you warm lodges and food. The yellow rocks that have captured your soul have been in those mountains since the Great Manitou himself walked this earth. They will still be there next spring, if you have not recovered your sanity by then."

I said, "All of us are very grateful for your kindness, Chief Ouray. I will speak to my people. Perhaps they will agree to stay here for the winter."

Powder Face said seriously, "It is a simple decision, Alferd. Anyone who goes into the high country this time of year will surely die. I do not believe gold will be of much use in the Spirit World, even for the white men."

I smoked that wonderful cigar and mulled things over

in my mind. I had not had any tobacco other than the smoke Powder Face had given me earlier since my supply of long nines got washed away with the red mule. One thing I learned to admire about Indians was how they never seemed to get into a dither over making decisions.

What bothered me most of all was the fact Ouray had agreed to that treaty. This meant any simpleton could stumble across my rich strike, remove my claim papers from the rock cairn I had built, and replace them with their own. From Israel Swan, I had learned that to make my claim legal I needed to have filed it with the courthouse in Saguache. I did not feel it prudent to mention the fact I hadn't already done so. I'm rather certain this small detail might have upset Frank Miller to the point he could have balked at financing our expedition.

While I held no doubts the entire San Juan Mountain range would be crawling with prospectors next summer, I could see no harm in resting here among these friendly Indians for a while and building up our strength. The more I thought of the lovely Chipeta, the more sound-minded the idea of lollygagging here for a while became.

"Yes," I said at length. "I am convinced of your reasoning. We shall stay here at least for a while. But we must leave at the earliest possible time. The snows aren't very much at all around here. I can't see where the mountains could be *that* bad."

Ouray kept his stoic face. "If you were up there in those mountains you would know the truth. The People have lived here for many centuries. We know the mountains in winter and we respect them." He stared at Powder Face. "I must tell our medicine men to work extra hard."

Powder Face said to me, "I will show you the lodges

we have prepared. But first I must tell you of our most sacred rule that we cannot allow to be broken."

I said nothing and watched while Chief Ouray fished a cigar box from beneath a bearskin. His expression displayed no emotion when he opened it and displayed the contents.

Inside that wooden box were at least two dozen black and shriveled male members with the scrotums still attached.

"We know that you and your friends are crazy," Ouray said. "Our women must be protected by any means. To have a child by a man that has lost his mind is a terrible thing. Sometimes talk is not enough to convince our guests to avoid lying with our women. The problem is a simple one to cure. Most men recover within a few days."

"Make sure your group understands our rule on this matter," Powder Face said. "Indians do not employ lawyers, simply a very sharp knife."

My throat had become parched. "Please rest assured that I *will* tell them to leave your women alone."

Powder Face patted me on the shoulder and smiled. "Then come with me and I will see that you and your men are settled."

Chief Ouray remained seated on the stack of hides. "We will smoke again and talk of many things."

"Thank you again, my Chief," I said as I turned and left the tepee with Powder Face.

Chipeta stood smiling when I passed close by. Now I could see the crow's-feet at the corners of eyes and wrinkles in her face. It amazed me the tricks that light can play on a woman's beauty. Chipeta, I decided, was not pretty at all, and I wondered deeply how I could have been so mistaken earlier.

Nineteen

"What do you mean that ve must stay here all winter?" Frank Miller growled. "I haf put my money and my faith in this mine of yours, Packer, and now you say ve do nothing while others might steal from us our gold."

All twenty-one of us were jammed together in the lodge I had been given to share with my five partners. This made for mighty close quarters. A few thousand cooties that had called the mass of animal hides inside the tepees home had removed themselves and taken up residence in our beards and hair or inside our clothing. The resulting itching tended to shorten everyone's tempers considerably.

I nodded agreeably at the butcher and decided to soothe his ruffled feathers. "Miller is absolutely right about the fact that we need to get after the gold. However, every single one of us is plenty worn out since we were forced to walk here after that ramshackle Mormon ferry caused us a disaster. I say we rest up for a spell. It's only getting on the first of the year. From what Powder Face tells me, there's likely to be too much snow up there to do much mining anyway."

James Humphreys said, "Those Injuns are treatin' us pretty good. I can't see where a breathing spell would hurt us any."

"There sure ain't much snow hereabouts," Alf Rankin

commented. Then he added, "But I can't see where we need to go runnin' off up there right away. Likely enough there won't be any other prospectors hittin' those mountains for a few weeks or so."

We were forced to halt our meeting until Israel Swan worked his way through a coughing fit. When he finally got his wind back he said, "Boys, there ain't no way any of us can do any good at chasin' gold veins until we can see the dad-blasted ground. I say we stay right here until the weather turns warm."

Frank Miller snorted, "Then ve will find others haf already gotten to the mine and ve are too late. I haf paid much and I say ve go soon and ve be *there* when the snow melts."

"Okay, men," I said. "We seem to be in agreement to rest here for a while. I'm certain you know that we will need a good supply of food and warm clothes before we head out. Start sticking back what you can. In a few days I'll see if I can bargain with Ouray, maybe trade him a rifle or such for a supply of jerky and pemmican. We'll be at the mine before the rush starts, but we need to be prepared before we leave here."

"The Utes have been plenty decent toward us," George Noon said.

Wilson Bell squeaked, "They ain't got a lot of choice. The calvary'll come and wipe 'em out if they mess with white folks."

I glared at Bell and forced back a grin. "And don't forget just how pretty and available those Ute girls are. I'm betting you'd enjoy dipping your wick with one of them a whole bunch."

All of us had a good chuckle. Then after some small talk, Alf Rankin's group retired to their tepees for some much-needed rest.

* * *

A few cold snaps and moderate snowstorms kept everyone content to remain in Ouray's encampment the entire month of January. While I had stayed in camp and kept Chief Ouray and Powder Face entertained by smoking with them and telling them stories of my sea-faring years—they were both captivated by my tales of the ocean—other members of our group had joined in hunting parties. The Utes were most generous in dividing up the meat to be smoked into jerky or pounded with dried berries and fruits into pemmican.

The Indians were most fascinated by Frank Miller's ivory-handled knife. The manner in which the thin razor-sharp blade sliced thin strips of lean meat for curing caused the butcher to receive many offers for his stiletto. He dismissed them all with a shrug and grunt. Many comely squaws smiled and offered other incentives to obtain his knife. Since the lead had gone out of his pencil, he paid them no mind. I found this disappointing, even more so that Wilson Bell still had all of his equipment intact. Occasionally people just refuse to act in a manner you wish they would.

The first week of February was a restless time for my five partners. Game had been very plentiful and we had managed to lay in a store of food that would last us for many weeks. This fidgety feeling was enhanced by clear blue skies and a return of warmer weather.

Alf Rankin and most of his group had become lazy from eating too much and lollygagging around. They had voiced to me that they were quite content to hang around the encampment until Chief Ouray said it was safe to head into the white peaks to the south that beckoned with a siren's song.

A full moon was hanging low and bloodred on the

night of February Eighth when my partners and I held a clandestine and fateful meeting in our tepee.

"Men," I said as we sat in a circle around the flickering fire. "From the looks of things we're going to have an early spring. If we want to get a jump on everyone that's going to be heading into the San Juans, I believe we ought to plan on leaving."

"I haf been worried,' Frank Miller said. "I tink Al Packer is right about ve should go now. The snow is melting and ve haf much food to eat."

"What about the others?" Israel Swan said. "Alf Rankin and those boys have stuck with us this far."

I said, "They aren't ready to leave just yet. If those men go and change their minds they can follow our tracks. It isn't like I haven't asked them to go along. Chief Ouray simply has them frightened is all."

Israel Swan said, "I have been around gold rushes all of my life. From what I know, those mountains will have prospectors crawlin' around on them thicker than cooties in a tepee. If we've got plenty to eat and warm clothes, I can't see a problem. We can use my hatchet to make us a hut once we get there that'll be dang near as good as what we're stayin' in now. I say we vamoose an' be the first ones on the ground. That way we can stake some more claims without having to argue with anyone else."

Wilson Bell squeaked, "I'm with my partner. Let's go get rich an' protect our gold mine."

I looked around at George Noon, who had remained silent. "What do you have to say. We are *all* partners on this venture."

Noon poked worriedly at the fire with a stick. "That Ouray seems to think we oughtta wait, but if Mister Packer says we head off, I'm goin' along."

"Then it's agreed among us all," I said firmly. "We'll bundle up our foodstuff and head off before sunrise.

That full moon will give us enough light to travel by. I can't see why we need to let everybody in the whole camp know we're leaving."

"*Ja,*" the butcher said. "I am happy to go to our gold."

We made small talk for a while, then slid between elk hides to get the last comfortable night's sleep we would likely get for many days.

I had my own reason for wishing to leave as quickly as possible and it had nothing at all to do with gold. Chief Ouray had a most comely young sister with the unlikely name of Susan. Like Chipeta, this maiden had alluring eyes and a most striking figure. Using the wiles of a woman, she had induced me to visit her lodge the past two nights.

Never in my life have I ever encountered a more voracious woman. The term "wild Indian" had likely been coined by the first man to crawl beneath her blankets. My back was still raked raw by her sharp fingernails. The young lass kept insisting that her brother would approve of our union if we were to be married. I weighed living my life among the Utes with all of my equipment intact against my adding to the contents of that cigar box the chief was so proud of. I made my decision quite rapidly.

It was time to go after my gold mine, posthaste.

Twenty

Luckily, the entire Ute village slept through the chorus of yapping dogs that bade us farewell in those early morning hours of the Ninth day of February. I shared Powder Face's opinion that those mongrels are only good in pemmican. I confess to worrying a tad that Susan might encourage a war party to come after some items I treasured very much, but this never occurred.

As I was the leader of our small band, I kept to the front and guided us along the Gunnison River, which we encountered three days into our easterly trek. I was gratified the weather continued in our favor and, with few exceptions, we were able to navigate around snowdrifts with little difficulty.

Rabbits and deer were plentiful, as they had been near Ouray's camp. Each evening we roasted fresh meat on sticks held over a crackling fire. This enabled us to conserve our two deerskin bundles of jerky and pemmican for a time when we might need them.

In spite of Israel Swan's incessant wheezing and coughing fits and Frank Miller suffering recurrent attacks of gout, we made good time. Drawing closer to that shining white mountain of dreams seemed to have a salutary effect on us all.

The sixth day we passed by those three black monoliths where I had been forced to bury my sacks of gold ore when Trevor's stupid horse broke its leg. Of course, I kept silent about this, but I knew now my course was true. Since I had had the foresight to blaze those trees, the fact that my map to the mine had been lost during the disaster we suffered at Green River Crossing did not concern me at the time.

We struck the Lake Fork of the Gunnison River around noon of our eighth day out of Ouray's camp. I was still somewhat concerned about the Indians following us, so I had forced a rigorous pace.

"Dang it, Packer," Israel Swan wheezed. "We need to make an early camp. I'm plumb tuckered out an' Ole Miller's had to slice open one of his boots so his big toe could stick out. That gout's painin' him somethin' powerful."

I went and eyeballed the butcher's foot and had to agree with Swan. Frank Miller's toe was swollen to the size and color of a purple plum. The cantankerous German would likely slow us down even more if he didn't take it easy for a while.

There was no sign we were being pursued by any of Chief Ouray's braves, and I too felt an urge to rest before we headed south into the rugged San Juan Mountains where our fortunes lay.

A bitter cold wind bit at our cheeks and frosted every spoken word. The sky was like blue ice covering the heavens. I admit to having had difficulty even recognizing the Lake Fork River, since it was frozen solid and blown over with a light covering of snow. I also knew the country into which we were destined to traverse was much steeper and rougher than anything we had yet experienced. Since the elevation would increase steadily, I feared deep snow might become a severe problem.

"Boys," I said, "in view of everyone's desire to rest and Frank Miller's malady, let's make camp and build up a warm fire."

"That sounds good to me," Humphreys said. "There ain't a cloud in the sky an' the sun's shinin' away, yet I'm freezing my nuts off."

I quickly scanned the horizon again for Indians, but saw nothing.

"This sure is dang cold country," Wilson Bell said. "If a storm catches us without shelter I don't know what we'll do."

"Come along with me," George Noon said to Bell. "We'll gather in some wood and start a fire. It don't look to me like it's gonna snow nohow."

Shortly all six of us were gathered around a crackling fire. We had warm elk or bear hides borrowed from Ouray's camp draped over our shoulders. Felt coats pale in comparison to animal skins when it comes to retaining body heat. We wore thick cozy hats to keep the heat from leaking out the tops of our heads, and had mittens made from beaver pelts. The only real failing turned out to be our boots. The blasted bitter cold that had struck numbed our feet, then worked its way upward from there.

"I tink when I am a rich man," Frank Miller said staring at his swollen purple toe, "I vill live in California. This weather I do not like."

"The summers up here are really nice," I said.

James Humphreys grinned. "If you're not here that week, Packer, I'd reckon you'd miss the whole show. I agree with the butcher. California, especially down in the southern part along the coast, is where I want to hang my hat."

"That's where I'm from originally," George Noon said, drying out his mittens against the fire. "My father was in business in Los Angeles. He died suddenly when I was in Bingham City an' I just didn't know what else to do but stay there. My brother's taken over running the business an' my pa was already buried when I got the word."

"What about your ma?" Israel asked. "I'd reckon she's plenty worried about you."

Noon shook his head sadly. "Nope, that's the reason I left home. My pa an' my brother, Sawyer, never said nothin' to me directly, but I knew they hated me and rightfully so. You see, my mother died bringing me into this world."

The long silence that followed was numbing as the air. The kid had never said anything about his past. Usually he simply sat around and listened to us talk.

"There weren't no sign of game when we gathered up the wood," Bell piped, changing the subject. "We never even saw a track."

"Well, don't fret it any," I said with a wag of my head toward our supply of foodstuffs. "We can make it until spring with what we've brought along with us."

"I reckon that's a fact," Humphreys said. "Still, it's a worry that all of a sudden we ran out of wild game for some reason. Last night there was deer an' elk ever where."

George Noon stood up and slid his mittens on. "I reckon I'll do some hunting." He nodded at Bell. "Why don't you bring that big shotgun of yours an' come with me. Maybe we might find some birds like ptarmigan or maybe even a porcupine."

"Yeah," Bell answered. "We'll go hunt up some food while the old fellows rest."

That idiot Bell was really getting under my skin. Since having him gone for a spell would be a pleasure, I simply poked another stick into the fire and kept my silence. My only regret was that I might miss out being there the first time Bell pulled the trigger on that shoulder cannon he was so darn proud of. I knew that would be a wonderful piece of entertainment.

* * *

The sun was lowering along with the temperature when Noon and Bell came puffing back into camp leaving small white clouds of frozen breath hanging in the still air. I had heard no gunshots and was not surprised to see them return empty-handed.

"It's cold enough to freeze the balls off a brass monkey," Wilson Bell squeaked, beating his mittened hands over the fire.

"I'm sorry, Mister Packer," George Noon said. "There weren't a sign of anything out there. I can't figger out why ever animal seemed to have up an' skedaddled."

"Don't worry about it," I said. "We'll be following the river the rest of the way to our mine. Likely enough there'll be plenty of game further up. Fill your belly with some pemmican and get a good night's sleep." I glared at Bell. "While you fellows were out hiking and enjoying the scenery, us old folk laid in a supply of wood to keep your tootsies warm."

"*Ja,*" Miller said, "tomorrow ve vill kill us a deer and good ve vill eat."

I tossed a couple of large dead logs onto the fire, then rolled up in my elk skin and awaited the darkness. Listening to any more of Bell's insipid whining would certainly upset my night's sleep.

A deep guttural grunt shook me from my slumber. The first thing I noticed was that my idiot partners had let the fire burn nearly out. Then, only a dozen or so yards away on a slight rise, I made out a large brown boulder that had not been there earlier.

I blinked sleep from my eyes and focused on the dark hulk by the wan light of a partial moon. My blood ran cold as the night when I was certain what I had first taken for a big boulder was moving about.

This was a bear, and from its immense size I knew it must be a grizzly. I thought of reaching for my Sharps rifle, then remembered back to the monster bear that had attacked Gidd Trevor and me. I had learned first-hand a grizzly can soak up a lot of lead and still rip a man to shreds. From the snoring coming from the bed-rolls that contained my addle-brained brothers-in-arms, I knew I could expect little if any help from them. Most likely one of them would pull a pistol and shoot that bear just enough to piss him off. Then we would be in deep shit.

My quandary as to what to do became answered when the beast simply ambled off into the darkness. I lay there and stared at the stars until my heart began beating normally again. Then I sat up and began poking the fire to life.

"Vat *ist* going on?" Frank Miller said, rolling out of his bedroll. "My foot hurts so bad I am not able to sleep."

"Then you should have kept the fire going," I growled at his statement, for I was surprised I had heard the bear's grunting over that butcher's incessant snoring. "We had a bear in our camp."

"Oh, God!" he screamed, loud enough to wake the dead. "A bear hast come to kill us all."

Everybody but Wilson Bell bolted awake. That squeaky-voiced simpleton was able to sleep through a war without waking up.

"Where's the bear?" Humphreys yelled, pulling his little pocket pistol that I knew would only make a grizzly mad.

"A bear," Israel Swan wheezed. "That can't be. They hibernate all winter. Everybody knows that."

"Reckon everybody might know that, but no one told

this bear," I said. "Because I got a real good look at
the thing and it was a bona fide high country grizzly.
At least it took off before you popped it with that little
gun of yours. Those things take a lot of killing. Believe
me, I know that for certain."

I fed the growing fire some finger-sized branches and
it blazed against the night. The cold had increased with
a vengeance. My nose and cheeks stung from an icy
wind that had arisen from the north. I thought that if
I had a thermometer the temperature would surely read
well below zero.

Israel Swan coughed deeply, then said, "Come to
think on the matter, I've heard that bears can come out
of hibernation if they get hungry or just take a mind
to. Reckon that's a true fact. It might explain why the
game around here has taken off. A grizzly runnin'
around would be a good incentive to leave, for sure."

"At least it's gone now," I said. "If we keep the fire
built up, likely enough he'll leave us be."

I noticed Swan kept staring and squinting at the slight
rise behind me. He tossed off the hide he was using as
a blanket, then bent down, pulled a long blazing limb
from the fire to use as a torch, and stood. The north
wind whipped the flickering flame, but we then could
see what had attracted his interest.

"That bear got away with every bit of our food!"
James Humphreys sputtered. "How in the hell did it
manage to cart off both of our parcels an' not any of
us know about it?"

"Grizzly bears are awfully big, but somehow they can
move quiet as a ghost," I said. My knees were nearly
knocking. Not from the frigid weather, but because our
missing food had been only a dozen feet from where I
had been peacefully sleeping.

George Noon's young face looked pale and frightened

in the yellow light. "What'll we do, Mister Packer? Now we ain't got a thing left to eat."

"Don't worry, men," I said. "Once we get up the river a ways I'm sure there will be plenty of game. After we shoot an elk or deer there will be lots of food for us."

Israel Swan wagged his head worriedly. "I don't know. Maybe we oughtta head back toward Ouray's camp. The weather has turned on us an' we know for certain there's lots of game in that direction."

The temperature seemed to drop even more. Chief Ouray was absolutely the last person in the world I wanted to set eyes on. "I'm going on to my mine. We have guns, knives, and warm clothes. In a day or two we'll have our food supply replenished. If anybody wants to head back, I'm not going to stop them, but as far as I'm concerned they forfeit their share if they do so."

"*Ja,*" Frank Miller agreed. "Ve go with Packer. Jerky ve make more of when ve shoot a deer."

Israel Swan tossed his torch back onto the fire. "All right then, I guess we'll go ahead. I only wish I had a better feeling about this."

"You fellows get some sleep," George Noon said. "I'll keep the fire goin' in case that grizzly decides to come back. Reckon I've already slept enough myself."

Wilson Bell continued to snore as we covered ourselves against the bitter cold. I finally drifted off to sleep beneath a gray and starless sky.

Twenty-one

I could barely move my arms and legs when I awoke the next morning. In fact I was covered over with a good two feet of snow that had buried me during the latter part of the night. I fought my way to the surface and surveyed our camp through what had become a raging blizzard.

Alongside where our campfire had been I noticed a lump in the snow that I figured to be George Noon. I made it to my feet, waded over, and kicked him awake. The kid bolted up like he'd been shot. He quickly understood why I was a tad upset with him.

"Gee, Mister Packer, I'm sorry. I reckon I must've dozed off an' let the fire go out."

"Don't fret it any," I said calmly. "Likely enough the blizzard would've put it out anyway." I waved my hand toward the other white lumps. "We had best see if they'll all wake up."

In a few moments my keen and perceptive partners had dug themselves out and were pawing around in the snow trying to find their guns or whatever else they had left lying about before they went to spend time in the arms of Morpheus.

James Humphreys stamped his feet to get the blood flowing, then batted snow from his beard. "Dang it all.

The only good thought I can come up with is the fact that blasted grizzly didn't show itself again."

"It was too smart," Israel Swan said. "Right now that bear's in a cozy den somewheres digestin' our food."

"My foot," the butcher whined as he attempted to stand. "I cannot feel my foot. I tink it be frozen."

I sat Miller down on his bedroll, held up his gouty extremity, and looked it over. His swollen purple big toe protruded further through the slit he'd cut in his boot than it had before. I held no doubt it was frostbitten. He should have wrapped it up in a warm blanket rather than leaving it out to freeze.

"It'll be okay once you get the circulation back into it," I said, trying to comfort him.

"I cannot valk," the German moaned when he attempted to move about. "I must haf help."

Wilson Bell came struggling to his side. "I'll help him along. We just won't make good time for a spell."

"Which way do we go, Mister Packer?" Noon asked.

I squinted into the swirling, raging snowstorm. "Upriver, men," I said with conviction. "That's where the gold is."

Israel Swan sputtered through another coughing fit. "I just hope we're still alive when we get there."

Around midday the snow abated, yet the sky remained pewter. With me being the strongest of our group, I broke the trail through drifts, some of which were over four feet deep. Following close in my wake were George Noon and James Humphreys. Israel Swan kept coughing so much he even held back Wilson Bell, who was dragging along Frank Miller. By my best estimate we had traversed over a mile.

"I sure wisht we could see some of that wild game

you was talkin' about last night, Packer," Humphreys grumbled. "Things are getting mighty hungry out."

"Don't dwell on it," I advised. "That's the worst thing you can do. Now that the snow's quit falling, I'm sure we'll find something to eat in a while."

"Yeah," he snorted, "or something will come along and eat *us.*"

For supper that night, George Noon and I took Swan's hatchet to the riverbank, chopped through the hard frozen earth, and dug out a goodly supply of cattail roots. Thoughtfully, I had brought along several waterproof containers of Lucifer matches, and the rest of our party had a cheery fire going when we returned.

Roasted cattails are quite nourishing, if not very tasty. All of us had a full belly when we rolled up inside our warm bedrolls to get a good night's sleep. It hadn't snowed anymore and the temperature had even risen slightly.

I couldn't explain why everyone seemed so upset with me over the way things were going.

For the next three days we were forced to subsist on more roots, rosebush pods, or the inner bark of aspen and pine trees. All of these, however, make for wholesome and healthy fare. We had brought along a couple of light frying pans, which came in handy for melting ice for drinking water. No one should eat snow to quench their thirst. Not only will a person become dehydrated, the cold snow will lower your body temperature considerably. I also employed a skillet we had bought from the Mormons to cook up tree bark that had been pounded into a paste using the handle of my bowie knife. While this is not a very tasty meal, by adding a sprinkle of salt it is palatable and keeps one's energy up.

I knew in my heart that if we kept our wits about us everyone would be fine. The single biggest problem I faced, which became more obvious to me every day, was the fact that all of my partners were quite short on wits.

Frank Miller kept moaning and complaining about his foot hurting. The higher we climbed into the frozen and rugged San Juans, Israel Swan had increasing difficulty with his breathing. Most days he cost us over an hour's traveling time because of his coughing fits. On a couple of occasions he had dropped to his knees and spewed a sprinkling of bright red blood onto the snow. I knew now his lungs were in far worse shape than probably even he had realized. I grew severely worried about his health.

"How much further is it to that mine of yours, Packer?" James Humphreys growled at me as I fried up a skillet full of tree bark for supper that evening. "We sure oughtta throw up a shelter an' let the butcher an' Swan rest up for a time."

"At the rate this bunch is traveling," I said rather testily, for I was becoming rather tired of being the brunt of everyone's abuse, "we might get there a day or so after the Second Coming. But to answer your question, I estimate we're only about ten or twelve miles from it. When we get to that big lake I told you about, the strike is only about a mile or so above there. We'll build us a good shelter once we get to the lake, just like we've planned all along."

"There'd better be some game about shortly," Wilson Bell piped with that shrill voice of his. "We're gonna need some meat to keep goin'. You've always said there'd be plenty an' we ain't found nothing at all to eat that's any good. I wonder just how well you know this country."

"You're welcome to go back to Ouray's camp any darn time you feel like it and lose your share of the gold," I retorted. "There will be game up by that lake for certain. If you'll do more helping out than complaining we'll get there sooner."

Bell was saved from picking a fight with me, which he would have lost rather badly, when Frank Miller raised his head toward the gray sky that had covered the sun for days and began praying loudly in German. The butcher had never seemed to show good sense, and lately he'd been losing more ground in that area.

"Let him pray, Mister Packer," George Noon said, placing a hand on my shoulder. "I'd reckon everyone's gettin' plenty worn out. Tomorrow I'll take my rifle an' scout around a bit. If I can shoot some game that'll brighten all our spirits."

"Yes," I said as I flipped over the tree bark in the frying pan. "I suppose that would help all of us."

Two days and about eight miles later, young George Noon came up dragging a big porcupine behind him with a short rope. We immediately made an early camp and built a roaring fire. I rolled the prickly animal by using a heavy stick up close to the flames, and began the process of burning off the sharp quills.

I must say the kid's earlier prognostication was correct. The wonderful porklike meat had the effect of raising all of our spirits. We ate every delicious morsel, then broke open the bones and sucked out the marrow.

That evening we bundled up for a good night's sleep with full bellies, and for once were not subjected to Frank Miller's bawling and praying incessantly in German.

By my best recollection we arrived at the lake that is now named San Cristobal on a cloudy afternoon, the

Twenty-Sixth of February. The sun had not shown its uplifting countenance for many days now. We had been able to find nothing to eat but tree bark or rose pods since we had eaten the porcupine. All of us were haggard and tired. Tempers flared at the slightest provocation.

While the cold sky remained pewter, only a few flakes of snow had fallen since the earlier inundation that had buried our camp. As we made our way through the increasingly rugged country to the lake where we intended to make a permanent camp, snowdrifts, some of which were well over eight feet deep, impeded our travel greatly.

Frank Miller now had to be carried along by two men. George Noon found it in his heart to help out the old man. At least Miller's running out of steam had slowed down his caterwauling considerably. Israel Swan puffed, wheezed, and coughed, but he kept moving under his own power.

I must admit that this expedition was not going as planned. Nothing, however, that had happened thus far even began to prepare me for the shock of what I saw when we finally made our way to the valley that held the iced-over lake that had shimmered so beautifully in the autumn sun last fall.

My heart sank in my chest when I surveyed the blackened tree stumps that protruded through the harsh expanse of snow that lay around the lake and extended into the mountains to the east as far as my eyes could see.

A late fall thunderstorm must have struck after my departure and a bolt of lightning started a forest fire.

I silently cursed my luck. If only the notebook with the compass bearings I had made with such precision had not been lost at Green River Crossing, I could easily have returned to that mine.

Now, with my trail of blazed trees destroyed, I noticed every canyon and jagged mountain peak were maddeningly similar.

I did not have a clue where to look for my rich gold strike.

Twenty-two

James Humphreys surveyed the devastation the forest fire had wrought and clucked his tongue. "Well, now we know why all the critters took off. There weren't nothing' left for 'em to eat. That was one heck of a big burn from the looks of things."

"There's no way we can make a permanent camp hereabouts, Packer," Israel Swan growled. "There sure ain't any game left in these parts. That blasted fire likely ran 'em miles from here."

"Maybe we could chop a hole in the ice over the lake and catch some fish," Wilson Bell piped in what was likely the first idea he had ever come across.

"Does anyone have any fish hooks or line?" I asked. "And what're you planning to use for bait?"

Bell cocked his head and made an attempt at thinking while I studied on our dilemma and tried to get over being shaken by the disaster that had befallen me. Until recently I had thought the Ute Indians to be my biggest problem.

Things certainly had not gone as I had planned. I was stuck here in the high country of Colorado, with five idiots who owned half interest in a gold mine I doubted I could find again without weeks of searching once the snow melted. The only way to recognize the place would be that rock cairn I had built. But after the fire, would it still be standing? Nothing about the area struck a familiar chord.

Israel Swan took me from my thoughts by dropping to his knees and coughing a spray of bright red blood onto the snow. When he regained his breath he asked the same question I'd been pondering.

"Where's your mine from here, Packer?"

I had no answer except the truth. "I blazed a line of trees from the lake here to the vein."

"There ain't no more trees," Wilson Bell observed with stunning brilliance.

"Alferd Packer," James Humphreys snarled. "Are you tryin' to tell us, after all we've been through, that you've gone and lost the mine?"

"I can find it," I said firmly. "There's a claim monument built out of rocks up there. Don't go and try to blame me. I didn't cause the whole damn forest to burn up."

"We're plumb outta luck 'til spring," Swan wheezed. "This snow's so blasted deep nobody could find a piano, much less a pile of rocks, until the stuff melts."

Israel's observation had an effect on us all that was more chilling than the cold in which we stood. Here by the lake, even tree bark was not available. A quick glance about did not show that any wood small enough to build a campfire had been spared by the conflagration that had seized the area.

Frank Miller leaned heavily on George Noon and began bawling, "My money *ist* gone—all *ist* lost—*kaput*. All *ist kaput*. Damn you to Hades, Packer!"

As I have mentioned before, I do not tolerate abuse well.

"Listen here, Miller," I said loudly. "And this goes for all of you. There is no way I or anyone else could have foreseen this. I accept no blame, but if we're going to survive this you must listen to me."

James Humphreys said, "We're listenin', Al. Just like we've done all along. It's just the results that I'm concerned about."

I decided to ignore his insulting attitude. A true leader of men does not stoop to base behavior. "There is an Indian agency over that pass to the east that Gidd Trevor and I passed on our way up here to the lake last year. That's where Chief Ouray and his tribe spends the summer. It's called the Los Pinos Agency and there will be plenty of food once we get there, for that is what I say we do. The game has been driven off by the fire and we have no choice. Just remember, I put a claim on that mine, and when the snow's gone we can find it and mine the vein just like we'd planned all along."

"We coulda stayed right there in Ouray's camp an' saved ourselves a passel of grief," Swan observed.

I did not share Israel's views on the "passel of grief" part. However, I could see where he'd come up with the feeling. There was not a single morsel of food left for us to eat and by my best estimate, the Los Pinos Agency was likely a good thirty or forty miles distant by taking a shortcut through the pass. We could not tarry here any longer.

"Daylight's burning," I declared. "I'm mighty sorry that God went and started a fire, but if you want to stay here and blame me for it, go right ahead, for I am going to the Indian agency."

"We're comin', Packer," James Humphreys spat. "And if you can't lead us straight to where that agency is, I plan to kill you."

"If I can't find the place," I said, cold as the air, "you may as well save your bullets, Humphreys, because we'll all be dead real soon."

I did not bother to look behind me as I trudged off through the waist-deep snow toward what is now called Slumgullion Pass.

* * *

The forest fire had not crossed west of the Lake Fork River of the Gunnison, nor burned much below Lake San Cristobal, which explained why I did not notice the lack of trees until we came to the valley where the lake is.

I still felt the stings of my partners' insults even though I had led them to firewood and cooked up three heaping skillets of tree bark for supper that night.

Little would have been gained by argument. I endured their slings and arrows with stoical indifference. This disaster, while not of my doing, had understandably caused my partners distress. I knew once they had berated me sufficiently, they would feel better. My goal was simple and clear-cut; if I did not see to their safety, no one else in our party had the intelligence or fortitude to do so.

That night I was taken aback and became concerned when Wilson Bell joined Frank Miller in howling prayers to the starless sky. Bell, of course, did not know German, so he mostly sniveled in gibberish.

The fact of the matter was, Wilson Bell had just lost what little mind he possessed. I simply did not know this at the time.

The next day we had started up the rugged mountains from the bottom of Slumgullion Pass when those pewter clouds that had been keeping us company began dropping flakes of snow larger than chicken feathers. Around an hour later, a terrific wind began thrashing at us from the north. Fortunately I found a ledge of rocks surrounded with trees in which we took shelter.

We had been caught in a blizzard. I could not see

ten feet ahead. For anyone who has never been caught in such a situation I must describe our plight.

Howling winds whipping around trees and rocks picks up snow from the ground and adds it to what is falling. The resulting frigid melee renders any sense of direction impossible. Men have been found frozen to death only yards away from a cabin or even a town, but were unable to find safety in the icy whiteness that stings a person's face and eyes like a thousand scorpions.

To build a fire is impossible. All we could do was hunker together beneath blankets and share the warmth of each other's bodies to keep from freezing to death.

I remember hoping that God understood German. Maybe Miller's praying might help get us out of this fix yet.

Twenty-three

We lay against that rock ledge, hunkered beneath our hide blankets, for two days while the storm screamed and wailed unabated among the craggy peaks like a vengeful hellhound.

Driven by an icy and furious breath, the snow built quickly over our makeshift shelter. I forced sleep from my weary body in order to stay awake and brush away the accumulated white death before it choked off our air and suffocated my poor partners.

Frank Miller, bless his soul, prayed his fervent German prayers for an entire day before he grew silent and went to that realm where he could find out firsthand if God had gotten his message.

The worst of that matter was, Wilson Bell then took over the praying and yelling. His primitive, guttural screams blended with the howling of the blizzard and continued until he eventually tired. Bell then dropped his chin to his chest and began staring around with darting, wild, animal eyes.

As do all storms, this one eventually ceased on the morning of the third day. Almost as if offering an apology, a glaring sun that gave no warmth appeared when the clouds departed and the wind stopped its howling.

George Noon and James Humphreys helped me dig ourselves out and level a flat spot on which we could build a fire, for the weather was dreadfully cold. Israel Swan attempted to help, but was too weak to do so. He was forced to sit and watch, his face pale as a ghost. Every short while he would break into a racking fit of violent coughing and sprayed more blood onto the glistening snow.

Wilson Bell leaned forward, rested his weight on the knuckles of his closed fists, and surveyed us with darting, wild eyes while we worked. He looked for all the world like some ferocious beast waiting to pounce. With the death of his partner, what little mind he had to work with had snapped like a rotten rope.

I have wished a thousand times hence that I had followed my instincts and tied him up hand and foot. But, alas, fate dictated I would not.

The storm had caused me to remain without sleep or even some tree bark to soothe my hunger pangs for three days. Now, my stamina and strength were becoming quite taxed.

Snowdrifts had blown so deep that to obtain wood for a fire we found it necessary to lie flat and struggle up to the high dead branches as if we were swimming in water.

Should all of that snow been spread out evenly on a level plane, I estimate it would have been ten or twelve feet deep. The howling winds and jagged mountain peaks had conspired to cause drifts, some of which would have buried a three-story building, to barren strips that showed only scoured gray rock.

Once we had a warm cheery fire crackling away, four of us crowded around it and took stock of our dire situation. Wilson Bell remained crouched on his knuckles, and had added to his menacing demeanor by uttering an occasional growl.

His dead partner was by his side only a few feet away. When I tried to drag the butcher's body off, Bell had crouched low and roared at me like a panther. I decided to let things be.

I had attempted to move Miller by grabbing on to his bad foot. The gangrene that had developed must have been worse than I thought for foot, boot, and all came off in my hands quite easily. This seemed to be what set Wilson Bell to growling.

"I've seen a passel of lunatics in my time," James Humphreys said. "All bartenders have to put up with 'em, but Wilson Bell would take first prize if they ever held a contest."

"Leastwise we got that big shotgun and his knife away from him," I said. "If he don't go and bite anyone he shouldn't be too dangerous."

"We have to have food," Israel said. His voice was pathetically weak. "None of us can make it much longer without some meat." He turned to me. "Al, you're the likely one to save us. Not only are you the strongest, you're the only man here who knows where the Indian agency is at."

"Do you think you can make it over the pass, Al?" Humphreys questioned. Since the storm he had become quite friendly and agreeable toward me. "That was a real booger of a snowstorm. I'd reckon it'd be a struggle at the very least."

"I must try, boys," I said. "I am weary to the bone, but time is something we do not have to spare for we will all grow weaker by the day without sustenance."

George Noon bravely volunteered. "I shall go with you, Mister Packer."

"No, young sir," I told him. "You need to remain and help Mister Humphreys construct a shelter in case another storm should strike. There is wood to be gathered and tree bark to be sliced off for food. Perhaps you might become lucky by hunting and find another tasty porcupine."

"I reckon Swan oughtta keep a gun on ole cracked-brain," Humphreys said, handing him his small pocket pistol. "We're gonna be too busy with our own mess cookin' to keep an eye on him."

"That is a good idea," I answered. "For I estimate I may be at least two weeks in returning with supplies and help. I simply do not know how bad the snow will be crossing the pass."

"Go get help, Al," Humphreys said. "Before you go I want to apologize for some of the things I've said to you. We all pushed our way into your mine and that forest fire wasn't your fault. I suppose those rich gold samples made us all a little crazy with greed."

I draped my elk-skin blanket over my shoulders and grabbed up the Sharps rifle. "Take care, and I hope you will find something to eat besides tree bark before I return."

I struggled through waist-deep snow to where the wind had left only bare rock. The sun was shining so brightly on the snow that I could see but a short distance ahead. The trek I faced was a long one and my condition was precariously weak from lack of nourishment. I breathed deeply ten times to add air to my lungs, then started up that rugged and icy canyon.

As I progressed I could not help but think of Frank Miller's foot coming off in my hands like it did.

Was it edible?

Being forced to bypass deep snowdrifts, I do not believe I made more than a mile before darkness called a halt to my climb. There was no wood with which to build a fire, so I wrapped up in my blanket on a snowless ledge of rock and stared at the myriad of twinkling stars above until sleep claimed me.

I was jolted awake before the crack of dawn by a

nightmare of what had happened aboard the *Mary Celeste*. I never allow myself to return there when I am awake. The memories are far too painful. Only during the dark of night can they find their way into my head.

In spite of the bitter cold I was perspiring. My heart throbbed like a steam engine. Once I regained my composure I lay until the light became sufficient for me to begin climbing once again.

I tried unsuccessfully to not think about food.

Dear God, I was starving. My strength was fading with every foot I managed to gain up that icy canyon. Only the thought of my comrades depending on me for their very lives prompted me to continue.

I found a rosebush that had a few dead and dried buds on it. I ate every morsel of them along with much of the stems. I then used my bowie knife to chop through the hard frozen earth to get at the roots, which I devoured as if they were some delectable foodstuffs.

It was not good. My stomach began hurting terribly, and I became so nauseated I lost my meager rations. I rested for an hour or so, then began my struggle anew.

I believe it was around noontime when my journey ceased to have any meaning. I faced not only my own doom but also that of my poor partners.

Glinting ahead of me in the cold fire of a heartless sun was a sheer wall of wind-driven snow at least a hundred feet high that stretched across the rugged canyon I was following like an icy fortress.

It would be impossible to cross. I knew in my breaking heart that I did not possess the strength to try to find a way around this impediment. The sheer walls of rock on both sides were ice-covered and far too treacherous for a man in my weakened condition to attempt to scale.

There was no choice I could have made but that of returning to my starving comrades and hope they had been lucky and shot some wild game for food.

Descending from the mountain was much easier than my climb had been. I also had the trail to follow that I had made on my struggle upward. The furrows through the higher drifts and areas of deep snow lessened my efforts considerably.

The false sun had lowered behind the white peaks to the west, and darkness was beginning to enshroud the craggy mountain valley when I encountered the aroma of roasting meat.

I knew our camp to be some distance away, yet, unmistakably, I smelled what could only be the savory fragrance of pork roasting over an open fire drifting up the canyon on an icy breeze.

My partners had been successful in their hunting efforts! I envisioned a fat porcupine dripping grease onto a crackling fire as it was being rotated on a stick.

I quickened my pace and my heart was uplifted. We were going to be saved after all. My failure to cross that snow-clogged pass had thankfully not doomed us.

I could not control my drooling as I fairly ran into the camp.

Twenty-four

I shudder to put pen to paper to tell of the ghastly scene that awaited me when I returned to our makeshift camp.

The cold sun had hidden itself behind rugged peaks to the west, and the yellow, flickering flames of the campfire cast shadows from rocks and trees that danced about upon the snow like specters in a nightmare.

The first thing I noticed with alarm was the blood that appeared to be everywhere. Patches and sprays of crimson winked at me through the gathering darkness while the specters moved silently about.

My foot brushed against what I thought to be a round rock. Only it rolled too easily. I glanced down and beheld the severed head of Frank Miller.

Then, as my horror-filled eyes adjusted to the flickering wan light, I made out bodies lying about as if they were rag dolls that had been tossed aside by an angry child.

Before I could absorb the enormity of what had transpired, the monster was upon me.

Wilson Bell sprang from the shadows and swung a bloody hatchet at my chest while screaming like a panther. Strange, how I remember noticing his eyes. I swear they were glowing bloodred and the pupils were slit vertically, like those of a cat—or a demon.

Instinctively, I brought up the Sharps Rifle and thwarted his blow. The wood stock splintered and I was knocked over backwards by the sheer force of Bell's attack with the hatchet.

I used my feet and propelled myself away from this blood-covered, screaming apparition that seemed to have superhuman strength. The Sharps had been destroyed and was unusable. I threw the broken rifle at Bell and attempted to reach my pepperbox pistol, but it was no use. To protect myself against the bitter cold I had buttoned my felt coat to the top button. The pistol was in my pocket beneath it.

I caught a glint of something metallic out of the corner of my eye. I chanced a second and rolled toward it. What had caught my attention was Bell's big eight-gauge shotgun leaning against a snowbank.

Was it loaded? I wondered with distress. At least I could use it as a club. I grabbed the wood stock and swung the huge weapon around, cocking the hammer as I did so.

For some inexplicable reason Wilson Bell halted his assault. He simply stood there stone still in the flickering light with that bloody hatchet held high over his head. He rolled his tongue hungrily around his lips, all the while surveying me with those beastly eyes of his.

Then with the scream of a banshee he leapt toward me.

I pointed that huge shotgun at his middle and pulled the trigger.

The explosion was deafening and the terrific recoil of that cannon against my shoulder felt as if it had smashed bones. I was gratified to see the damage inflicted on the other end was much worse.

Wilson Bell literally flew up and back through the air. When he dropped back to earth, I could see the campfire glowing through the huge hole that had been blown in his belly.

He still stood! I watched in pure horror when he actually grinned at me. Bell looked about for his hatchet. Then he focused on the gaping hole where his middle used to be.

"Oh, my," was all he said as he crumpled into a heap.

I lay there for a long while, ignoring my throbbing shoulder. I knew that any moment Bell would come back to life and renew his attack on me.

Of course, he was stone dead. However, I took the precaution of taking out my pepperbox pistol before I approached his motionless form. Keeping the gun pointed at him, I kicked his worthless body several times with my hobnail boots. When I had finally convinced myself the monster was destroyed, my heartbeat returned to normal and I began to take stock of the situation.

I quickly came to realize that of our original party of six men, I alone was still within this mortal coil. Frank Miller had died on his own from blood poisoning. Wilson Bell, in his insane state of mind, had somehow gotten hold of Israel Swan's hatchet and viciously slaughtered him with it.

James Humphreys and young George Noon I found hacked to death on the other side of the campfire. I did not notice their bodies right away.

I focused on the leg of a man that was spitted on a stick and dripping grease into the fire. The little sizzles from the hot coals were giving off the aroma that had earlier garnered my attention and started me to drooling.

Good God, was I hungry.

It all boils down to what is edible, doesn't it? Meat is, after all, meat.

The drooling and salivating returned uncontrollably.

I fought it down once again. I dragged all of the bodies of my slain companions, except for the demon-infested Bell, to the fire and laid them out. I even retrieved Frank Miller's head and placed it back on his frozen torso. That was when I realized it was the German's leg cooking over the fire.

Drip, sizzle. Drip, sizzle. Drip, sizzle.

My good God, it smelled just like roasting pork.

The sweet, wonderful aroma that drifted and hung on the frigid air became unbearable.

Roast pork, tasty and filling. That's all that really matters— filling and tasty. There are only two choices; survive by any means or die.

Good God in heaven, I had not had a thing to eat for days.

I am not a stupid man like many others. I had learned from Billy Kincaid's dying after eating that prairie dog.

I roasted Frank Miller's leg very thoroughly before I ate it.

The morning broke bright and blue over the pass to the east. The mountains remained caught in the icy embrace of winter's talons, yet for the first time in a very long while I did not notice the cold. I had enjoyed a dreamless night of perfect sleep and felt refreshed. And I was not hungry.

There is no way I can possibly convey the euphoria and sense of peace and calm that enveloped me like a soft warm cloud.

I went to the fire and added more fuel. It blazed wonderfully. After I had eaten my breakfast, I sat there by those bright flames and I felt, well, as if I were *becoming* . . .

Turtle John, Fritz Kenyon, and I had visited many islands of the South Seas. There we had found many civilizations that not only practiced cannibalism, but openly embraced its merits.

In many cultures it is considered an honor to be consumed by one's friends. By doing so, those of the living add the spirits of the departed to themselves. In this manner, the dead live on.

The euphoria I enjoyed, I knew, was due to the spirits of my comrades becoming part of me. They were asking—begging—me to consume them so that they might yet live on.

I vowed I would honor their wishes fully.

Then I bolted upright. My heart throbbed in my chest wildly.

Wilson Bell's evil spirit was here too! It had to be destroyed, lest it infect me. I knew where the spirit lived, however.

I quickly cut out his foul heart and burned it to ashes in the fire.

The feeling of tranquility returned as the smoke from Wilson Bell's charred heart drifted away along with his demon soul.

My four remaining friends were most proud of me. I know this because they told me so many times during the long nights and weeks I spent there on that snow-covered mountain honoring them.

The flesh and spirits of my comrades sustained me until the ice and snow began to melt and run clear and cold in the creeks.

I am no fool. I realized how the narrow minds of those who enforce the law would likely view my actions. Even though I had done absolutely nothing wrong.

Taking with me as much jerked meat as I could carry along with the gold coins Frank Miller had sewn in his coat and the money from the pockets of my friends, which totaled over six thousand dollars, I once again headed up into the high mountains to cross the pass and return to civilization.

My friends accompanied me, although no one would believe me if I told them.

Twenty-five

I felt a great deal of trepidation about stopping by the Los Pinos Indian Agency, but I really needed to. I had to begin planting seeds of an alibi to defend myself should evidence of what had occurred in those rugged mountains come to light. The camp where I had spent many weeks was well away from any likely trails, but I figured some snoop would likely find it anyway.

It is a terrible cross to bear when one has done nothing wrong, yet he knows the narrow-minded folks who enforce our laws will probably take offense at his actions, no matter how necessary or altruistic they might have been.

The possibility Chief Ouray and that rascally young sister of his, Susan, might be at the agency increased my discomfort as I walked along what is now called Cochetopa Creek. I was amazed as to just how little snow was about, and wondered deeply what month of the year it was. Time, since I had begun honoring my companions, was like looking back into some strange and foggy dream.

I caught a scent of smoke—my sense of smell had become quite acute—and retreated into the towering pine trees so that I might survey the agency without exposing myself to undue peril.

When I saw the solitary peeled log and chink building

that was the Los Pinos Agency, I relaxed. If Chief Ouray were there, the place would have been covered with te-pees galore instead of the half dozen or so that were in evidence. There would also have been a goodly sup-ply of mongrel dogs yapping away at me, for Ouray liked to eat dog very much.

I tossed away the meager supply of smoked meat I still had with me into some bushes with much sorrow. Lean strips of breast are *so* sweet and tasty.

I remembered the words to a popular slave song that I felt appropriate to the occasion, and began singing them.

Nobody Knows the Trouble I've Seen.

I kept my cheerful attitude until I came to within a hundred yards or so of the front door. There was little doubt in my mind that I would have some tolerable explaining to do as to why I had come back from the mountains short five partners. If not this time, certainly someone would bring up the blasted question later on. I had to prepare.

My beard was long and matted. I knew I must look a fright, for many long months had passed since I had bathed or been able to clean up any. It was exactly the way a man would appear after being abandoned by his friends and left to fend for himself.

I rubbed my eyes with my fists to make them red and watery. Then I put a hangdog expression on my face and walked the short distance to the Indian agency.

"My God, man," the first fellow to set eyes on me exclaimed. "You look like you just lost a fight with the Devil! Take a seat and I'll fetch you a cup of coffee and something to eat."

I marveled at the gentleman's intuition. Actually I had *won* a fight with the Devil, but felt it prudent not to mention that fact. I stumbled, then sagged into his arms once I was close enough to do so. He scooted out a chair from a long wooden table with his boot, then eased me into it.

"Thank you," I gasped. "I never thought I would ever make it to a settlement. I—I've been caught in the high mountains most of the winter. I can't tell you how glad I am to be alive after what I have suffered."

"You are safe now, sir," the man said as two others who seemed to be the only persons in attendance came to my aid. "I am General Charles Adams, agent in charge of the Los Pinos Ute Indian office, which is where you are. What is your name, my friend?"

"P-Packer—Alferd Packer," I answered haltingly. "I was part of a prospecting party heading into the San Juan Mountains. There were six of us. I—I don't remember just how long ago it was that I twisted my ankle and could not go on."

A burly short man with a bushy brown beard placed a hand on my shoulder. "I'm Larry Dolan and I own The Tiger Spit Saloon over in Saguache. Are you tellin' us that those so-called partners of yours up an' left you to fend for yourself in the middle of winter?"

"Y-yes, sir, I'm afraid that's what they went and done, all right. I told them I would make out fine, so I can't rightly go blame them for it."

"I don't know what this world is coming to," General Adams said, rummaging around in the kitchen. "Alonzo's going to have his work cut out for him now that the San Juans are open for prospectors. Greeners and tinhorns always make for problems any time there's a gold rush. Everyone is always in too big of a hurry to get rich to care for their fellowman and live by the teachings of the Good Book."

"Wish I could get you a shot of whiskey, Mister Packer," Larry Dolan said, patting my shoulder. "I surely do, but this bein' an Indian agency and all, they ain't none allowed hereabouts." He chuckled. "Well, I reckon

I shouldn't complain because I catch 'em good later on when they get to Saguache. After goin' without bein' able to enjoy what makes life worth livin' for months on end, they sure make up for lost time."

"Come on, Dolan," the slender man who I had yet to meet growled. "This poor fellow's been through enough without you trying to talk him to death. I'm sure he's plumb starved."

"Yes, sir," I said, turning toward the clean-shaven fellow who I noticed right away sported a silver badge on his tweed vest. "I have certainly been forced to subsist on whatever I could find."

"Alonzo Walls," he said, extending his hand. "I'm the sheriff around these parts. Dolan an' me just drove out a wagon load of supplies from Otto Mears' store. Chief Ouray an' his bunch'll be showin' up fairly soon an' likely they'll need some vittles."

"Why don't both of you two pound on each other's ears and let this man eat?" General Adams said, sliding a steaming bowl of beef stew along with a plate of buttered bread in front of me. "He's been through enough perdition without listening to a bunch of gum-rattling."

I took a moment to survey this so-called general. After the war it seemed that everyone I met who had been in the Army, especially the Confederate, was at least a colonel. Anyone who claimed to be a major, I knew, was either a truthful man or hadn't gotten the ambition to raise his rank. With all of the generals and colonels running about, I wondered who actually did any of the fighting.

Charles Adams, however, I decided might be an actual general. There was something about his bearing that spoke of familiarity to command. He was a decidedly natty fellow who wore a gray suit, white shirt with a black bow tie, like one of those ghastly things President Lincoln used to wrap around his neck. Adams had short brown hair, neatly trimmed, and a walrus mustache that drooped at his cheeks, making him appear sad. The small wire-rimmed glasses that perched on the end of his beak spoke of a career government man, for certain.

I sipped from the steaming cup and smiled. "It has been a long while since I've tasted coffee, sir. I thank you for your hospitality. Might I ask what month this is?"

An expression of concern crossed the general's face. "Why, I suppose you wouldn't know after being abandoned in those terrible mountains. This is the Sixteenth day of April. Do you remember the date when you were left on your own?"

I drew down my brow in puzzlement. "It was sometime in February. I—I can't remember for certain. The sky was always gray and the cold was terrible. Most of the time when I wasn't gathering wood, I huddled under my hide blanket next to a fire to keep from freezing to death. Sometimes I'd drop off to sleep and when I'd come around the fire would be cold. I can't rightly say for sure now how long I was up there."

"You're just plain lucky to be alive," Larry Dolan said. "There ain't a lot of game about in the dead of winter."

That blasted lawman focused on me. "Just what *did* you find to eat up there?"

I blew a cloud of steam from my cup. "Luck was with me for you are quite correct about there being a lack of game. My partners had left me with enough rations for about a week. As I have mentioned, my ankle was too swollen for me to move about much."

"Those bastards that left a man in that condition oughtta be hung," Larry Dolan interjected.

Alonzo Walls nodded coldly. "Let Mister Packer continue."

"Fortunately I had my fifty-caliber Sharps rifle when a sow grizzly came into camp after me. I shot the beast right in its open mouth just as it charged. Bears take a while to know they're dead. This one swatted my rifle away and broke the stock before it dropped dead at my feet. That bear provided me with meat for a long while."

"I never heard of a grizzly comin' out in the wintertime," Dolan said.

General Adams looked at the saloon keeper and snorted, "Bears can come out of hibernation whenever they please. Any person who spends time in God's great outdoors knows this is a true fact. I would venture Mister Packer is a lucky man, a *very* lucky man indeed."

I stared longingly at the plate of beef stew before me. "I want to give thanks to the Almighty for this food and my deliverance. What I wished for more than anything during my tribulations was a Bible to read."

General Adams' lower lip quivered slightly; then he went behind the counter and returned with a black leather-covered Bible. "Here, my good man. Keep this and may you find comfort within its pages." He glared at Dolan and the sheriff. "Come with me and let this poor Christian eat his food."

I patted the Good Book and attacked the stew as I knew they expected me to. The meat tasted dreadful, but I choked it down while smiling broadly at my benefactors. I felt gratified that blasted sheriff seemed to have had all of his suspicions allayed with my story of the grizzly bear. Lawmen, being basically dullards, are sometimes easy to sway.

At the time I had no idea as to just how much good I would get out of that Bible.

Twenty-six

It was getting onto dusk of the next day when that freight wagon I rode in the back of creaked down the dirt streets of Saguache, Colorado. Alonzo Walls did the driving while Larry Dolan sat crossways on the seat alongside the sheriff, yammering away as he had done all day. The saloon keeper would have made a natural congressman or senator, for he could talk the spots off a guernsey cow without saying a single word about anything that mattered in the slightest.

Nevertheless, I was very grateful they had asked me to come along. Should Chief Ouray have shown up while I was at the Los Pinos Agency, I knew in my heart that he would most likely resort to more than harmless banter.

It felt so good to be clean and shaved. Last night I had luxuriated in a copper bathtub full of hot soapy water. Afterward, General Adams had shown considerable tonsorial skills with shears and razor. Due to those blasted cooties that had taken up residence in my beard and hair when I was among the Utes, I had opted for a very short haircut and only retained a trim goatee. Not having my hair crawl around on its own was a blessing.

Dolan waved his hand about and said proudly, "This town will be bigger than Denver one day. The location is ideal to service all of the boom towns that will surely bloom as spring flowers in the majestic San Juans. Why, over in Baker's Park, which ain't much but a few shacks nowadays, they claim to have found silver by the ton."

Somehow, the sheriff got a word in. "Those partners of yours, Packer. I wrote down their names and come to think on it, you never said where you all were headed. Since you ain't dead, I reckon they didn't break any laws, only I was wonderin'. It takes a powerful motivation to cause anyone with even half a brain to head into the high country in winter. Hell's bells, the snow won't be outta there for another month or so."

"Baker's Park," I said without hesitation. "Like Dolan just said, there's been a lot of rich strikes in that area. We wanted to be among the first there when the snow melts."

Alonzo shot a sardonic glance at the distant white peaks where the sun was hiding its face. "You could still leave next month and do that."

"Here we are," Larry Dolan fairly shouted as the lumbering wagon groaned to a halt when the sheriff set the brake. "The Tiger Spit Saloon. There ain't a better house of relaxation and sporting within a hundred miles."

I hopped down, then grabbed my blanket from the wagon bed and surveyed what Dolan was so blame proud of. So far, what I had seen of Saguache reminded me of Bingham City, only being here on the flats, the wind blew all of the smoke toward Kansas instead of its being trapped in a canyon.

The Tiger Spit Saloon was a false-front, two-story affair built, as were most Western towns of the day, of unpainted clapboard. It sat on a wide, dusty street that seemed to serve as the main part of town. I noticed the usual trappings of civilization; stores that sold hardware, dry goods, and groceries; restaurants, livery stables, hotels, and barbershops.

When I saw the office of Samuel R. Quitman, M.D., I thought of poor Gidd Trevor, but as there is nothing to be gained by wondering what might have been, I turned my attention to Larry Dolan's saloon. In great contrast to the dreariness of the building and Saguache in general, there was the huge painting of a snarling tiger done in bright orange that covered the entire upper story of the structure. The name THE TIGER SPIT SALOON beckoned cheerfully with three-foot-high bloodred letters.

"Nice place," I commented cheerfully. "And I don't notice any competition either."

Dolan cocked his head at Alonzo. "My cousin don't allow any riffraff in Saguache."

"Gentlemen," I said, "I believe the least I could do is buy you a drink. What do you say?"

"Thanks, Packer," the sheriff said. "I'll take you up on that later. Right now I'd best get back to my office and see if ole Wade, my deputy, is awake."

Larry Dolan slapped a hand on my shoulder. "Come on in an' I'll show you around. A man who's been through what you have don't buy no drinks, though." He grinned devilishly. "At least not the first one."

In spite of a growing cold, only batwing doors swinging in the wind impeded our entrance. I was taken aback by the number of men inside. There were three poker tables in action and two faro layouts where grizzled miners were attempting to buck the tiger. Along one wall was a huge bar, behind which were mirrors interspersed with paintings of nude women. After the winter I had just spent, this place was like entering paradise.

"Ed," Dolan shouted over the tinkling piano to a portly bald-headed man behind the bar. "Set up two shots of the usual for my friend Al Packer and me."

The big man rolled the stub of a cigar around in his mouth for a moment while glaring intently at me, then bent down and came up with an amber bottle and poured two glasses full.

"Ed Whitmore don't take to smilin' much," Larry Dolan said when the surly bartender set out our drinks. "He thinks it ain't a good idea with his other occupation bein' what it is an' all."

I eyed my whiskey. "I'd reckon he must be the local undertaker."

"Nope." Dolan grabbed his glass. "Ed works for Alonzo when there's need for a hangman."

Suddenly I really *needed* that drink.

"Here's to any man who can survive like you done," Dolan said, holding up his glass. "You're one tough and lucky cuss, Alferd Packer."

I slugged down the whiskey and nearly dropped to my knees. Until now I had thought that rotgut they distilled in the Everglades to be the most potent coffin varnish in the world. On that point I was sadly mistaken. If a man was smoking a lit cigar and took a drink of this stuff, it would likely ignite and blow his head clean off his shoulders.

"Bumblebee brand whiskey," Dolan said proudly while I attempted to breathe. "My favorite, it has a sting to it an' will make your head buzz."

"You forgot to mention how smooth it is, too," I wheezed.

"Bumblebee is an acquired taste. You'll find it's more of a sippin' whiskey than you might be used to."

"I reckon you're right on that point." I fished a five-dollar gold piece out of my pocket and laid it on the bar. "Give Mister Dolan another," I told the petulant bartender. "I believe I'll stick to something that's less apt to be fatal."

The bald barkeep chewed on his cigar without hinting at a grin.

"Give my friend some Old Crow," Dolan chuckled. "That's a good drink for beginners. Here at The Tiger Spit we'll even serve sarsparilla if'n that makes a cusomer happy."

"Old Crow sounds good," I said as the plump Ed Whitmore waddled off. It was then that I caught sight of a door opening into one of the several rooms upstairs. My heart fluttered when I encountered a brief glimpse of a naked raven-haired girl blowing a kiss at some departing cowboy.

"You know something, Dolan?" I said, keeping my eyes fixed on that door. "I have suffered through a terrible long and cold winter."

He sipped some of that awful Bumblebee whiskey without flinching. "A man needs to dip his wick once in a while. That's my philosophy and the little ladies in those rooms upstairs goes along with it—for a price, that is."

"How much?" I asked without looking at him.

"One of the best things about livin' in Saguache is the cost of the necessities of life are reasonable. Two dollars for an hour check, or I can brass you in for all night for only ten bucks."

"What do you mean brass me in?"

"It's a system that keeps the girls from screwin' a customer more ways than one. I sell you a brass token an' you give it to the little lady. This way the girls' ain't bothered with havin' to handle money so they can concentrate better on their work."

"I think I'd enjoy a full night of female companionship," I said, plunking down a gold eagle. "There were lots of times I wondered if I'd ever get another chance to do so again."

The bartender returned with our drinks. I took a sip

and nodded in satisfaction. This was excellent whiskey. Now if only the women were of the same quality.

"Ed," Dolan said, "bring over an all-night check for room three." He turned to me. "Letticia Le Dew is her name. She's a chunky blonde, but you get more lovin' for your money with a biggun and Letty sure is big where it counts the most."

"The black-haired girl up there in the room at the head of the stairs sure looked cute."

Larry Dolan leaned close to not be overheard. "Since you're my friend, and have suffered through a rough winter, I must tell you. Her name is Adelaide an' she simply can't seem to get rid of the clap." He chuckled under his breath. "I'm always honest when I tell folks she just saw the doc."

"Letticia," I said. "That's a nice name and I really do like blondes."

I picked up the round brass token with a big number three stamped on one side and the words "All Night Check" on the other. I paid Dolan another five dollars for a bottle of Old Crow, then went up the wooden stairs to where I would thoroughly enjoy my first night in Saguache.

As in Bingham City, not everything about the place turned out to be dismal.

The next morning I took a room in the Alhambra Hotel. Then I visited the First National Bank of Saguache, where the fawning cashier gladly accepted my deposit of over six thousand dollars in gold coins. Those things are terribly heavy to move about with. After packing them for days, I wondered anew how Frank Miller had kept from drowning in the Green River.

My other honored partners had also insisted that I take their money, for in the realm they now inhabited

it was of absolutely no use to them. Israel Swan had
donated six hundred dollars. James Humphreys, five
hundred and change. George Noon, the poor young
chap, had only fifty dollars to give me. Wilson Bell, the
demon-infested idiot who caused all of my problems,
had one hundred dollars in eagles. I was spending his
money first just in case some of Bell's evil might have
somehow attached itself to it.

I visited Lehman's general store, where I purchased
a new suit of fine-quality clothes along with new boots,
for mine were decidedly worn out after the trek across
Utah. I added a new Colt revolver of forty-five caliber
along with a holster and a box of shells.

After tallying my money over dinner at a Chinese
chophouse, I found I had twenty-five more of Bell's dollars to rid myself of. This would present little problem.
I rested the afternoon in my comfortable hotel room,
then went to visit my good friend Larry Dolan.

As usual, The Tiger Spit Saloon was enjoying a booming business. I had found there were nearly fifteen hundred souls about Saguache. Most of them were awaiting
the spring thaw to enable them to get rich by prospecting in the San Juans. I thoroughly intended to join in
the rush, only I already had a rich strike that would
likely present only minor difficulty to locate again.

I had decided it would be a prudent move to take
along a pack mule with a pick and shovel. These items
would certainly not raise any eyebrows. Only I needed
to bury some things I had rather not have found. Then
I could employ those tools to unearth the rich vein,
which, of course, was now solely my property.

"Well, you're lookin' mighty chipper," Dolan announced, eyeing my new clothes. "And from that grin
on your face, I'd reckon little Letty treated you good."

I plunked another of Wilson Bell's tainted eagles
down on the bar. "I think another night would tell the

tale. She certainly is a wildcat between the sheets, that's for sure."

"Like I told you," Dolan chuckled, "you always get your money's worth in Saguache and The Tiger Spit Saloon."

Ed Whitmore waddled over chewing on what was likely the same cigar he had yesterday. "What'll you have?" he grumbled, tossing down the brass check for room three.

"Just a beer," I said. "Even good whiskey gives a man a headache the next morning."

Larry Dolan chuckled. "When you grow up, switch to Bumblebee. It only stings once, and that's on the way down."

"I'll keep that in mind." I motioned toward the door where a few flakes of snow had begun falling. "Looks like a storm's blowin' in."

"I love it when that happens. Keeps folks inside spendin' money. There'll be a passel more shortly 'cause Chief Ouray's back. Him an' a bunch of 'em will be here in Saguache shoppin' up a storm shortly. Indians like their whiskey an' this is the only place they can get served."

"Chief Ouray's coming *here?*" I choked.

"Yep, we only missed 'em by a day. What's wrong with you, Packer? You don't look too well all of a sudden."

"Oh, it's nothing," I said. "Just a tad too much whiskey last night."

"You'll like Ouray," Alonzo Walls said, who was standing alongside Dolan. "He's a real card for an Injun."

"That's the truth," Larry Dolan said. "He even packs around a cigar box full of dried up tallywhackers he shows off to greenhorns as bein' chopped off men that mess with Ute women."

The sheriff took a long drink of beer and laughed. "Can you believe some fools actually think he's tellin' the truth? Land sakes, that box has nothin' in it but deer an' elk privates. Some of those Injun gals like doin' it better than a man. Ouray knows that, an' his cigar box ain't slowed things down a bit for anyone but Dolan's girls upstairs."

I forced my teeth to unclench. "I have met Chief Ouray before. You are right about him showing off that cigar box. It is just that I have a difficult time accepting the idea that anyone would be fool enough to believe him."

"Hell's bells, hardly anyone does," Larry Dolan said. "Drink your beer, Packer. You look like you could use it."

James Humphreys had been absolutely correct when he said Indians were mighty tricky to deal with.

Twenty-seven

It is never wise to irritate the man who owns the only saloon in town, even more so if his cousin happens to be the sheriff. I realized ahead of time just how upset Larry Dolan would likely become when I rented a small frame house on the outskirts of Saguache and moved Letty Le Dew in with me. I had rightly guessed she was one of his biggest moneymakers.

Dolan turned red as a beet and was so angry he hissed like a rattlesnake when I went to The Tiger Spit Saloon to see him. "Dang you, Packer, I treated you square an' now I ain't gonna serve you in here no more. If'n you so much as miss a cuspidor, I'll see to it that Alonzo gives Ole Ed the job of hangin' you. Here in Saguache we take the law mighty serious."

I noticed the ponderous and stoic bartender kept his gray eyes focused on my neck as if he was deciding what size of rope would work best to stretch it.

"Now, Larry, my friend," I said quickly and sincerely, "I would never do anything like that to upset you. It's just that I have a good month or so before I can go prospecting and it's a nice feeling to have a woman to cook for me and all."

Dolan's eyes bugged when I handed him three hundred dollars that I had just taken from my account at the bank.

"What the hell are you pullin', Al Packer?" Dolan chirped.

"I'm simply renting Letty Le Dew for a month," I replied. "Thirty days at ten bucks per comes to three hundred dollars to my way of counting. By then I reckon the snow will be melted and I'll be on my way and she won't be any worse for the wear."

Ed Whitmore wagged his bald head sadly. I could tell he really would have enjoyed hanging me better than serving me drinks.

Larry Dolan looked puzzled. "Nothin' like this has ever happened before. This is mighty strange, but dang if I can find anything wrong with it." He spun to the bartender. "Ed, give Packer a beer on me an' you can forget what I said earlier about not servin' him. It's just that I've never had anyone rent a whore for longer than a night before. Kinda upset my thinkin' an' threw my good disposition for a loop, but I'm better now."

I tossed a five-dollar gold piece on the plank bar. "Give Mister Dolan one of those Bumblebee whiskeys he enjoys," I told Ed. "And pour one for yourself. It's the least I can do since you've been deprived of the joy of hanging me."

The bartender actually came close to smiling, but caught himself in time to avoid the embarrassment. "Yes, sir," he grumbled as he waddled off to fetch our drinks.

Dolan turned and stared over the batwing doors at a raging electrical storm. "It's gotta be the blame weather. I never saw such weird weather as we've been havin'. First off it snows, then it sleets. After that's all done with, I'll be switched if we don't get us a thunderstorm with more thunder an' lightnin' than a body would find in Hades. That's sure enough to cause a sane man to rent a whore for an entire month."

I started to say something to him when suddenly

those doors swung open and my blood turned to ice water. Chief Ouray himself and four of his braves along with General Adams came inside dripping water. From the stern expressions on their faces I knew right away something was terribly wrong. My first thought was that Ouray had decided to add the genuine article to that cigar box of his for what had transpired between his little sister and me. You can imagine my surprise and relief when he ignored me completely.

General Adams hollered loudly, "Bring him in, boys, and one of you go for the doctor."

The Indians moved aside to allow Alonzo Walls and some fellow dressed in buckskin to carry a limp man in out of the storm. Two tables were quickly slid together and the listless figure was laid out on top of them.

I stepped close and gasped in surprise when, even though half of his head was fried, I recognized who it was. "Why, that's Powder Face!"

"We were just ridin' along into town," the old buck-skin-clad man with a white beard said. "When a bolt of lightnin' plain came outta the clouds an' struck him square on his noggin. Kilt his horse, to boot. Here I was no more'n five feet away an' didn't even git singed."

Larry Dolan came over and felt Powder Face's neck. "Reckon we can save a doctor bill. He's deader than a doornail."

I looked at the stricken Ouray. "I am sorry. Powder Face was a good man."

Ouray said, "Do not mourn for the remains before you. He has been summoned by the Great Spirit, who apparently had need of him."

"This is a great tragedy," General Adams intoned. "He was a friend to all who knew him."

"We will leave with him now," Chief Ouray announced. "The mountains are calling."

"It's stormin' like blazes out there," the sheriff said. "He'll keep 'til it blows over."

"No," Ouray said, turning to his braves. "Take him and we go—now."

I and everyone else stepped back and watched as the Utes picked up their dead companion and melted into the raging storm.

"That is one thing the Indians have a lot of experience with," the general said solemnly.

"What's that?" Dolan asked him.

"Burying their dead."

"Reckon he's right about that," the old man said, staring at the closed doors. "It seems like they do get a lot of practice at it."

"If'n the gov'ment had enough sense to pour sand outta their boots, they'd go run the blame Mormons outta Utah instead of wastin' efforts messin' with a bunch of good Injuns," the old man with the bushy white beard said to me over a drink later on.

"The Mormons sure aren't worth a hoot at building a ferry," I said in agreement, and then introduced myself to him.

"I'm Bridger, Jim Bridger," the old man said, giving me a firm handshake that belied his skinny frame. "I've had a bellyful of Brigham Young an' his bunch. If'n they tried to bury me in Utah, I'd dig my way to the top of the ground an' make it to Colorado before I went an' died all the way dead."

"I have heard of you, sir," I said. "I would say most folks have. Why, you are a famous mountain man and Army scout who pioneered the opening of the West. I would be honored to buy you a drink."

"Thankee, Mister Packer," Jim Bridger said. "I truly enjoy a good whiskey when I get the chance."

"Hey, Ed," I hollered to the still-unemployed hangman. "Bring over a shot of Bumblebee for Jim Bridger here. On second thought, make it a double."

I watched as the mountain man rolled the amber liquid around in his glass, sniffed at it, then slugged down the entire contents with one gulp. I waited for him to begin gasping and fall to his knees. To my utter amazement, Bridger simply smacked his lips and said, "Not bad whiskey, but I prefer Taos Lightning or something with more of a kick to it."

There was no doubt in my mind how men of his ilk had managed to open the frontier. Bumblebee whiskey would raise a blood blister on a potbelly stove. "May I ask what brings you here to Saguache?" I said.

"Chief Ouray an' poor ole Powder Face asked me to help negotiate that treaty where they give up the mountains. I say it was outright thievery by the gov'ment, but those Injuns had no choice as I could see it."

"Didn't you have a trading post on the upper part of the Green River?" I asked, changing the subject, for I was still disturbed about what had happened to Powder Face.

"Yep, I surely did. Then Brigham Young got the religious piles over my sellin' a gun or two to the Injuns so's they could get somethin' to eat once in a while."

"The Mormons ran you out of business?"

"Oh, no." Jim Bridger took out a plug of Bull Durham chewing tobacco, whacked off a big chunk with his bowie knife, and plopped it into the middle of his beard. "Fair an' square ain't in the Good Book *he* reads. Brigham Young sent down a passel of Zealots he calls 'Avenging Angels' dressed up like Injuns and burned the joint down. Kilt all my livestock an' stole whatever they could pack off that wasn't ruined. I figger I lost nigh onto a quarter of a million dollars. Nowadays, I'm broker than a trapper leavin' a whorehouse."

"I'm sorry," I told him. "Perhaps you will recoup your fortune one day."

"If'n I do," Jim Bridger said, "I intend to hire me an army an' kick ole Brigham's butt clean into the Pacific Ocean. But it won't happen. All I got is a dirt farm back in Missouri an' a daughter to marry off if'n I can ever find a suitor for her that's blind in one eye an' can't see good outta the other. Blanche is kinda short on looks."

"I wish you good luck, Mister Bridger," I told the famous man. "I will be proud to buy you another drink, then I must go. Letty will have dinner fixed shortly."

"Thankee, sonny." He glared at the bartender. "Hey, baldy. You got somethin' to drink that ain't sissified like that other stuff was?"

Ed Whitmore bit the end clean off his cigar. "I got a jar of Snakehead Whiskey that even the freighters are 'fraid to drink," he growled.

"Now yer talkin'." Bridger grinned. "Bring it on."

The bartender set out a wide-mouthed jar of straw-colored liquid that had the head of a big diamondback rattlesnake floating around inside. Ed's eyes flashed a surreptitious smile as he poured a glass and slid it toward the mountain man.

Jim Bridger slugged it down like he had done the glass of Bumblebee. He spit a wad of tobacco in the general direction of a cuspidor and shook his head. "I thankee, Packer, fer the taste, but I reckon I'll pass on any more milk."

"You're more than welcome," I said. "I have enjoyed meeting you and wish you well. Now I must be off."

Larry Dolan came over. "You're welcome to the bottle, Mister Bridger, if you want the stuff, 'cause no one else will ever touch it."

Jim Bridger grabbed the jar and fished out the snake head using his fingers. Then he held it up and stared at the thing for a while. "He looks purty well pickled. Reckon I'll finish it, an' thankee, sonny boy."

"You take good care of Letty," Dolan said to me.

"That's yer wife?" Bridger asked.

"Nope," Dolan spoke up. "She's a whore that works upstairs. Packer here has gone an' rented her for an entire month. I never had nothin' like that happen before."

"I knew I liked you, sonny," Jim Bridger said to me after taking a gulp from the jar of whiskey. "I plain admire a man that can make a lengthy commitment to a woman."

Before I stepped out into the still-rainy night, the old mountain man had drained the whiskey. The last time I ever saw Jim Bridger, he was spinning that snake head around on the bar while complaining about Mormons. I can truthfully say he was a very singular man and I am glad to have made his acquaintance.

Twenty-eight

Two weeks can pass by mighty fast when a man has a home to spend time in when he's not in a saloon. Letty Le Dew certainly knew how to make a fellow happy more ways than one. Not only was she some pumpkins, that lady could cook!

Every morning after I had gotten my money's worth, she would drape a frilly chemise over her tempting body, toss some wood into the cookstove, and go to work. Plates of sourdough pancakes smothered under mounds of fresh butter and syrup, surrounded by heaps of crispy bacon and fried eggs, started our day.

Then I would lie on the bed and read while my breakfast digested and Letty cleaned the place up. I had become quite fascinated with the novels of Jules Verne. I thoroughly enjoyed *From the Earth to the Moon* and his latest book, *Twenty Thousand Leagues Under the Sea*. There was really nothing I could do until the snow melted from the mountains. Considering my last experience up there, I was certainly in no big rush to push the matter any.

After a sumptuous dinner, I usually napped to rest up for an evening of playing poker at The Tiger Spit Saloon. I had never really enjoyed games of chance before, but as I had both money and time, this was a great way to while away the days until I could take care of cleaning up a potentially embarrassing mess I had left near the bottom of Slumgullion Pass. Then set about becoming a rich man.

Letty turned out to be a real peach to live with. That lady never once uttered the word *no* to me. I also found out that her real name was Letty Morgan and she was French as sauerkraut. I understood fully her need to form a fantasy in a man's mind, for in this world, every one of God's creatures are forced to get by in whatever manner they can. She was quite fortunate to have found an occupation that she was not only adept at, but enjoyed as well.

The Eighth day of May had been an unusually warm and cloudless one. It was the type of day that turns snow into babbling steams and sends prospectors heading off into the high country. Restlessness welled in my being like an unquieted storm. I had been unable to nap that afternoon, and tried to read an unfathomable novel about some idiot named Ishmael chasing off after a great white whale, but could not stay interested in it. Anyone who had ever sailed the oceans, as I have done, knows full well there is no such thing as a white whale.

I uncorked a bottle of Old Crow, sipped at it, then tickled Letty's fancy for a spell, which I found much more enjoyable than reading a book about some blasted whale.

I was dressing to go The Tiger Spit and play poker when Letty, naked as the blue sky outside, ran to me and wrapped her arms about me.

"Oh, Al," she cooed after planting a steamy kiss on my check with her ruby lips. "I have been so happy lately. Please stay home with me. There is a strange feeling I have that something bad will happen to you."

"Now, Letty," I said, "don't go and get all worried about nothing. I'm just going to play a little poker."

"No, Al, my love, I want you to take me away from

here, from Saguache and the life I've been forced to live. You are a good man and I'll be satisfied just to stay with you. I would never ask you to marry a—whore, for that is what I am."

I embraced her tightly and felt her shivering as if she were cold. "Letty, my dear, I must return to the mountains and make my—our—fortune before we can speak of such things. A beautiful lady such as yourself deserves a mansion on a hill, not some little cabin to call their home. Trust in me and give me time."

"Do you mean it?" she sobbed, her pitiful shivering subsided. "Will you actually have me, knowing what I am—or rather what I was?"

I gave her a firm squeeze. "Just trust me. Now you quit worrying your sweet self and think about fixing supper, for I will come home to you after I win us some money."

"It—it's just that I wish you would stay here with me. I really like being with you."

I stepped back and daubed tears from the corners of her deep blue eyes with the back of my finger. I drank of her beauty, for I had become quite infatuated with Letty Morgan. While Larry Dolan had described her as chunky, I simply thought of her as being large in all of the right places. Letty was only eighteen years old and sweet of disposition, a lady who should be allowed her dreams.

"Now don't you fret any. I will take care of you. The Tiger Spit is a right nice saloon and there hasn't been anybody shot thereabouts lately. I'll be fine and will be home early."

I gave her another kiss, pulled on my boots, and grabbed up my coat on the way out. While it was nice and warm at the time, once that sun set it got plenty cold.

The bank had not closed, so I dropped in and ruined

the cashier's day by taking out five hundred dollars. It wouldn't do to upset Larry Dolan more than necessary until I had taken care of a rather delicate situation or two.

I couldn't fathom why it would take me longer than another month to get rich. I still had Letty paid up for another two weeks, but to be on the safe side I decided to give Dolan another month's rent for her anyway. As I have said, I was truly infatuated with that little blonde.

A wave of trepidation struck me when I entered The Tiger Spit. There were not nearly so many customers in attendance as usual. I knew the warm weather had given impetus to the great San Juan gold and silver rush. It really wouldn't be wise for me to lollygag about Saguache much longer.

"Howdy, Dolan," I said to him as I bellied up to the bar. "It's kind of quiet in here this evening."

"I'll be darned, Packer," he grumbled. "I'd have never noticed that fact if you hadn't gone an' pointed it out to me."

"Hey, Baldy," I hollered to Ed Whitmore. I had taken to calling him that ever since Jim Bridger had shown me how much the term upset him. "I'd like a mug of beer and a shot of Old Crow whenever you can find the time."

Larry Dolan rolled his head and sadly surveyed the half-empty saloon. "I didn't reckon on folks headin' out so blamed fast. It's that new place goin' up over by Baker's Park that's done it to me. They've found some mighty rich silver over there. So much of it, in fact, they're already callin' the town Silverton."

I ventured, "Maybe you ought to think of opening a saloon over there. That way you can catch 'em there in the summer and here in the winter."

Dolan sighed, took a deep drag on a long nine cigar, and blew the smoke out his nose without so much as a

slight cough. I assumed the Bumblebee whiskey had calloused his windpipe. "I've been thinkin' on that an' it's
a good plan if I had the money, which I don't. Ever
blasted dime I got is sunk right here in The Tiger Spit."

"I've got a lead on a rich strike," I said, capturing
his full attention. "If Dame Fortune smiles on me,
maybe I can help you out fairly soon."

Ed brought my drinks, glared at me with his usual
snarling expression, and said, "I sure hope somethin'
hits. Dolan jus' told me I'm gonna be out of a job if
things don't pick up."

"Maybe Alonzo'll come up with someone that needs
hangin'," Larry Dolan quipped. Then turned to me. "I
appreciate the thought, Al, and I sure hope you do
make a find. If you strike it rich, I'd be more than
happy to set down and work somethin' out with you."

"You can count on it," I said sincerely. "Now I'd like
to talk with you about Letty."

Dolan pinched his eyebrows together. "I'm sorry, Al,
but I can't take her back. There ain't enough business
for the three whores I got left. You will tell her that
real nice-like, won't you? She done real good for me
when things were poppin'."

I downed the Old Crow quickly to keep a smile from
my face. "It'll break the little lady's heart right in two,
but since you're my good friend, I'll give her the sad
news."

Dolan cocked his head and bit hard on his cigar when
a thought struck. "Now I can't go givin' no refunds.
You went an' paid for her for an entire month an' a
deal is a deal."

I brushed my hand against the five hundred dollars
in my pocket. "Why, the thought never crossed my
mind," I said truthfully. "Alferd Packer's word is always
good as gold."

"I can agree with that," Dolan said. "How about we

go sit in on a game of poker? I've got to make a livin' somehow."

Night had fallen along with the temperature. Through the front windows and over the batwing doors a myriad of twinkling stars hung like jewels against a black sky. Overhead, on wagon wheels suspended from the ceiling by chains, dozens of smoking coal-oil lamps illuminated The Tiger Spit Saloon while we played five-card stud by their flickering yellow light.

I had lost nearly a hundred dollars, giving me reason to wish that I had listened to Letty's good advice and stayed home. A burly freighter by the name of Bum Hicks and Alonzo's deputy, Selman Wade, a skinny runt with a pockmarked face and shifty eyes who eerily reminded me of the demon-infested Wilson Bell, were picking both Larry Dolan and me clean.

If I drew three of a kind, one of them would come up with a full house. When I held a full house, I would lose to four of a kind. I knew full well that those two scallywags had conspired beforehand to cheat us, but for the life of me couldn't figure out how they were doing it.

The simplest and best method of handling those cardsharps would have been to employ the law firm of Samuel Colt, spend the price of two cartridges, and retrieve our money. Since Selman Wade had a tin star pinned on his dirty wool shirt, coupled with the fact Ed Whitmore was looking for work, I decided it prudent to let bygones be bygones.

"Well, boys, I reckon I've had all the fun I can afford for one night," I said, folding my cards. "I'd better head for home while I've still got a coat to keep me warm."

"We'll be here agin tomorrow night," Bum Hicks drolled. "Then the next day I'm makin' a run to Cañon

City for a load of picks an' shovels, gold pans and minin' stuff. All the stores hereabouts are plumb sold out already."

I felt a twinge of concern. Of all the men in the area, I likely had more need of a pick and shovel than any of them. "Dadgum it, I was hoping to head for the high county myself," I said. "I suppose now I'll have to wait until you get back to buy an outfit."

Selman Wade giggled like an idiot and raked in the pot. "If you've got enough money left to buy one with, I'd reckon you're right about havin' to wait. Also, the prices are headin' nowhere but up. Folks who mine the miners always make out when there's a gold rush on."

I scooted back my chair and stood. "I'd venture that my luck prospecting might be better than playing poker. Have a good evening, boys, but hang on to your money, for I intend to win the next time we get together."

"Take care, Packer," Larry Dolan said. "One more night of losin' like this one an' these two yahoos will own The Tiger Spit. I can't think of a worse trick to play on 'em."

I chuckled and turned to leave. That was when I realized when a woman has an intuition about something, a man is a fool not to listen to her.

My smile fled quicker than my money had gone and my knees felt wobbly when I saw striding through those batwing doors none other than Alf Rankin.

Twenty-nine

"Alferd Packer!" Rankin exclaimed loudly. "All of us figgured you an' your bunch had gone an' froze to death lookin' for that mine of yours, especially after that big storm struck." He looked about the saloon. "Just where are your pardners anyway?"

I was so taken off guard that I stood there thinking on the matter until Larry Dolan spoke up.

"Those fellows you call his pardners," Dolan growled, "went an' left poor ole Al to fend for himself up there in the mountains when he twisted his ankle. He's just dang lucky to have lived through bein' abandoned all hurt an' with no grub."

"What the hell are you talkin' about?" Alf Rankin said, tramping toward me. "Packer was their guide an' the only man among them that knew where he was goin'. Old Man Miller an' Israel Swan were too stove up to leave anyone. What's goin' on here?"

This was turning out to be the bad day Letty had feared. I hadn't really expected someone from the Utah bunch we had left in Chief Ouray's encampment to show up here in Saguache. In retrospect, I could see where I had been somewhat remiss in my judgment. When a person is forced to tell an untruth, however noble his motive might have been at the time, he must follow through with it.

"Whether or not you believe it, Alf Rankin," I said, facing him square on, "does not mean it didn't happen. I made the mistake of showing those so-called pardners of mine a map I had made to where that gold was. Then when I went and slipped on a patch of ice and hurt my ankle, those fellows didn't think they had any further use for me. They took that map in exchange for leaving me a rifle and a few bites to eat. I never saw them again."

"That's a crock," Rankin spat. "Those fellows bought into your story of findin' gold an' Frank Miller put up the money 'cause you were too broke. What I'm askin' you straight out, Packer, is what became of those men?"

"Most likely they're mining my gold," I fairly shouted. "Why don't you go look for them if you are so blasted concerned?"

"I'll do just that," Alf Rankin snapped. "I know something has to be terribly wrong for you to be here playin' poker when you was dead broke before. I also intend to take the law along with me." He stared at Selman Wade. "Are you the sheriff hereabouts?"

"No, sir," the deputy answered. "You'd be wantin' my uncle, Alonzo Walls."

It was becoming quite plain to me that every solitary soul in Saguache was related somewhere down the line.

Larry Dolan kicked back his chair and stood. He was already in a tolerable bad mood over losing money in the poker game. "Now just what gives you cause to come in here makin' accusations at one of my good customers?"

Alf Rankin introduced himself and basically gave a disgustingly factual account of our trip from Bingham City, Utah, to when my five companions and I had left them at Chief Ouray's camp.

While I listened to him rattle on about how I had cajoled folks into coming out to Colorado on the basis of some rich gold specimens along with a good story, I noticed Ed Whitmore staring at my neck again.

The worst part of Rankin's yammering was his pounding away about just how broke I had been. Larry Dolan's Tiger Spit Saloon had received several hundred dollars of my friend's donated money since my arrival here. I could see how the law might interpret this in a bad light.

The ponderous bartender draped a towel over his shoulder and walked around the end of the bar to say, "Packer told folks plain as day that his pardners were headin' for Baker's Park. I ain't never heard nothin' about any gold mine, that's fer sure. But Ole Al here has spent a passel of money. Hell, he even went an' rented a whore for an entire month."

Alf Rankin shook his head in puzzlement. "Ain't none of us ever heard tell of Baker's Park afore. Packer had a claim that he said was mighty rich an' convinced us all to come to Colorado with him. I reckon he owes an explanation of what really became of his pardners an' how he got his money."

That dang Rankin should have been a politician or at least a lawyer, for it was painfully obvious to me that he had gotten folks' curiosity up.

It occurred to me that a quick departure might be in order. Then I realized it was my word against his. I sincerely doubted the little mess I had left behind would be found before I could take care of the matter. What I needed to do most was keep my wits about me. I remembered a wise saying that the best defense is a good offense. Since I was caught between the Devil and the deep blue sea, this was a time to test the theory.

I turned to Larry Dolan. "Now see here, this fellow is just out to cause me problems. He simply doesn't realize that those pardners of mine *did* leave me just like I've said. Also, Rankin had no way of knowing that when I couldn't go on, Frank Miller went and paid me for my share of the claim. That German wasn't *all* bad. This should explain where I got my money."

Dolan rolled a long nine cigar between his lips. "Al, you did mention earlier that you had a lead on a gold strike."

I said quickly, "And I surely do. When I was prospecting the area up there last fall, I found another vein. It's my intention to open it up just as soon as the snow melts. There are lots of good leads in that country besides the one I sold when I was forced to do so."

"How about it, Rankin?" Dolan said to him. "If you don't have any proof against Packer here, I'd reckon you oughtta keep your trap shut an' go about your own business."

Alf Rankin shrugged his shoulders. "I only know that I have a really bad feeling that something's terrible wrong here. But to answer your question, I can't prove a thing—yet."

"And you won't either," I said happily. "Why don't you let bygones be bygones and I'll buy us a drink."

"I reckon not," Rankin said as he spun to leave. "I've a busy day ahead of me tomorrow visiting with the sheriff. I believe his name was Alonzo Walls."

"You take care now, Alf," I hollered after him. "Because I'm not going to hold a grudge against you for being mistaken."

"That man seems plenty determined," Bum Hicks said.

"Oh, he's just a sorehead," I said. "Let me buy us all a drink and then I'm calling it a night."

I downed a shot of Old Crow and left The Tiger Spit quite quickly. The way Ed Whitmore kept staring at me was downright unnerving.

* * *

When the bank opened the next morning I closed out my account. I had slept but little the past night, and as the possibility that I might have to leave in a hurry kept recurring to me, I took all of my money in easily carried fifty- and hundred-dollar paper notes.

After leaving the bank I dropped by Stein's Livery Stable, where I was forced to pay the exorbitant price of one hundred dollars each for two very mediocre horses. I would have much preferred mules, but the rush to Silverton had made them unavailable. I bought one riding saddle, tack, and a pack for the other horse. I also paid to have them stabled and reshod. I remember staring at the shining white mountains and wishing deeply the warm weather would continue so that I might be able to quickly accomplish my mission.

I knew in my heart that if I got back to the camp and buried a few things I had left strewn about in the snow, I would be fine. Alf Rankin's whining would come to naught when my five pardners simply vanished. In the turbulent frontier it was not an uncommon occurrence for men to simply never be heard of again.

When I walked down the dirt street from the livery heading back home, my stomach dropped and I felt my heart begin racing.

Alf Rankin and Alonzo Walls were heading into The Tiger Spit Saloon chatting away like old chums. I darted into an alleyway to keep from being spotted. I had done absolutely nothing wrong, yet having the law become interested in you is always unsettling.

I hurried home to my sweet Letty. I realized, should things take an unfortunate turn for the worse, her aid could become valuable. I also wanted her to know the truth of the matter before her judgment became tainted by lies and unfounded rumors. It is *so* comforting to have a lovely woman to rely on in times of crisis.

* * *

The next few days passed splendidly. As usual, I kept spending my evenings in The Tiger Spit Saloon. It would have appeared that I had a valid reason for concern should I have not done so. Thankfully, the weather remained warm and sunny. I knew that I would now be able to head back over that steep pass on horseback with little difficulty.

Alonzo Walls, of course, had questioned me again about my five pardners. I held fast and he seemed quite satisfied with my stance, as rightly he should have. I was furnishing his cousin with business, while Alf Rankin, it turned out, was nowadays almost a teetotaler.

Bum Hicks had returned with a wagon load of mining supplies. I purchased a much needed pick and shovel, for which I paid the unbelievably high price of ten dollars each. Then, to appear as if I were going prospecting, I bought a gold pan, some drill steel, blasting powder, and a roll of Bickford black fuse.

I made my plans to leave on the morrow, for those shining mountains were now showing patches of gray streaking up their sides. Now that Hicks was back, I had invited Selman and him to another round of poker. I had lost another fifty dollars to them and had given considerable thought to their winning so easily.

Selman Wade always wore a bright silver ring on the third finger of his left hand. I was certain he was using it as a "gaper" or mirror to read the cards as they were dealt. The fact that he was a deputy made his cheating more likely. All lawmen are basically dishonest or they would be in another line of work.

The sun was lowering behind the mountains when we took a table by the window. Larry Dolan brought over a fresh deck of cards and deftly spread them on the green cloth.

"I'm feelin' lucky tonight, boys," Dolan remarked as he raked in the cards and began shuffling. "Five-card stud okay to lose with?"

"Name your own pizen," Bum Hicks said with a grin.

I kept my eyes glued to Selman Wade's grimy hand. "That sure is a mighty pretty ring you got there. Do you mind if I see it?"

The deputy turned six different shades of red, but eventually he managed to get his mouth to work. "Why, uh—no, I reckon not."

I grinned, and started to grab up that ring and kindly ask the cheating deputy to put it in his pocket until the game was over, when I froze in my chair.

The batwing doors flew open and in marched Alonzo Walls, Alf Rankin, Chief Ouray, along with two of his braves, and, of all people, General Charles Adams. The party had a grim expression pasted on their faces as they came straight towards me.

"Alferd Packer," the sheriff growled. "You are in a lot of trouble."

"And just what is this all about?" I asked.

Chief Ouray held out some long strips of meat that I quickly recognized. My legs grew weak and I could not speak.

"White man's meat," Ouray said. "We found this on a hill above the Los Pinos Agency. This is from where you came."

General Adams spoke up. "The skin is still on it, Packer. These strips were cut from a human being. There is no way to deny the fact."

"We searched your cabin," Alonzo said with a sneer. He took a thin-bladed ivory-handled knife from his pocket and showed it to me. "Mister Rankin identified this knife as belonging to one of your pardners, a German butcher by the name of Frank Miller."

I took a deep breath. "Miller left me that knife—I could use it to survive with, he said."

"Not this time, Packer," Alf Rankin said. "No more lies, you killed those men, then—my God, you ate them!"

The sheriff took a pair of manacles from his back pocket. "Alferd Packer, I'm puttin' you under arrest until we can get to the bottom of this."

As the cold steel fastened about my wrists, I kept staring at those strips of flesh.

Where in the hell are coyotes when you have need of them?

Thirty

The lowest form of life that infests God's good earth is not a venomous reptile, a poisonous spider, or some vicious four-legged varmint. I found out the hard way it's a dad-blasted writer. Just one of those blamed idiots can cause a man more grief than all of the lawyers and sheriffs in the entire country would be capable of.

But I am getting ahead of myself.

After I was arrested, Alonzo Walls lodged me in the Saguache jail. This was a dreary earthen dungeon with one solitary barred window that gave a splendid view of the sheriff's office and a sturdy-looking gallows that had been built on a vacant lot alongside.

I was not unduly concerned by the scaffold at the time. Alf Rankin had just turned out to be a sourpuss who was trying to cause me problems. There was simply not more than a few shreds of evidence against me, and, of course, my conscience was perfectly clear regarding my actions this past winter. Any right-thinking man would have done as I had given the same set of circumstances.

Even in the nepotistic town of Saguache, I did not expect Ed Whitmore to find gainful employment until I had received a fair trial, at which I would surely be acquitted.

I really did need to get out and take care of some items that required tidying up. The weather continued in its warming trend, and I felt a growing concern at the number of men who were heading into the mountains. Fortunately, most of the talk I overheard told me most were leaving in the direction of Silverton, while my destination was more northerly. Still, there was a chance some flaming idiot might stumble over some things that could cause me considerable grief.

I took comfort in the fact that aside from the sorehead, Alf Rankin, and a bald hangman looking for work, most folks were quite sympathetic toward me. Sweet Letty Morgan, God bless her, stood by my side with the firmness of a mighty oak tree. She visited me every day bringing along some of her delicious cooking, for the food Alonzo or Selman brought in from the Chinese chophouses was of decidedly poor quality.

After two weeks of being so unfairly imprisoned, Letty came to the window of my cell one afternoon wearing a cute smile on her freckled face.

"Oh, Al," she said, "the lawyer you wanted, Hamilton Beesley, telegraphed from Denver that he will take your case. He will require a fee of one thousand dollars upon his arrival here in Saguache. The way folks are talking, I'm certain that lawyer will have you out of jail real fast. I simply can't understand why that mean ole sheriff went and locked you up in the first place."

"Now, Letty, my love," I said, pressing my face against the steel bars, "Alonzo has simply been swayed by a demented man who bears me ill will for some strange reason. Please telegraph Lawyer Beesley to come at once. I fear it would be disastrous for our future if I do not make it into the mountains quite soon. There is always a possibility some prospector might stumble across my—our rich gold mine and claim it as their own."

"I will not let that happen to us. I'll send a return message to the lawyer telling him to hurry quickly. Mister Conroy at the telegraph office told me that with the

new stage roads that have been built the trip should
only take him a couple of days at the most."

It irked me to have to pay a thousand dollars of my
hard-earned money to some suited shylock to free me
from a cage in which I had been so unfairly imprisoned.
The problem being, summer was fast upon us. With all
of the recent attention I had received from the law,
should some idiot stumble across the mortal remains of
my five deceased comrades, I knew full well Ed Whitmore would find work stretching my neck. This was not
a good time to be cheap.

"Go, my little dove of freedom," I said cheerily. "Take
care of our future, for it is in your hands, my sweet.
The sooner I am released from here, the quicker I can
go and assure our fortune."

Letty blew me a kiss from her open palms, then spun
and ran toward the telegraph office. While I smiled
broadly at her, I must confess that my heart was heavy
with foreboding. Each day that I languished in this
squalid cell, the more likely my problems could increase
to the point where any lawyer, no matter how expensive,
would cease to be of much benefit to me.

I returned to the flea-infested cot that was my sole
place of repose and lay down. I clasped my hands behind my head and watched by wan light as a black
widow spider spun its web on the ceiling. My dear
friends James Humphreys, Israel Swan, George Noon,
and Frank Miller visited me often in my dreams. Wilson
Bell, of course, having no soul to linger, never made so
much as an appearance.

From these spectral divinations I knew full well that my
old companions wished me well and bore me no malice
whatsoever. My conscience was clear as the finest crystal
on the matter. It was with the narrow-minded living members of law enforcement that my difficulties lay.

Letty had been allowed to bring me some books to

read. I had even managed to wade through most of the ghastly *Moby Dick or the White Whale* by Herman Melville. It amazed me how some novels ever got published.

The black leather-covered Bible given me by General Adams I kept under my pillow. It was from this Good Book that I derived the most comfort, as the general had prognosticated I would.

When Letty had brought me the Bible, the Book of Exodus had been hollowed out to allow room for a key to the cell door.

My little love had pilfered a key from Selman Wade's pocket while he was otherwise entertained. It had been a simple matter for her to make a wax impression and get the thing copied, for it turned out to be only a skeleton key. While the deputy blissfully slept away, Letty had returned it to the ring and the idiot was none the wiser.

It disturbed me deeply that Letty had had to soil her loveliness by lying with this pock-faced, soulless, card-cheating, hooligan of a lawman.

I could not, however, allow myself to rely on the mechanisms of law alone to keep me from being hung should those bodies be found before I could inter them beneath the earth.

Planning ahead has always served me well, otherwise I would have long before shed this mortal coil along with Turtle John and my other shipmates aboard the *Mary Celeste*.

I briefly glanced at the copy of *Moby Dick*, then returned my attention toward that black widow spider. I found its web-weaving to be much more absorbing.

"They found 'em, Packer," Alonzo Walls yelled at me through the bars that evening. "An' you ate ever last one of 'em. Damn it all, from what that writer fellow said, you killed your partners an' then stayed alive for weeks eatin' on their dead bodies. I never heard tell of nothin' like this before."

I bolted up from the cot. "What the heck are you talking about?"

"He even made a sketch of 'em, Packer. It was plain awful."

"Now calm down, Alonzo," I said, "and tell me what has you so blasted worked up!"

The sheriff took a deep breath and glared at me. "There was a writer and sketch artist by the name of John Randolph sent out here by *Harper's Weekly* magazine to cover the rush to Silverton. Well, sir, him an' his bunch got a little mixed up an' went the wrong direction. When they was gettin' their bearings, one of 'em came onto a camp with dead folks that had no meat on 'em strewn all over the place."

"Now, Alonzo, I had nothing to do with that."

"They was *your* pardners, Alferd Packer. Hell's bells, their names was still in their grips, but not their money. Reckon you'll hang for sure now."

I swallowed hard and dropped back on that filthy cot. This was not what I wanted to happen at all. Leave it to some idiot writer to get himself lost and cause me problems. "I—I can explain, Alonzo, trust me."

"Ain't up to me none." His voice was calmer now. "Judge Carver's been sent for. When he gets here you'll get a fair trial an' Ole Ed'll get ten bucks for a proper hangin'. That poor fella's been outta work for quite a spell, y'know."

I said, "I have my own lawyer coming from Denver."

"He'd better git here afore tomorrow afternoon, because the judge'll be here around noon an' the hangin's set for square at five."

"This isn't right, Alonzo. I only killed Bell and that was in self-defense."

"Ain't me you gotta convince, Packer. If I was you, I'd save my wind for Judge Carver. He's known fer listenin' good before he hangs folks."

I decided to simply keep quiet. There was nothing to be gained by trying to talk sense to a lawman. After a few moments of glaring at me by the fading sunlight, he moved back from the bars to be replaced by the gloating, bloated countenance of Ed Whitmore.

"Tomorrow mornin'," the ex-bartender-turned-hangman said, "Alonzo an' I'll chain you up and take you over to the gen'ral store. I need to get you weighed proper so's I can figger the drop. I'd hate to see you wiggle around on the end of a rope for a spell. I have a reputation to protect."

I grinned at him. "I always knew you were a kindly sort."

"Gotta snap their necks good an' hard. That way it's over with before God gets the news, an' I promise you won't feel nothin' a'tall."

"I appreciate your concern, Ed," I said. "Could you ask Alonzo to step back over?"

"Sure, Packer." He nodded. "An' no hard feelin's? I'm just doin' my job."

"None whatsoever."

Alonzo's ugly mug reappeared at the bars. "Now whatta you want from me?"

I grabbed up the Bible, taking care to keep a firm grip on it. "I would surely appreciate a lantern or candle to read by."

He seemed taken aback. "Why, sure, Alferd, I'll send Selman by with a coal oil lamp. I suspect that Bible will be a great comfort to you."

"More than you know," I said.

Thirty-one

A full moon hung high in a silky black, jewel-studded Colorado sky. The yellow orb furnished wonderfully sufficient light for Letty and me as we rode our horses along the sagebrush-lined road that headed northeast from the dreary town of Saguache.

I was quite relieved to be on my way, and expected to be a goodly distance from town before anything amiss was discovered. Should that idiot deputy, Selman Wade, try the door to my cell, he would find it was still securely locked.

In case he or some other dolt peered through the bars, I had cleverly filled the sheets with dirt scraped from the floor and placed them on the cot and draped them with a blanket. This made it appear that I was facing the wall and reading my Bible by lantern light, steeling myself for the hereafter.

All in all, I thought things were going rather splendidly, and doubted anyone would note my departure until Alonzo Walls and Ed Whitmore came by to feed me breakfast, then get me weighed on those brass scales at the general store for my hanging.

I could not contain a smile of satisfaction from crossing my face when I realized those dunderhead lawmen would soon show themselves to be as stupid as they actually were.

Of course, I really owed much of my being clear of Saguache to the lovely Letty Morgan. If she had not successfully managed to pilfer that key and kept the horses stabled at our home in anticipation of such an emergency, I likely would have been in for a very bad experience on the morrow.

Another thing added considerably to my happiness; I reached down and patted the leather saddlebag that held over six thousand dollars, all of it in easily carried paper bank notes. My sweet Letty had donated her life savings toward our future together.

It was also uplifting to know that expensive lawyer, Hamilton W. Beesley, would have made a long and tiring trip for naught. Anytime a man can screw a lawyer and outwit a sheriff along with a hangman, he has good cause to feel joyous.

"Al, dear," Letty said as she rode by my side. "It broke my heart to hear all of those terrible things folks are saying about you."

"Saguache is a town full of ignorant and unenlightened people, my dove. Just be thankful we are leaving there."

"Oh, I'm *so* glad we're together. I know you couldn't have killed anyone. I simply can't understand how the law and that writer could be so mistaken."

"People can often be cruel and narrow-minded," I said with a sigh. "What troubles me the most is the fact that I will be unable to go for our rich gold mine until after the *real* killer of those poor men is apprehended."

Letty turned in her saddle and studied me by the pale moonlight. "Yes, Al, I know you—we—are wanted fugitives. I have given the matter some thought. In what—used to be my line of work it was often necessary to look like an entirely different person. Some of the men who used to come to my room were so drunk they thought I was a new girl whenever I dyed my hair a different color, or cut it. New merchandise always gets more business, for some men like to brag about being the first ones to sample the goods."

It hurt me deeply to hear little Letty talk about her past, yet the idea of changing my appearance seemed like a wonderful plan. I had little doubt that before the sun set again, my description would have been telegraphed to every sheriff for hundreds of miles. Any man with long black hair sporting a goatee and traveling with a young blond lady would be instantly suspect wherever we showed up. I also felt a chill in my spine when I realized the horses we rode, a roan and an Appaloosa that were both branded, would be far too easily recognizable for comfort.

"What do you have in mind to color my hair with?" I asked her.

"I brought along some bottles of hair dye. For you I have ochre and for me, I'll become a brunette. Tomorrow at first light, when we are by water, I will shave your beard and then trim your hair. Within a few minutes, you'll be a neatly trimmed redhead," she tittered. "After I've finished, I'll bet you could ride right past that awful Alonzo Walls and he'd never recognize you."

But he certainly would identify the horse, I thought. It was best not to worry my Letty. I knew that somehow, some way I would come up with a solution to the dilemma.

When I studied my new mien by using a small hand mirror Letty had thoughtfully brought along, I knew she had been correct when she said even the sheriff would not recognize me. I scarcely could recognize myself with burnt red hair and matching eyebrows. I did not care, however, for having my beard shaved. I thought it made me appear unnecessarily harsh, but as my lady said the coloring could run should I accidentally get it wet when I drank, I understood her reasoning perfectly.

We had stopped to rest alongside the rippling waters of the San Luis River. The position of the sun indicated it to be around nine o'clock in the morning. I knew that by now the town of Saguache was a hornet's nest of activity. There were many roads out of that town, but I knew Alonzo would be so angry he would put together posses for all of them. For this reason I had decided keeping to the back country and away from all well-traveled roads would be a healthy move.

"Letty, my love," I said happily. "Not only do I look like a totally different man, but we have many hours of head start on any lawmen. Come to think on the matter, I have not properly thanked you for everything you've done to help me. Why don't you get that blanket of yours and lay it out on a soft patch of grass and let me show you my appreciation."

"Oh, Al," she giggled as she went to do my bidding. As I have said, the word no simply wasn't in that sweet lady's vocabulary.

"Where are we going, my love?" Letty asked later that day. We were riding cross-country along the western slope of the Sangre De Cristo Mountains, heading north.

"I have given the situation a lot of thought. My idea is to encounter the Arkansas River and follow it to Cañon City and Pueblo. From there we can travel by stagecoach to Denver and on to Cheyenne in the Wyoming Territory. We can lay low there until things quiet down. Then before the snows hit, I will return to the San Juans and stake out our gold mine."

"But how will you file the claim? You cannot do so under your own name."

I grinned. "Oh, you must be thinking of that wanted man Alferd Packer. I haven't seen him for quite a spell." I turned toward her and tipped my hat. "I wish to introduce to you the dashing young John Swartze."

Letty giggled and brushed a wild strand of brunette hair from her face. "Why, I'm very pleased to make your acquaintance, my good sir. I have the feeling we are going to get along fabulously."

"I *know* we will," I said, spurring my horse into a faster gait.

The sun was lowering in the west and we were setting up a camp next to a small stream, for we were both exhausted, when tragedy struck and once again my dreams came crashing down around me.

Sweet Letty Morgan, the apple of my eye, was out gathering some wood to build a fire with when she was bitten in the throat by a huge green timber rattler. The little lady had not seen the coiled viper and bent over the snake, which struck upward and sunk its fangs into her lithe neck. No person who is bitten in that manner lives more than a woefully few pain-racked minutes.

I rushed to Letty's aid when I heard her scream, but sadly there was nothing I could do to save her. I grabbed up a limb and smashed the life from the vicious reptile; then I held her in my arms while she gasped and sobbed piteously.

"Oh, Al, my love—carry on without me," were Letty's final words.

I clutched her lifeless frame close to me and cried for the longest while. I have never felt so distraught. Eventually, however, all tears must dry. Remembering my lost love's last request, I laid her out in a brushy area and cut some bushy green saplings to keep the buzzards from finding her.

Just before darkness claimed the valley, I led her horse, the easily recognizable Appaloosa, to alongside Letty's resting place. To save the sound of a gunshot, I pulled my razor-sharp bowie knife from its scabbard and sliced open the animal's throat. It died very quickly. I also covered the horse with green branches, for circling vultures have a tendency to attract attention.

Later, I fried up some salt pork and potatoes for supper even though my appetite had long since fled. I needed to keep up my strength, for I owed it to my little lost love to do so. Before retiring, I filled my hat with water and dashed it on the flames. After everything Letty had done to get me this far, it would have been a shame to allow myself to be captured for something so foolish as leaving a fire burning.

That night Letty visited me in my dreams, as do many of my fallen comrades. She bade me her fondest farewells, told me of her undying love, then, after once again encouraging me to carry on without her as best I could, she departed to the place from where no one has ever returned.

When I awoke the next morning, my eyes were matted with dried tears.

It took me nearly a full week to arrive at the point where the Arkansas River cuts into the unbelievably steep and rugged Royal Gorge. Being forced to stay off all beaten paths had slowed my progress considerably. From here, however, the rough terrain would force me to travel a well-used wagon road to reach the town of Cañon City.

Over the past several days, I had plenty of time to think on my future and ways for me to preserve my hold on this earthly coil. Nothing that had transpired of late was in any way my fault, yet I knew that most certainly a hangman's noose awaited me should I become careless. And sometimes even lazy, half-wit lawmen can get lucky.

Here, alongside the gushing clear waters of the Arkansas, I was alone, and as I would soon enter a sizable town, this would be my last time to prepare myself.

I removed the saddlebags from my lathered roan and allowed the animal to drink greedily while I took stock of my appearance. Thankfully, sweet Letty's mirror, comb, and her hair dye were coming in quite useful. I scraped the whiskers from my face with a folding straight razor, using a bar of soap and cold river water for a lubricant to avoid cutting myself. A man of my calling would never appear unkempt.

Carefully I inspected my appearance, admiring how handsome John Swartze looked with red hair. Letty's dye had worked perfectly. I washed my hands and face and combed my ochre hair. I tucked my money away deep inside a saddlebag after counting it once again. Six thousand three hundred dollars and change would carry me for a long while once I got decent employment, which I now planned to do upon my arrival in Cañon City.

I retrieved my horse and unsaddled him, then quite carefully checked my surroundings to make certain I was alone. The animal seemed to still be thirsty, so I led him closer to the rapids and fired a single shot from my .45 into its left ear. Luck was with me and the horse bolted away from the blast and into the deep water. The last I saw, it was tumbling over and over in white water, heading into the abyss of the Royal Gorge. Should it wash up miles downstream I doubted the animal could be identified, for the boulders in that river were giving the carcass a severe pounding.

I picked up the saddle and walked oh-so-carefully on wet round boulders, and threw that saddle with all my might into the strong current. Absolutely nothing that could possibly be connected with Alferd Packer remained to cause me problems.

The Bible General Charles Adams had so thoughtfully given me was to serve yet one more purpose. While the center of the Book of Exodus had been removed, I decided that enough of the book remained to carry out my task. In a very short while I would burn this Bible in a cookstove and replace it with one that was intact.

I remembered some words to a religious song that I had overhead echoing from an open church door while I was lodged in jail in Saguache. I felt it appropriate to happily sing a few lines.

> Free from the law, O happy condition,
> Jesus has bled, and there is remission;
> Cursed by the law, and bruised by the fall,
> Grace has redeemed us once for all.

I draped the pair of saddlebags over my shoulder, tucked the black Bible underneath my arm, and strode off.

The Reverend John Peter Swartze, a Baptist preacher whose mission on earth was to stop the Devil in his tracks and save souls from perdition, was on his way to Cañon City, Colorado.

After all, I mused, *since I was already filled with the spirits, the calling was a natural one.*

Thirty-two

I could not contain a gasp of astonishment when the lumbering freight wagon I rode in the back of passed around the edge of a steep, flat-sided sandstone cliff that reminded me of an eagle's wing and I first beheld the gray stone buildings of the territorial prison.

If I had known earlier that this establishment was here, I surely would have decided to go to other, more agreeable environs. Then it dawned on me that this was likely the last place on earth any dunderhead sheriff would expect me to show up, for I was certain the town of Cañon City would be infested with lawmen.

The burly freighter noticed my eyeing the prison, and spat a wad of tobacco on the wagon seat as he turned toward me. "Reckon there's a passel of work fer you inside there, preacher." He chuckled and added, "Of course, I'm sure a man of the cloth can find plenty of sin that needs curin' 'bout anywhere he goes."

"Amen, brother," I said. "The Devil is everywhere and often goes around in sheep's clothing. I simply did not know this prison was here."

The freighter laughed and sprayed tobacco juice about. "Why, hell—uh, sorry, parson—I mean why, shucks, that place got built some years back. It was in Sixty-Nine the good citizens hereabout was given the choice of havin' a college or a prison. That sure didn't strain any brains. They's a lot more folks attend jail than some durn school an' they stick around longer, to boot." He eyed me strangely. "That is lessen they get themselves a hangin' date. Reckon when that happens, you gotta work mighty quick to grab up that soul before ole Satan gets his claws on it."

I swallowed hard. "I do not believe it is right for the law to execute people, and I shall oppose it at every opportunity."

"Folks round here will 'spect that from a preacher. I wouldn't 'spect a lot of progress along those lines, however. Hangin's is always good fer saloon business."

"Could you recommend a decent hotel?" I asked. The subject of hanging was causing me discomfort and it needed changing badly.

"Hell—ah, shucks, yes, I surely can. There ain't but one choice fer a gentleman like yerself. I'll drop you off in front of the McClure Hotel. Ole Sam Sowers sets out a good table an' has a right decent saloon with no whores about." He turned and flicked the reins. "A body's gotta walk two whole blocks fer one of them."

The wagon gave out a groan when the freighter set the brake in front of an attractive three-story redbrick building only a short distance from the prison. I had made note of the sheriff's office that was less than a block to the south. It was gratifying that Alferd Packer was nowhere to be seen; the law could walk him to prison from here.

"Thank you, brother," I said as I swung down from the wagon and retrieved my saddlebags. "And may God bless you for your kindness toward me."

"Weren't nuthin', preacher. I'm just sorry to hear yer horse up an' died on you suddenlike."

"The poor animal was quite old, my friend, but I shall miss him nevertheless."

"Yep, reckon I know what ya mean. I get rather attached to 'em myself. Well, I gotta head over an' git a load of coal for Saguache."

I was too taken aback to do more than nod at the freighter as he flicked the reins on his four-horse team and started the wagon lumbering off. A drink to steel my frayed nerves would have been nice, but since I had chosen to pass myself off as a Baptist preacher, this would not have been a wise move. There were many good points about their religion, however, which would make my task easier.

Baptists don't rely on a lot of ritual or wear odd clothes. From what I had seen of their preaching, it consisted of simply lambasting sin in all of its forms. This generally meant loose women and whiskey, both of which I had a fairly good knowledge of. If I were to make a success of passing myself off as a preacher, I couldn't be asked too many fussy religious questions as are Catholic priests or Presbyterians. Becoming a Baptist was an excellent choice.

I took a deep breath, draped the saddlebags over my left shoulder, and strode into the McClure Hotel. I rented a room with board for a week. At this time I had no real plans other than to relax and allow time to pass while the law scoured the country looking for Alferd Packer.

The cadaverous desk clerk acknowledged me with a grunt when I plunked down a nickel for a copy of the *Pueblo Democrat* and headed up the curved oak stairs for my second-story room. I wished to read the headlines announcing the jailbreak in Saguache of some person by the name of Al Packer who was not only being sought for murder and robbery, but also the crime of cannibalism. It was a comfort to be many miles from that terrible place. Later, I would purchase a new suit of clothes, bathe, have a scrumptious steak dinner, and relax. I had plenty of money and the town of Cañon

City was not as bad as I had feared. The McClure Hotel had much better accommodations than the Saguache jail.

I wound up lollygagging there in the hotel, leaving only for occasional walks or to shop, for an entire two weeks. This behavior did not seem to cause any eyebrows to become raised. I also took the precaution of informing the skinny desk clerk that I had been ill. I paid for everything with cash and spent much time in my room reading and recuperating from my exhausting experiences of late. Summer was well upon us, and I spent many relaxing hours leaning back in a very comfortable chair with a warm breeze blowing through an open window and getting caught up on the news of the world and current literature.

I studied the contemporary magazines, *Scribner's Weekly, Popular Science, Illustrated Police News,* and perused most carefully several old issues of *The National Preacher* that I had found in the downstairs reading room.

I also read a couple of recent novels, *The Story of a Bad Boy* by Thomas Bailey Aldrich, which I found quite entertaining, and *The Fair God* by Lew Wallace, which bored me nearly as badly as *Moby Dick* had.

I was growing exceedingly fidgety, for I have never been one who enjoys being in one place for long. Around a dozen years ago, only three years after its discovery in my native Pennsylvania, oil had been found north of Cañon City. From conversations I had overhead in the lobby, these fields were being extended to the east of town near the juncture of Four Mile Creek and the Arkansas River. The idea of investing some money there seemed more to my style than being a stump preacher.

I had decided to hire a carriage and scout out the

countryside where the oil had been found when my plans were once again changed like a winter wind. You may well imagine my emotional upset when I answered a polite knock on my door one afternoon only to open it and find two uniformed men wearing guns and shiny sliver badges.

"Reverend Swartze?" the lankier of the two lawmen asked nervously, holding his hat to his chest. This gave me time to quiet my throbbing heart and get my mouth to engage.

"Uh, yes, I am he, officer," I answered at length. "How may I be of service to you gentlemen?"

"Well, sir." The same officer nodded to his decidedly corpulent companion. "I'm Officer Garrett and this here's my partner, Captain Brennan. We're here at the request of Jack Goode. He's the prison warden, as you likely already know."

I said shakily, "I have heard of the gentleman."

"We were informed that you've been ill, sir," Officer Garrett said apologetically. "And we hate to bother you, but we were told that you're a Baptist preacher?"

"Yes, I am a minister of the Gospel."

"Well, sir," Captain Brennan piped up, his voice was chillingly cold. "We have need of your services in the morning, if you're up to it, that is."

I coughed long and deep, then extracted a handkerchief and dabbed at my eyes, taking care not to rub my ochre eyebrows. "How may I be of assistance to you gentlemen?"

"We're sure sorry about your being sick an' all," Officer Garrett said. "But we've got ourselves a horse thief and a stagecoach robber by the name of Crocker Stonebridge that's gettin' himself hung at ten in the mornin' down in front of the prison."

"Yes, sir." I coughed again to get the point across.

"All the regular preachers are either out of town or

busy doin' weddin's or such," Brennan replied. "Crocker's asked for a parson to walk up the gallows with him and say a few good words from the Bible before he gets dropped."

This time I did not need to fake my cough. When my mouth could once again form words, I said shakily, "It is the poor soul's right to have comfort in his last moments of life. I shall be there, gentlemen, and may God bless you for asking."

Officer Garrett spoke. "I'm sure ole Crocker will appreciate havin' you there. It's a mystery to me how you preachers can find anything decent to say about the likes of scallywags like him, but I reckon you'll manage. They always seem to, somehow."

"All men are equal in the eyes of God," I said firmly. "Our blessed Savior forgave the thief on the cross as he shall forgive Crocker Stonebridge."

Garrett turned to the captain. "Like I just said, preachers can find good in anyone."

Brennan snorted. "If we get that Alferd Packer in here, it'll be a strain for the best of 'em. I'm plain lookin' forward to that hangin'."

I became racked with a terrible coughing fit that would have done justice to Israel Swan's best efforts.

"You up to this, preacher?" Officer Garrett asked with concern.

"Ten o'clock in the morning," I said after catching my breath. "I shall arrive early to give the poor condemned soul as much comfort as I can."

"Parson," Captain Brennan said sincerely, "you are a good man."

"I shall see you on the morrow," I said, then closed my door and began the work of composing myself. I had not known for certain just what being a preacher would entail exactly, but *this* scenario I had not imagined in my wildest dreams.

I plopped heavily down in my chair and grabbed up the Bible. I had been remiss in not studying it earlier. There had to be some words I could read that were not in the Book of Exodus. I buckled down and began scribbling notes.

It was going to be a very long night.

Thirty-three

The orange glow of a rising sun found me still poring over the Bible attempting to come up with some words of comfort for the condemned Crocker Stonebridge and not betray my ignorance of the preaching business.

I was exceedingly nervous about the whole affair. From all of the revelry coming from the downstairs saloon and about town this past night, I knew full well the hanging would be well attended. Hundreds of eyes of both stewed and sober citizens and lawmen from all over the country would be focused on the Reverend Swartze. I had to carry this off or the next hanging I attended would be my own. A scenario I did not relish.

It was also exceedingly troubling to me that Stonebridge, who would drop into eternity at my very feet, had only robbed a few people. Alferd Packer would certainly draw a much larger crowd, should such a tragedy be allowed to occur.

I cursed aloud my decision to become a blasted preacher. A whiskey drummer, cobbler, or even a traveler from the East in search of health here in the high and dry climate of Colorado would have served me as well and caused a lot less problems. But, oh, no, I had to tuck a Bible under my arm and run about quoting scripture like some Zealot on a mission. Now, as the saying goes, my chickens had come home to roost.

I ordered breakfast to be brought to my room. After a huge plate of ham and scrambled eggs and several cups of black coffee, my body felt refreshed, but my nerves were still frayed. The hands of the clock on my nightstand moved with amazing rapidity. I assumed they were moving even faster for Crocker Stonebridge. It was now nearly nine o'clock. And I still did not have the vaguest idea of what I would say or read.

It dawned on me like being struck by a lightning bolt: *The Lord's Prayer!*

That always seemed to fit most any situation quite nicely. The problem was, I could not remember all of the words. And also, I didn't know where in the scriptures the darn thing was located. The Bible has an awful lot of pages to it and I was on a tight schedule. I grabbed up the Good Book and began thumbing through it with much speed. Thankfully, what I was looking for turned out not to be in the Book of Exodus, and I found the passage I needed in the Testament of Saint Mark.

Carefully and repeatedly I studied the text until I hoped I had committed it to memory. I then dressed in my new suit of clothes, checked my hair dye in the mirror, and adjusted my tie with shaking hands. I placed a marker for the Sixth Chapter of the Book of Mark, and took the added precaution of clipping the Book of Exodus closed so that Letty's handiwork would not cause me embarrassment at an extremely inopportune moment.

The Reverend Swartze departed the McClure Hotel with a churning stomach, and followed the lines of people heading west towards the imposing gray stone wall that surrounded the territorial prison.

"Mornin', parson." Captain Brennan met me at the edge of the milling crowd that was gathering around the wooden gallows, which had been built high on a large wooden platform where everyone could view the proceedings without difficulty. "Glad to see you were up to makin' it. Our prisoner ain't really takin' this well," he said as he escorted me through the mass of onlookers.

"I shall give him what little comfort I can from the Good Book," I intoned.

A long corridor had been roped off that led from the gallows to a massive steel door set in the stone wall. You may well imagine my discomfort of being escorted past dozens of badge-wearing lawmen. I was amazed, however, that none of them paid me any particular mind. I was hopeful this trend would continue.

The captain banged on the steel door with his nightstick. "Open up, Ralph, I brung the preacher."

The squeaking of that huge door opening reminded me of a wailing woman. I was quickly ushered through this portal and led to a nearby cell. Once inside, I was taken aback when introduced to the condemned. Instead of the hardened road agent I had expected, Crocker Stonebridge turned out to be a rather plump, beardless kid of nineteen with fear-widened, teary eyes.

Captain Brennan pulled out a gold pocket watch and studied it gravely. "You two have ten minutes, then we have to get on with it."

"Please, God, I don't want to die!" the boy cried out after taking a quick look at me, then buried his face in his hands.

"Courage, my son," I said with a pat to his trembling shoulders. "Soon your soul will be in a better place."

"Ten minutes," the guard repeated, then slammed the cell door closed behind him as he left us alone.

None of the questioning I had feared so much occurred. Crocker Stonebridge was in such a dither over being hung he simply sobbed and moaned for the entire time until the guards came for him. All I did was hold my Bible in my hands and feel sorry for him.

"I'm Warden Goode, Reverend," a hard-faced older man who sported a handlebar mustache and a potbelly said to me. "We'll be walkin' together, right behind the condemned prisoner."

"The young man's name is Crocker Stonebridge," I admonished. "A fellow human being."

Warden Goode studied his boots. "Yes, preacher, I am sorry about that."

A bevy of uniformed guards descended upon the sobbing boy, grabbed him up, and manacled his hands behind his back. The lad was so distraught he had to be carried from the prison and up the thirteen steps of the gallows.

I stayed by the warden's side and said nothing. Crocker kept bawling so loudly no one thought much about me keeping quiet. Everyone's attention was nicely focused away from me.

The noose was placed around the young man's neck and adjusted. Two burly guards kept him held up when the warden turned to me. "Okay, preacher, say your words."

With sweaty hands I opened the Bible. It amazed me that I did not have to read the Lord's Prayer, but remembered every word with clarity. My voice was strong and the crowd grew silent during my recitation.

Then I said the word "Amen" and, oh-so-suddenly, Crocker Stonebridge dropped from my side through the trapdoor that had been opened on my unknowing cue. The rope that was about his neck made a twanging sound when his weight jerked it tight.

"Oh, shit!" the warden fairly screamed when he peered down through the open trapdoor.

"My God in Heaven!" I heard a guard yell. Then a chorus of curses and hollering broke out amongst the crowd. Several men who had gathered close by the gallows on the ground below spun away to vomit their breakfasts.

I summoned my courage and ventured a peek down to see what was amiss, for I rightfully assumed things had not gone as planned.

Crocker Stonebridge's body lay next to a support post for the gallows, spurting blood from where his neck used to be. The young man's head was still held by the noose and swaying to and fro. The idiot hangman had misjudged the drop and decapitated the poor fellow.

Captain Brennan turned to me and shrugged his shoulders. "Well, I don't see a problem here. After all, he wasn't supposed to live through it."

I trust that by now you are coming to understand my intense dislike for lawmen.

While I could have easily pushed that corpulent guard through the trapdoor to wallow in the blood below, I simply and stoically tucked my Bible away and very calmly walked down the steps from the gallows, threaded my way through the crowd, and returned to the McClure Hotel.

The only good to come from this terribly botched affair was the fact that no one paid me any mind when I packed my grip and departed the illustrious town of Cañon City on the noon stage to Pueblo.

John Peter Swartze's preaching days were behind him. I needed to keep my head about me and Colorado did *not* seem like a good place to accomplish this.

Thirty-four

The stately city of Cheyenne, in the eastern part of Wyoming Territory, was quite a delightful place to spend time. There were wide, tree-lined streets along with numerous prosperous businesses such as banks, saloons, and houses of recreation. It is very possible, looking back on the matter, that I could have remained there for much longer than the seven months I did enjoy. Leaving Cheyenne became an excellent idea on the Eighteenth of January in the year of Eighteen Seventy-Five, for that was when I shot Wild Bill Hickok.

Of course, I didn't kill Wild Bill or even do him a lot of damage. Jack McCall was to perform that public service a couple of years later up in the gold rush town of Deadwood. My problems stemmed from the fact that Hickok had bad eyesight and an even worse disposition. If the famous gunman was possessed of the slightest sense of humor, we might have turned out to be friends, but he was as arrogant and unforgiving as a skinny banker.

I had come straight to Cheyenne without tarry when I departed Cañon City after that terrible experience I had with the hanging of Crocker Stonebridge. The last thing I wished was to be a preacher. During a layover late at night while the horses were being changed, I made the pretense of warming myself against the huge kitchen stove inside the way station. I then very stealthily slid that Bible into the firebox. This put an end to my career as a man of the cloth. That line of work I cheerfully bequeathed to others.

During the rest of the long and dusty trip to Cheyenne I pondered my future employment to avoid any suspicion falling upon me. I knew I must appear to be gainfully employed, even though I had plenty of money. As I had learned so well in Cañon City, I also needed some occupation that would keep me from the public eye.

My dilemma was answered when that stage rattled down the dirt streets of Cheyenne and I spied a sign posted in the window of the High Plains Hotel advertising for a cook. As I had some fair experience along this line I applied to the manager, a fat, ruddy-faced Irishman by the name of Ward O'Neill, who hired me on the spot.

To my great joy, not only did I receive a wage of ten dollars a week, I was also given a pleasant room in the hotel along with all of my meals. This arrangement, which kept me from prying eyes for most of the day, suited me wonderfully.

Irish cooking, for that was what the restaurant served, turned out to be very simple to prepare. The first and most important ingredient is a potato; from there a man can do no wrong. Stews were quite popular fare. I would start with a big pot of whatever meat I felt appropriate for the day. Then I tossed in cabbages, carrots, or whatever else was handy along with a ton of potatoes, and everyone, including me, was always quite pleased with the results.

At nine o'clock sharp every evening, including Sunday, the restaurant closed its doors. Then it took me around an hour to scrub the pots and pans, wash dishes, and generally clean the joint up to make ready for the next day's stew. O'Neill allowed me to order bread, cakes, and pies from a Chinese bakery in the next block, which eased my work considerably.

My long day's work done, I would wash up in the bath at the end of the hall, change my clothes, and walk to a cheery saloon to wash the taste of potatoes from my throat.

The Tam-O-Shanter was a nice saloon just across the street, so it was handy. Miles O'Neill, my boss's brother, ran the place and a glass of beer only cost me a nickel there. Accordingly I gave them most of my business. I have never fully understood why one nationality of people seem to congregate together, but they always do. One good thing I can say about the Irish outside of their questionable tastes in stew; darn few of them ever seem to become lawmen. This delightful trait was to earn the entire species my heartfelt respect.

Occasionally, however, wanderlust would cause me to venture to what passed for the downtown section of Cheyenne. The block east of The Cricket Club theater sported a row of businesses that offered a much more interesting form of recreation than any stage thespian could ever hope to compete against. There was The Yellow Dog Saloon and, not showing too much imagination, across the street stood The Red Dog Saloon. I chose to avoid these dives and while away an occasional evening enjoying the delights of The Green Lantern, which held, I believed, the best-looking soiled doves Cheyenne had to offer.

Out of respect for my sweet departed Letty Morgan, I formed no relationships here other than those of the quite temporary sort. I knew in my heart that she would understand more than most the basic urges that a man is forced to realize on occasion.

Everything was going along rather splendidly for me until that fateful night I decided, for some reason, to drop by The Cheyenne Club, which was the largest and most well appointed of all of the gambling houses, and play a few hands of poker.

It was somewhat past midnight and the always present wind was whipping up a skiff of snow that had fallen a few days ago and taking it for another pass through town. The frigid temperature combined with the blasted howling wind made it cold enough to put goose flesh on a penguin. I suppose after the winter I had suffered through last year, I was getting fairly tired of cold weather in general.

I stepped inside The Cheyenne Club, shook the snow from my longcoat, and hung it on a peg, then went to warm myself by a huge potbelly stove that sat square in the middle of the building. It was always wise to check out a new saloon or gambling joint for deadbeats or troublemakers before deciding to stick around. I certainly did not want any sheriff to come around for the purpose of quieting some ruffian. I had been around enough lawmen in Colorado to last me for quite a spell.

This place was downright pleasant. A piano player who managed to bang the right keys most of the time was at one end of a great, curved mahogany bar that must have been a hundred feet long. There were a good dozen gambling tables in operation and everyone seemed to be having a grand time. Drinks were served to men at the tables by pretty waiter girls who wore skirts high enough to show off their ankles. I held no doubts what the rooms at the head of the stairs were used for. All in all, I thought The Cheyenne Club to be a delightful establishment.

That was when I noticed a bunch of men about one poker table and I first set eyes on Wild Bill Hickok. During my job at the restaurant I had overheard many people talking about Hickok's being in town, so his presence came as no surprise.

Wild Bill was a living legend who had cut quite a reputation for himself in Kansas cow towns as a shootist. He apparently enjoyed his fame for he dressed like he was in a parade. Long blond hair cascaded down his shoulders. He wore fringed buckskin clothes, while around his rather ample middle, a bright red sash kept twin ivory-handled pistols with the butts turned inward quite handy.

Bill sat leaned back in his chair with his back to the wall, studying his cards with squinting eyes. I was quite surprised to note an empty chair at the table, so I beat some life into my cold-numbed hands and went to take it. Not everyone gets a chance to play poker with a legend.

"Gentlemen," I said politely as I placed a hand on the back of the chair. "If this seat is not taken I wish to play."

Hickok cocked one of his blue eyes at me. "You have made a mistake, my friend."

"I'm sorry, sir," I said, jerking my hand away from that chair.

"Go ahead and sit down," Wild Bill said, breaking into a chuckle. "I was referring to the 'gentleman' part. You used the plural and far as I know, I'm the only one hereabouts that fits the description."

A chorus of guffaws broke out among his band of hangers-on. I held real doubts Bill was joshing me any, he seemed to be mighty fond of himself, but I took the seat anyway.

I made a hasty introduction, then stacked up a few double eagles on the green cloth in front of me while Wild Bill shuffled the deck and filled me in on the rules of five-card stud as if I was some greenhorn. I decided that he was likely used to folks who didn't know beans about gambling sitting in on one of his games simply to be able to say they had lost money to Wild Bill

Hickok. I, on the other hand, had every intention of cleaning out the pretentious galoot.

An hour or so later I was ahead by nearly five hundred dollars and Wild Bill Hickok's temper was growing as short as the stack of gold coins in front of him. I really believe the idiot thought I was supposed to lose to him just because he was famous.

Looking back on the matter, I likely should have lost a few dollars and retired to my room. Only, back then I was three days shy of my twenty-seventh birthday and did not have the wisdom that comes with age. I had made up my mind to break Hickok's purse.

"Luck seems to be with you tonight, Mister Swartze," Bill said as he lit a big cigar. He rolled it between his fingers, then blew a cloud of smoke into my face. "What do you say to a man's game?"

"What do you mean?" I asked him.

"Everything in front of us is bet on one hand. No draws, no one but us will be in on the deal. To be fair about it, I'll even let you shuffle the cards. Whoever has the best hand wins the pot, then we can retire for the night."

I eyed Wild Bill's purse and could see his reasoning; I had a good two hundred dollars more than he did.

I said, "That's a mighty sporting offer, and the hour is late. I agree to everything but one."

"Spit it out," Hickok grumbled.

"You shuffle and I'll do the cut."

The famous gunman grinned and cracked his knuckles. He was always doing that for some reason. It did cause me to notice he had the longest, daintiest fingers I have ever seen attached to any human.

"Ante up, Swartze," Bill said as he deftly shuffled the deck, then set it in the center of the table.

I slid my pile of gold coins to the middle of the table.

I could tell Wild Bill was taken aback when I simply tapped the cards and said, "Deal them."

The Cheyenne Club grew quiet as night in the Utah desert. Bill slowly dealt each card faceup. The first to me was the ace of diamonds. Hickok dealt himself a ten. Murmuring swept the crowd when I received another ace and Bill the king of spades.

"Well, well," Bill said coldly. "This is looking very interesting."

My next card was an eight. Bill drew another king and grinned from ear to ear. Then Hickok tossed me another eight, and his smirk fled when he drew a trey.

"Three of a kind'll beat that Swartze's hand," someone murmured aloud to Wild Bill. He ignored the man and then tossed me another eight and the color left his face as he squinted at my cards.

"Why, that's another ace of diamonds," he growled, staring square at my eight of hearts. That was when I realized Wild Bill was nearly blind.

"No, sir, Mister Hickok," one of his buddies said. "Swartze's holdin' a winnin' hand fair an' square."

Wild Bill slid another card from the deck and tossed down another king. "Sure looks like a misdeal to me," he boomed.

"Swartze has plumb gone an' beat out ol' Wild Bill fer sure," some burly idiot standing behind me yelled. Then he slapped me on my back so blamed hard it knocked the pepperbox pistol from out of my pocket. The thing fell to floor and must have landed on its hammer, because all six barrels fired and Wild Bill Hickok flew back in his chair and grabbed at the side of his head with his right hand.

I held out my hands palm up as quickly as I could.

Wild Bill glowered at me as a trickle of blood ran from his ear.

"Someone's shot Hickok," people began yelling at the tops of their lungs.

Now for a man who did not wish to attract attention to himself, things were *not* going well for me.

"Go fetch a doc," I heard someone call out.

"Git the sheriff," another dunderhead hollered.

I simply stared at the famous gunfighter for a long moment, then decided he really hadn't been damaged too badly by the accident. "Let's take a look at that ear."

"You stay put, Swartze," Bill hissed, and turned to a man next to him. He pulled a bloody hand from his head. "How bad is it, Charlie?"

The man named Charlie stepped close and eyed the wound. "It ain't but a nick outta yer earlobe. Reckon the blood makes it look worse'n it really is."

Wild Bill Hickok folded a handkerchief and stuck it against his ear. He surveyed me with reptilian eyes.

"John Swartze," he said coldly. "This is a misdeal. Take back the hundred bucks you started with, pick up that damn pistol of yours, and leave here. Tomorrow at noon, if you are still in Cheyenne, I will kill you."

Bad eyesight or not, there was something about Wild Bill Hickok's demeanor that told me I had best do as he asked. I didn't relish being cheated as he had plainly done, but should I have faced him and won, for I am also quite handy with a pistol, I would have been subjected to much unwanted scrutiny.

I nodded at Wild Bill. "Thank you for a most entertaining evening."

The man named Charlie grabbed my pepperbox pistol from the floor and handed it to me. "I'd reckon Bill's feelin' mighty generous tonight. Most times he'd a-plugged you."

I slid the gun in my pocket and carefully extracted

five double eagles from my winnings and stuck them in with it.

"Noon tomorrow, Swartze," Wild Bill growled, leaking blood on the floor.

"Yes, sir, I understand," I said. I got up and went to retrieve my coat while suffering the abuse of laughter from many quarters.

Winter in Cheyenne, Wyoming, was far too harsh for my tastes. Come noon the next day I was on a train bound for Salt Lake City. From there I intended to head south by stagecoach to the Arizona Territory and do some gold prospecting.

I am truly happy that Hickok must have found the incident quite embarrassing to him, as I have never read or heard any more on the matter. For me to have been known as "The Man Who Shot Wild Bill Hickok" would have been a terrible cross to bear.

Thirty-five

Back in those days stories of new gold strikes were bandied about like women's gossip at a church social. I made a point to keep abreast of those in the best possible manner; I checked out every saloon I could as I made my way south into Arizona Territory.

No newspaper that ever inked a page could hope to compete with the wonderful speed by which news moved from one saloon to the next. While I kept my ear to the ground about Arizona gold finds, I was also relieved to hear nothing of any new gold rush to the area around that sparkling clear lake in Colorado where my fortune lay.

I had in no way given up my dream of opening the rich mine poor, deceased Gidd Trevor had bequeathed to me. After the recent turn of events, however, I felt it prudent to postpone returning to Colorado for a while and trust that no one would stumble over what was very rightly my property.

It was simply dreadful the way I had been vilified by the press. The article in *Harper's Weekly* by John A. Randolph, the idiot who stumbled over my companions' remains, had been the worst of the lot. All of them, however, had me guilty of murder, robbery, and cannibalism. While all I had actually done was survive.

Should I make a misstep and fall into the hands of

some stupid lawman, I knew there was no way I could receive any kind of fair trial on the matter. The simple fact that I was there and they were not wouldn't be a very adequate defense.

One of the good things about gold is that it keeps quite well in the ground. People are also blessed with very short memories. All I needed to do was avoid attracting attention to myself for a while and I would be fine.

I was very gratified that I had not killed Wild Bill Hickok. The resulting publicity would certainly have had fatal consequences for me.

From all reports the town of Prescott seemed to be the hub of activity for the entire desert country. I disembarked the stage there on a bitterly cold afternoon toward the end of February. Snow lay in abundance about tall pine trees, which upset me greatly. I had come to Arizona to be rid of the white and miserable stuff. This place was no great improvement over Cheyenne, with the pleasant exception that Wild Bill Hickok wasn't about.

I rented a room for the night, then went to visit the area of town locals called "Whiskey Row." For some strange reason, the city's founders had insisted that all places where liquor or other delights were sold be limited to one block. I strongly suspected the Mormons were behind this idiotic plan, but was not interested enough to inquire if I were right or not.

The Gold Dust Saloon was ensconced in the midst of the "Row" and appeared prosperous, so I stomped the snow from my boots and went inside. In contrast to most mining camps, every saloon in Prescott was built with sturdy bricks. The Gold Dust had a magnificent walnut bar along with pictures of nude women hanging in abundance on the wall behind. I immediately liked the place so I bellied up to the bar, placed my foot on a brass rail, and ordered a whiskey.

Making friends has always come easily for me. I quickly struck up a conversation with a fellow about my age by the name of Dillon Jordan. It turned out that he was also a prospector who, for financial reasons, was forced to labor in a mine far south of here and explore the desert for new veins on his days off. Dillon was an expert miner and had been sent by the mine manager, Benjamin Phelps, to purchase supplies.

"Vulture City's what they call the town that's sprung up there," Dillon Jordan said. "Old Man Henry Wickenburg found the Vulture Mine back in Sixty-Three, but somehow he got it taken away from him. He still lives in a little shack by the Hassayampa River and thinks he still owns that mine."

I asked, "Is this Vulture Mine a rich one?"

Dillon gave out a chuckle, then stealthily slipped a few rocks from his coat and showed them to me. They were chunks of white quartz that had streaks of yellow gold laced through them like spiderwebs. The stuff was as rich as the specimens Gidd Trevor had taken from my Colorado mine.

"Most everyone that works there gets a 'bonus' once in a while," Dillon said with a sly grin. "The Vulture Company's already taken out a couple of million dollars from what the miners have left 'em. That vein's a real bonanza, for sure."

I plunked an eagle down on the bar and ordered us another drink from the surly-acting counterman who kept trying to listen in on our private conversation. "Do you reckon there's many more veins like the Vulture around there?"

"Thanks for the drink," Dillon said, then remained silent until the nosy barkeep had departed. "There surely is. I'm followin' some rich float, an' Ol' Man

Wickenburg's even rumored to have made another strike, only he's afraid to file on it, lest he get screwed out of it like happened with the Vulture."

I glanced through the front windows and noticed it was snowing hard. "I suppose a person will have to wait a while to do any prospecting with the weather like it is."

Dillon Jordan laughed until his eyes teared. "John," he said at length, "you really don't know beans about this country. When a person drops off Yarnell Hill, they leave the snow behind 'em. The area around Vulture City's nothin' but cactus, rocks, an' rattlesnakes. Snow's also got water in it. Down there in the desert that stuff's worth near as much as gold. Even the Hassayampa River's a joke. The only time the thing has water in it is once or twice a year, after a cloudburst."

"I have heard tell there's cactus that grows tall as a tree. Is that true?"

"The Mexicans call them saguaros. It ain't uncommon for 'em to get forty or fifty feet high. They're mighty striking when a person first sets eyes on 'em. Then you figger out they're worthless as tits on a turtle. A body can't use 'em for buildings or mine timbers like you can a tree an' they're too skinny to make shade when it's hot out, like most of the time."

"But like you said, there are some mighty rich gold veins around Vulture City."

"Yep, there sure are an' you're welcome to ride on the freight wagon with me if you'd like," Dillon said. "I'm leavin' at first light from Lenke's Hardware Store. I really hope the weather warms up a mite. I'm fetchin' back a hundred cases of Giant Powder an' that stuff gets plenty touchy when it freezes an' the nitroglycerine starts leakin' out."

"Thanks for the offer," I said quickly. "I need to buy

a mule and some supplies and my best guess is they'll be cheaper here in Prescott."

"Yes, sir, that's a fact. Skinner McCabe at the livery down there in Vulture City's came by his moniker from skinnin' folks, not mules. I won't be movin' too fast. You can catch up with me plenty easy. Just follow the main road headin' south. I'd be obliged to show you around once you get there. Vulture City needs some fine people like you in it."

"I'll get rounded up in the morning and be right behind you," I said.

Way, way behind.

More blasted snow was drifting earthbound from a dreary gray sky when I draped my saddlebags across the back of a decent red mule that I had paid a hundred dollars for and rode out of Prescott. I was seething over having had to pay such an exorbitant price for anything with four legs, but the varmint who ran the livery wouldn't budge.

"That's what things cost here in this neck of the woods, sonny boy," the white-bearded old codger had said with a snarl, causing me to shudder at what the price for a mule might have been in Vulture City.

I took my sweet time following the tracks of Dillon's wagon in the fresh snow. Dynamite or Giant Powder I knew to be plenty treacherous when it froze, and the weather hadn't been warmer than freezing since I'd been in Arizona. If an entire wagon load of the stuff was to explode, it did not seem prudent for me to be anywhere in the vicinity when the event occurred.

That afternoon the clouds cleared, exposing a beautiful deep blue sky. The weather became remarkably warmer. I realized the road had been dropping in elevation, but nothing I have ever experienced prepared me for what I saw when I passed through the shacks of Yarnell City and beheld the grandeur of the Mohave Desert from a viewpoint usually reserved for eagles.

I reigned my red mule to a stop amongst the multitude of huge, round, granite boulders that were strewn about the rimrock and peered downward with awe at the sprawling rolling desert that extended from the floor of the cliff a thousand feet below to the distant horizon.

This was inspiring country with not a patch of snow in sight. Somehow, a road had been chiseled out of that wall of rock. I flicked the reins and, keeping that stupid mule away from the edge, I began my descent. My Adam's apple bobbed in my throat like a boat on rough water whenever I ventured a peek over the edge. To drive a wagon loaded with dynamite down such a road would take a crazy man. At least I had sized up Dillon Jordan rather quickly; the man was a lunatic.

I rode into the town of Vulture City around noon of the next day. The experience of negotiating that precipitous road had exhausted me. When I encountered a stage stop at a little place called Congress Junction, I enjoyed a few shots of poor-quality whiskey, then rented a cot for the night. This also gave Dillon plenty of time to rid himself of that load of Giant Powder before I got there.

Vulture City consisted of a single long street lined on both sides with one- and two-story clapboard buildings of the same pallid grandeur that had graced Bingham City. At least the weather here was quite agreeable. I was pleasantly surprised to be able to remove my coat in comfort.

Those huge cactus plants were everywhere, along with abundant other strange varieties of plants that I had never before encountered. I was to find they all shared one thing in common: sharp thorns. Folks who call the desert home have a wise saying. "If it's green and growing, it'll have stickers. If it's moving about on its own, it will either bite or sting you."

On a low knoll at the south edge of town were the works of the Vulture Mine. This wasn't at all hard to figure out; a big sign attached to the top of the five-story-high head frame announced in bright red letters, VULTURE MINING AND MILLING COMPANY. The massive twenty-stamp gold mill shook the very ground beneath the town twenty-four hours every day, and gave off a din that reminded one of an approaching thunderstorm.

I rode to the far end of town and turned to watch as a large dust devil wound its way through town, spewing dirt through open windows and flinging clothes that had been hung out to dry onto cactuses.

All told, I liked Vulture City. There just had to be a lot of gold hereabouts to cause folks to hang around such a dismal place. I had made note of three saloons, and most agreeable of all was the lack of any visible law enforcement.

I stabled my mule at McCabe's Livery Stable at the unbelievable cost of one dollar a day. Then I was charged fifteen dollars for a week's room and board in the Vulture's Nest Hotel. This only served to buoy my spirits. No one could afford to live here if there was not a lot of money about.

The day was dying bloody on the western horizon when I awoke from my nap, splashed water in my face from a porcelain basin next to my bed, and wandered out to see how exciting nightlife in Vulture City would be.

I thought the Beachcomber Saloon to be a good place to start. Whoever had named the joint simply had to be a real character with a decent sense of humor. My spirits were high and I anticipated only an evening of merriment and relaxation.

Then, as I approached the batwing doors of the saloon, I heard loud yelling and cursing from within. I hesitated just long enough for the deafening blast of a shotgun to blow a man flying through the swinging doors and onto the boardwalk.

I noticed the poor fellow had caught several buckshot square in his breadbasket. In spite of his terrible wounds the bleeding man pulled a pistol from his belt and fired it through the batwings until it was empty. A scream of pain erupted from inside the Beachcomber.

That was when I realized the man with his belly full of buckshot was Dillon Jordan.

Thirty-six

I stepped close and ventured a peek inside the saloon. The fattest man I have ever seen, who wore a long silver beard and had a grimy apron tied around his ample middle, stood staring at a skinny fellow lying sprawled out on the floor in a pool of blood. The fat man reached down and grabbed up a double-barrel shotgun. That was when he noticed me.

"Come on in, stranger," the big man said in an oddly happy voice. "Reckon all the excitement's over fer a spell."

I swallowed hard and went inside. The man on the floor was nattily dressed and obviously quite dead.

"I'm Sam Cobb." The big man offered up a ham-sized hand. "I own the place an' I'll fetch you a drink once I get things tidied up a mite."

I shook his hand and shot a glance at the bullet-ridden body at my feet.

"Oh, pay him no mind," Sam said. "He's just a skunk of a lawyer that shudda been shot years ago. I gotta go look after Dillon, he's a regular payin' customer."

About a dozen men exited the saloon with us. I was the one who bent down and helped Dillon Jordan stagger to his feet. From the number of holes he was leaking from, I doubted he would live through the night.

"Hello, John," Dillon said hoarsely when he recognized me. He looked at Sam Cobb. "Did I get him?"

The barkeep nodded. "Carson Hewlitt's got more holes in him that counted. Sure too durn bad we ain't got Doc Simmons anymore. He mightta been able to cork those holes in yer belly."

Dillon attempted to laugh, but only succeeded in coughing up blood. "I reckon I could use a bed. Do me a favor will you, Sam?"

"Just name it," the saloon owner said.

"Plant that damn shyster afore I croak. It would pleasure me if'n he gets to Hell first."

"We'll start diggin' on the hole just as soon as we get you cared for." Sam Cobb looked at me. "You a friend of Jordan's?"

"Yes, sir," I said. "My name is John Swartze. We can take him to my room in the hotel and I'll see to him."

"Obliged to ya. Dillon's cabin is a fer piece," Sam said, then yelled, "Slim, you an' Hank help get him to the hotel and I'll give ya a shot fer yer troubles. There's a bottle of laudanum behind the bar, below the cash register. Fetch that along, too. I reckon Jordan'll have need of it."

The two men half carried the badly wounded man into the hotel and laid him out on my bed. Then they stared at me longingly.

"Go have your whiskey," I said. "And thanks for helping."

Both of them took off like a shot. Dillon Jordan moaned pitifully. I uncorked the bottle of laudanum and poured a healthy dose into his mouth. Too much of the opiate would be fatal, but I didn't see any point in measuring.

"Hang tough, Dillon," I said. "You'll make it through this in fine shape if you don't give up."

"You're a liar, John, but I appreciate what you're tryin' to do."

I asked, "What was all that shooting about?"

"A little disagreement over a minin' claim. I didn't tell you the truth in Prescott because I didn't know you that well. You see, I'd already found that vein an' staked it out. Then this lawyer jumps my claim an' tries to buffalo me by sayin' I hadn't followed the law right. He come in tonight with a shotgun an' demanded I sign a deed quittin' the claim over to him."

"I reckon you gave him a good answer."

Jordan wheezed. "A lotta help that'll be." He reached out and clasped my hand. "Listen, I'm in need of some help. I'm dyin' an' I don't know nobody round here that'll do what's right."

"You can trust me, just tell me what I can do."

"Sam Cobb." Jordan's voice was weakening. "He ain't a bad egg. Have him show you to my shack. It's about a mile down the river. Pull up the boards under my bed. You'll find a box there. Inside is some money I want sent to my wife." A rattling sound started building in his chest. "We have a good ranch up near Fort Fetterman in Wyoming. Wisht I'd a stayed there."

"How can I find her?"

"There's some letters there with her address. Hattie's her name." He coughed and more blood trickled from the corners of his mouth. "Gold is a terrible god to worship, John. I made a map to the strike. It's in that box along with claim papers. Go claim it 'fore someone else does, only don't go get yourself killed over it like I went an' done."

"I'll take care of the matter."

"I knew you were a good man the moment I set eyes on you. If that claim pans out, treat Hattie fair, won't you?"

"Don't worry yourself about it, I'll see to her."

Jordan moaned, and I poured some more laudanum into his mouth. His color was ashen. All I could do was ease his pain as best I could.

Dillon gave out a sigh. "I love her more than anything now that I'm passin' away. I could of stayed in Wyoming—we could have had kids—been happy. It's gold, John—the stuff is evil—don't let it . . ."

Dillon Jordan was dead. I closed his open eyes and headed for the saloon. The hawk-nosed old biddy who ran the hotel caught me in the hallway.

"That mattress is going to be ruined from all the blood. You rented the room an' had that man put there." The skinny woman stuck out a bony hand toward me. "Five dollars, right now, or I'll put you out."

I fished a half eagle from my pocket, showed it to her, then dropped it on the floor. "I'll see you in church."

"There ain't no church in Vulture City," she squawked.

"For some reason I expected that," I said.

When I left the hotel, that old woman was on her hands and knees poking round under furniture looking for her money.

Dillon Jordan's dying observation of gold was absolutely correct. That glittering yellow metal can cause simpleminded people to do most anything to possess it.

Sam Cobb read a eulogy over Dillon's pine box at nine the next morning. Aside from the bartender and me, only four men attended the brief service.

"Gotta plant 'em right away," Sam said to me after folding his worn Bible. "Bodies get ripe in these parts afore Saint Peter can tally up their souls."

I said, "Before our friend passed away he asked me to get some things from his cabin and mail them to his

wife. I was wondering, is there someone who could show
me to his place?"

Sam looked dumbstruck. "Dillon was hereabout fer
nigh onto a year an' this is the first I've heard of him
bein' married up." The portly barkeep surveyed the
desolate cemetery. "Reckon I can understand why he
didn't bring her out. This here's hard country fer a
woman."

"About Jordan's request."

"Oh, sure," Sam said as he turned his head toward
the grizzled old fellow who had helped out last night.
"Hank, you show Swartze here to Dillon's shack an' it'll
be good fer a shot."

"Yes, sir," Hank said. "Well let's get to it, I need that
drink before tha bugs come out."

Sam Cobb took note of my puzzlement. "Hank here
gets the deliriums an' sees bugs an' snakes when he
runs dry fer more than an entire mornin'."

"Well," I said, "let's not tarry."

I was beginning to wonder if folks went crazy once
they got to the desert or they were already crazy when
they arrived. I really didn't have time to ponder the
issue. I had a gold mine to claim.

I was taken aback when I studied the framed photogravure of Hattie Jordan. She was not all what I had
expected. This was the most beautiful woman I could
imagine. Even with the grainy black and white likeness
of her, I made out a delightful spray of freckles about
her high cheekbones. Curly locks of what I simply knew
to be auburn hair framed an angelic face and cascaded
down her lithe shoulders. I could understand full well
Dillon Jordan's bewailment at leaving such a lovely lady.

The box buried beneath that bed held little else of
value. Aside from around two dozen letters from his wife

that were bound together with a red ribbon, were fifty dollars in gold coins and of course, the map and paperwork for his strike. There was also a canvas bag full of high-grade like what he had shown me in Prescott. I knew now those samples had come from his mine, not the Vulture.

No wonder that lawyer had resorted to using a shotgun to obtain Jordan's claim. Gold as rich as what was inside that bag was enough to cause a lot of decent folks to use violence to obtain its source; let alone some greedy shyster.

I unfolded and studied the paperwork for Jordan's mine with the greatest of care. His fatal shootout with the lawyer had come about because of some supposed defect in filling out the forms, so I assumed a measure of improvement was necessary before I refiled on the vein in my own name.

The problem was, I could see nothing obviously wrong, but the legal system is notoriously picky. I pondered the situation and came up blank. Seeking out a lawyer of my own for help seemed to be akin to getting a coyote to guard the chicken coop. There sure was a lot more to the gold mining business than I had suspected.

At least the map to the mine was quite well done and easily decipherable. Best of all, the vein was only a little more than a mile from Vulture City. With the brass compass I had brought along I knew I could locate that mine within a hour or two. I decided after I got a peek at the vein I would figure out how to approach getting rich.

I stuck everything of value, including Hattie's letters, into my pockets and rode my mule back to the hotel. The first thing I noticed was that the old bat had actually put a new mattress on my bed, which surprised me greatly.

I extracted my writing supplies from the dresser, scooted back the chair, and penned a long, consoling letter to Hattie Jordan. From the letters to Dillon I found her address that turned out to be in the town of Casper in Wyoming Territory.

I was certain Dillon had said Fort Fetterman was their home, but then I remembered that aside from having nine buckshot in his belly, I had given him a lot of laudanum. I addressed the envelope to Hattie Jordan in Casper, Wyoming, and headed to the post office.

I sent it by registered mail, for I also not only included the fifty dollars, which I had changed from gold to paper money, I also, from the goodness of my heart, added another two hundred dollars. I told Hattie Jordan that I would do everything in my power to turn her poor dead husband's strike into a paying proposition and then, after expenses, we would share equally in the returns.

Since I was feeling quite pleased with the very fair manner in which I had taken care of Dillon Jordan's grieving widow, I decided to drop by the Beachcomber Saloon and relax for a spell.

My recently deceased friend's assessment of Sam Cobb had been quite accurate. He did seem like a good chap and I enjoyed my visit with him immensely. I left the bar that evening with a higher opinion of Vulture City. Not having a shootout in a saloon while a person is trying to relax always does a lot to improve one's attitude.

Sunrises in the desert can be stunningly beautiful affairs. The reddish glow in the east matched the fine color of my hair as I rode my mule, following the wobbling needle of a compass. The claim was only a short distance and I had hoped to inspect the vein, file new papers, and be back in town before noon.

I had just entered a low, rocky canyon lined on both sides with towering saguaro cactuses when suddenly a rifle shot split the still air and a puff of white dust indicated where the bullet hit the trail a few feet in front of me.

"Hold up there, hombre," a voice boomed from behind a large rock. "This is private property that you're trespassin' on."

I held my hands out in plain sight. "I reckon you're the guard Carson Hewlitt's got hired?"

To no great surprise he answered, "Yep, I surely am. What's it to you?"

"Just that the lawyer hired me to spell you for a while," I yelled out. "If you'd rather stay here, I'll be happy to go back to town."

A skinny galoot with a scraggly black beard showed himself. "Hewlitt ain't with you. He said not to let anybody come around if'n he weren't with 'em."

"He'll be along shortly," I said calmly. "You can point that gun somewhere else if you don't mind. I just come out here to help you."

"Git down off'n that mule an' we'll talk, but I ain't gonna trust ya none 'til Hewlitt shows himself."

"That's fine," I said, slowly dismounting. "It won't be but a short while until he's here."

The gunman walked down the rocky slope and surveyed me with cold eyes, all the while keeping his rifle aimed at my belly. "I ain't never seen you around these parts before."

"That's because I just came down here from Cheyenne to work for Mister Hewlitt."

"And just what might your name be?" he asked, stepping within my reach.

"James," I said with a grin, "Jesse James."

"No foolin'?" the simpleton said with obvious awe. "I've heard tell of you."

The second the idiot lowered his rifle barrel, I used a tactic I had learned from Turtle John; I tightened my fist into a knot, then with a single, savage blow to the chest, I burst his heart.

I buried the not-so-efficient watchman in a shallow grave to keep the buzzards away. I then scoured the area about the deceased's camp looking for a horse, but found nothing. My opinion of lawyers became strengthened when the sum of all the money the dead man had on him totaled a mere five dollars. The rifle he had kept pointed at my middle turned out to be a rusty old Volcanic. I doubted it would be worth my trouble to sell the thing, so I added it to the grave. Carson Hewlitt had certainly been a skinflint to hire such inept, poorly armed help. I was gratified Dillon Jordan had taken care of him so well.

After the unexpected delay, I set about checking out my gold mine. Actually the term "mine" was an exaggeration. All it consisted of was a hole in the rocky bottom of a ravine dug no deeper than what people set an outhouse over.

I checked about for rattlesnakes, then climbed down a rickety ladder to survey the vein. A thin seam of white quartz, not much wider than my thumb, ran down both sides of a shallow shaft. While this vein was not very wide, it was richer than sin. Spiderwebs of glistening yellow gold ran through it with great abundance. When that quartz seam widened with depth, as all gold veins do, it would become a veritable treasure house of riches.

Using a small pick I had found, I filled my pockets with as much high-grade as I could chisel loose. I then went to the pile of rocks that served as a discovery marker, removed the lawyer's paperwork, and tore it into shreds. I filled out my own claim, folded the form, and placed it in a can and securely buried it under more rocks. I now owned a very rich gold mine.

As I rode back to Vulture City that afternoon, it dawned on me I did not know the name of the man I had killed. There had been next to nothing in his pockets. I did not let the matter trouble me.

Any idiot who thought I resembled Jesse James would not be missed in the least.

Thirty-seven

"River Smith come by today to check out the shootin'," Sam Cobb said when I dropped by the Beachcomber that afternoon for a drink.

"Can't say I've heard of him before," I said. "Is he the local law?"

"Nope, Smith ain't local, thank goodness. Havin' the likes of him around would wreck the hell outta my business. He *is* about the biggest pile of law a body can find standin' behind a badge in these parts, however. He works for the territorial governor out of Tucson. Ol' River only shows up when someone gets plugged or a bank or stagecoach is robbed."

"Well, what did this sheriff have to say on the matter?"

Sam Cobb cocked his head in puzzlement. "You know I ain't rightly sure just what's stamped on that badge ol' River's so proud of, so I ain't sure if'n he's a sheriff or not. Reckon I'll check that out next time he's about. To answer yer question, there weren't much he could do but write up a report an' leave. Hell's bells, both the shyster an' poor Dillon Jordan's planted. When there ain't nobody left alive to stick in jail or hang, most lawmen head for greener pastures."

I hoisted and finished my mug of beer. "That's one

thing I like about Vulture City. It's a law-abiding town with absolutely no need for a sheriff."

"That's a true fact," Sam Cobb agreed. "Now if we can just attract us some good-lookin' whores an' keep out the stump preachers, this place'll be nicer than the Garden of Eden—a lot more fun at any rate."

"Amen, brother," I intoned. "If you include politicians and lawyers in that list, I agree that Vulture City *will* become a veritable paradise."

Sam Cobb clucked his tongue and set about refilling my mug. "Dag nab it, I sure missed a couple of the worst, that's a natural fact." He grinned as he slid another beer across the plank bar. "John, I hope you stick around. We need more good folks like you in these parts."

I wasn't ready to let out that I had claimed Dillon Jordan's mine and was going to work it. I wanted to make certain all of the claim corners were well marked and the thing recorded in Prescott before I risked attracting the kind of attention that had been fatal to the former owner of that claim.

"I reckon I'll stick around for a spell," I said. "I have a feeling things will be coming my way fairly soon."

I took the stage to Prescott the next day. There was no way I would ever ride a mule over that road again. The stagecoach was bad enough, but at least I could nurse a flask and not have to peek out when the thing went alongside that cliff at Yarnell Hill.

Considering the legal problems Dillon Jordan had suffered over that claim of his, I thought the matter over and finally went to consult a lawyer who had a sign in his window advertising himself as a mining specialist. I cannot recall the shylock's name, only that he charged me a hundred dollars to cross a T and darken a period or two. If preachers charged half as much for their time as lawyers do, I'd venture Heaven would be a mighty lonely place.

After I recorded the claim I decided to enjoy my time in Prescott before starting the grueling task of opening a gold mine. Vulture City had very little to offer in the line of recreation. As Sam Cobb had pointed out earlier, the soiled doves available there were built like a busted bale of hay.

I checked into the hotel, luxuriated in a tub of hot water, then dyed my hair to touch up some black roots that were becoming obvious. I must admit that every time I caught my reflection in a mirror I was astounded just how much different I looked with red hair. My sweet little Letty had been *so* discerning in matters such as these.

Ever since I had seen the picture of Hattie Jordan, I'd been dreaming of a lady who would look just as attractive as she did. I found her working out of a small crib in back of the Bradshaw Saloon. She told me her name was Alma and I became immediately smitten with the auburn-haired beauty. I paid twenty dollars for an entire night, and must say the little lady was worth every nickel of her fee, which was a lot more than I could say for a certain mining lawyer.

I lollygagged around Prescott for a week to rest up for all of the hard work that awaited me when I returned to my rich mine. I used some of my time to visit dealers of mining tools and machinery and obtained catalogues and prices for items necessary to operate my mine. Mostly, however, I whiled away my time either playing cards in a saloon on Whiskey Row or dallying with sweet Alma.

All good times must eventually come to an end. That gold was not going to crawl out of the ground on its own. It was with a degree of sadness that I quietly slipped from the little lady's feather bed to once again risk life and limb on that god-awful road back to Vulture City.

To this day I cannot venture how many souls must have lost their lives on Yarnell Hill. I can't honestly say I recall seeing any wrecked stagecoaches or freight wagons that had been dashed to smithereens on the rocks below. Of course, I did not check this out too closely. Heights and abuse are two things I have never been able to tolerate well.

The initial order of business upon safely reaching Vulture City was to soothe my frayed nerves at the Beachcomber Saloon. The next day I purchased a comfortable little home a block from the hotel for five hundred dollars. I had toyed with the idea of building a place at the mine, but that was a far distance from a decent bar.

Sam Cobb put me in contact with three men he said were excellent contract miners. Farley Fairweather was the oldest and most experienced of the trio, but like Israel Swan, his lungs were clogged with rock dust to the point where he could barely breathe. This left all of the hard work to his younger brother, Zack, and a burley nineteen-year-old farm boy from east Texas by the name of Spencer Willadee.

I hired them to open my mine at the rate of twenty dollars for all three men to work a ten-hour shift. Drilling, blasting, and shoveling is a very hard and dangerous job. Little Alma received the same amount of pay for simply lying on her back in a comfortable bed. Men are certainly not treated fairly in this world.

"We've gonna have to have a hoist an' head frame to go much deeper," Farley told me about a week after beginning work on the mine I had christened *Hattie's Hope* in honor of Dillon Jordan's lovely wife. "That windlass ain't gonna cut it for any production. If'n I was you, I'd bring in a steam boiler so's we can have a power hoist an' also run a blower to pump some breathin' air down the shaft. Things are gittin' too hot an' stuffy down there fer much work to git done."

It seemed to me that complaining about things was Farley Fairweather's main goal in life. "Can't you men at least blast out a shipment of ore to help with some of the cost? I really don't know if I can afford all of this equipment. I've already built a tool shed and brought out a blacksmith forge and coal to operate it."

"Ain't nobody can make a hole in rock without sharp drill steel to do it with," Farley grumbled. "Had to have that forge to temper it right. Fer as the rest of the stuff we're needin', Hammersmith's Minin' Company broke their pick an' is sellin' out everything. They got a boiler, hoist an' all. I reckon I could get the whole shebang fer maybe two thousand dollars. Won't take us but a couple of weeks to move it over an' git everything set up here finer than a frog's hair."

"What about *selling* some ore," I asked again. It was becoming quite obvious to me that Farley and his crew had lost sight of what we were out here to accomplish.

"I'd reckon we've got a ton or so of ore that oughtta pay to run through a mill if'n we had one."

"What do you mean if *we* had one? Can't we just load that ore on a wagon and take it to the Vulture Mill and sell it to them?"

Farley gave me a strange look. "Nope, that won't work. They only run their own ore. We could bag the stuff up an' ship it up to Prescott. Wyman Brothers has got a buyin' station there. The problem is, the freight'll eat up most of the profits an' the Wymans will steal the rest, most likely."

I was growing increasingly irritated with the direction the mining business seemed to be taking. "Are you telling me the only way to make the Hattie's Hope pay is to build my own mill?"

"If'n you don't want to get robbed by ever man Jack in the territory, it is. When you get your hands on gold bullion you can sell it straight to the gov'ment, or anyone fer a whole twenty bucks an ounce. That's the only way to make money in this business."

I took a took a deep breath and awaited what I knew was coming.

"Now Hammersmith's got a mill fer sale, too," Farley said with a smile. "It's got a Blake crusher an' a good Gilpin-type five-stamper. I reckon it'll come fairly cheap since they ain't nobody hereabouts got any ore to run through the thing."

"How much will it cost?" I asked through clenched teeth. "And how long will it take to move it out here and set it up?"

"Movin' that mill here ain't a good idea, Mister Swartze," the miner said, shaking his head sadly. "Ain't no water hereabouts. A mill needs plenty of water to operate as I'm sure you know."

I nodded my head.

Farley continued, "The mill's already set up on the Hassayampa an' has a decent well. I bet if a person offered 'em five thousand bucks fer the draw works an' the mill, they'd wind up ownin' it."

"That's more than I can afford." It was finally my turn to grumble and complain. "If they want to sell out, tell them I'll pay three thousand cash for all of the machinery *and* the mill. It's either that or I'll have to put the mine up for sale and lay everybody off."

Farley Fairweather broke into a coughing fit that made Israel Swan's seem like pikers. "I know Hammersmith an' I doubt if'n he'll take you up on it, but if you want me to, I'll go to Prescott an' see him," he wheezed.

"Three thousand dollars," I reiterated firmly. "He can take that or leave it."

"Yes, sir, I understand." Farley cleared his throat and stuck out his hand. "I'm gonna need some travelin' money an' stage fare."

I gave him fifty dollars, then hurriedly climbed back on my red mule and returned to Vulture City. At the rate I was spending money, I wondered if it took a gold mine to open another one of the things up. At least a beer only cost a dime in Sam Cobb's saloon.

The more I thought on the matter, the more convinced I became that the mining business was populated with idiots. The moment I had Hattie's Hope in production, I would sell out for a million dollars and return to the South Seas.

I was on my way to the Beachcomber Saloon to sip a few beers and ponder the state of my gold mining business when Emma Hawkins, a pleasant old lady who ran the local post office from a room off her laundry, saw me passing by and yelled through an open window, "Oh, Mister Swartze, there's a letter here for you."

This took me somewhat aback since I couldn't fathom anyone who would have sent me a letter. When Emma handed me the envelope I detected the faint aroma of lilacs. When I saw the delicate feminine handwriting and noticed the return address, I hurried home to read it. The letter was from Hattie Jordan.

My Dear Mister Swartze,

Words cannot express my sincere thanks for your kindheartedness. I would likely have never known of Dillon's death had you not written. I can now put a closure to his whereabouts as I have not heard from him in over six months.

The money you sent was greatly appreciated and has been of great help. The ranch here in Wyoming provides a marginal living, at best. I am forced to do much of the work myself, as my father who lives here with me is becoming quite feeble.

You mentioned my deceased husband had made a rich gold strike and that you were going to operate the mine and send me half of the profits. While I am most appreciative of your courtesy and compassion I cannot allow you to extend yourself to that extent in my behalf.

Therefore, I will use some of the money you so kindly sent to hire a man to help my father. I shall then travel by stagecoach to Vulture City and render whatever services I am able to assist you in this venture.

This is, I believe, simply being fair with you. As I pen this letter it is the Second day of April. I shall leave at the earliest opportunity and should arrive before the end of the month.

I am quite anxious to meet you and assist in any possible manner with your efforts. The fact that my husband made such a fine friend such as yourself gratifies me immensely.

Yours Most Sincerely,
Hattie Jane Jordan

I folded the lilac-scented letter closed and returned it to the envelope. Earlier on, I had believed that having to spend most of my hard-earned money on a blasted gold mill, along with a bunch of machinery that I had no real knowledge of, was the biggest problem I had to deal with. Now, I had a female partner to contend with, to boot.

A headache was building over my left eye. I placed Hattie's letter into a dresser drawer and hurried to the Beachcomber Saloon. Now, I *really* needed a few drinks.

Thirty-eight

It took three weeks of hard work in the increasing temperature of the desert to ready the Hattie's Hope Mine for production. I had decided by then that if I gave Farley Fairweather a hundred-dollar bonus along with a bottle of whiskey, he would find something wrong with my actions to whine and complain about, so I did nothing. The man's insipid sniveling had become insufferable.

Everything the grouch had demanded was in place at the mine. The big riveted steel boiler along with the steam hoist and air blower were readied for operation. Above the shaft itself a towering wooden draw works jutted three stories into the blue desert sky. This latter affair very uncomfortably resembled a gallows frame, which Farley mentioned they are actually called in some mining districts. Gold miners have a remarkably grim sense of humor.

My offer of three thousand dollars to Hammersmith's had been readily accepted, giving me cause to wonder if I could have bought the mill at a lower figure. At any rate, I now owned the mill and a five-acre plot of ground on what is laughingly called the Hassayampa River.

I shall not bore the reader with a long description of this mill or how it accomplished its purpose. Save to say, big chunks of ore-bearing rock were first broken into smaller pieces by a "jaw" crusher, then smashed into smithereens beneath six-hundred-pound iron stamps that were raised a few inches, then dropped on the ore until it had been beaten fine enough to amalgamate on mercury-covered copper plates.

The resulting amalgam was scraped off and placed into a cast-iron retort, which was then heated to drive off the mercury. This was done in the open air to allow the poisonous mercury fumes to be avoided. I am told that when a man inhales mercury gas, his teeth fall out. When the retorting was complete I would have a solid gold "button" to sell.

The milling process itself was accomplished among a thunderous din best described as having a tin washtub over one's head during a hailstorm. The very ground beneath my feet trembled as if an earthquake were in progress. Conversation of any type was an impossibility and hand signals were resorted to for any communication.

I left the milling of my ore to a pair of supposed experts that Farley had hired along with two very grimy but muscular helpers. All told, the cost of operating this mill amounted to over fifty dollars every day, with the mine itself costing me about the same.

Both of those huge boilers consumed an unbelievable amount of cordwood, all of which had to be freighted down Yarnell Hill from Prescott. I surely do not need to expand on how much this added to my costs.

At the time all that had been done with the mill was to run a few tests to assure the thing would work. I had all of the ore that had been extracted from the mine shipped to the mill, and studied the pile with a jaundiced eye. I was very much disturbed as to how much worthless brown granite was mixed in with the high-grade.

"There's a lot of gold in that ore you can't see without a magnifyin' glass," Farley assured me. "The mercury plates'll git it all, trust me."

I said, "The assays that Frank Simmons ran on the samples we took from the mine showed a gold content of one hundred ounces all the way to nothing. How can we judge what the mill will put out?"

Farley clucked his tongue. "Ever minin' man knows the mill will tell us that after we've run a few tons through 'er."

"Yes," I answered with a butterfly in my stomach. "I guess that *will* tell the tale."

I had just under fifteen hundred dollars left to my name. With the cost of running that mine and mill being over one hundred dollars a day, I sincerely needed to have some gold to sell shortly. As I didn't wish to hear Farley Fairweather complain or come up with some other item he couldn't live without, I beat a hasty retreat to Sam Cobb's saloon. It was a lot cheaper to hang around there than my mining operation.

The impending arrival of Hattie Jordan weighed heavily on my mind. Having the company of such a vision of loveliness, which I knew she would be, was quite desirable. However, I really needed to focus my attentions on the mine and mill until they were running profitably.

Aside from that, Vulture City offered no accommodations for a lady of quality. First shot at a tub of bathwater cost a dollar at the hotel. Second chances were fifty cents, dropping to a quarter for all of those who bathed later. I knew Hattie would want a dollar bath at least every few days or so.

To be a gentleman, I decided to move back into the hotel and give her my house to live in. There was a well with a hand pump over it where she could fetch all the water she needed by expending only some elbow grease. Money was something that I feared would run short before I was selling gold on a regular basis. I could live in the hotel much cheaper than she could.

"Fer some dad-ratted reason that gold or yours won't catch on the merc'ry plates," Farley Fairweather told me in his usual whiny voice after he had run the mill for three days. "I ain't never seen the like before. *Normal* gold sticks right away. The blasted stuff outta Hattie's Hope's got a coatin' of somethin' on it that makes it run right out in the darn tailin's and get lost."

"You didn't recover *any* gold in three days?" I was too aghast to shout.

"Nah," Farley said with a shrug. "Of course I got some gold, but sure not as much as what we shudda had. Can't figger it out a'tall. I used everything I could think of to clean them plates, but that gold of yours is a strange woolly-booger fer sure."

"The next gold mine I find, I'll make sure it's up to your standards before I do anything with it," I replied testily. "Tell me, just how much *did* you manage to recover?"

Farley broke into a coughing fit trying to gain my sympathy, then reached into his pocket and handed me a round gold button that filled the palm of my hand.

"It's a little more than seven ounces," he said with a pitiful wheeze. "From the color of the doré, I'd guess it's about four hundred fine."

"Huh?" I was both angry and dumbfounded. "Explain yourself."

"All minin' men know that gold is figgered on fineness. A thousand fine is good an' pure as it gits. Four hundred fine's about forty percent gold. The rest of that doré's likely silver or some such metal."

I resisted pulling my pepperbox pistol and improving the quality of people who claim to be experts on mining. "You are telling me that I spent over three hundred dollars to get back sixty?"

"Yep," Farley agreed. "That's 'bout the way I figger it, too. Now don't go a-blamin' me fer your problems. I didn't put that sick gold in the ground. If'n you'll let me, I'll bring over a good mill man I know in Prescott. I'm bettin' Ol' Kelly Herman'll figger out what's wrong in short order."

"How much?"

"Oh, Kelly's a good friend of mine. I reckon he'll come down an' work a week fer a hundred bucks an' expenses."

I closed my eyes and nodded. "All right, send for him. But I want you to lay off the mill crew until they're needed again. Keep pushing the shaft deeper at the mine. I want to open up that vein better in case I am forced to sell."

"Yes, sir," Farley said. "If'n that's what you got in mind, why don't we put the mill hands to work in the mine, too? This way we'll git that shaft deeper in no time a'tall."

I did not bother to add up how fast my money was disappearing. I told Farley to keep digging on the mine. Then I stuffed the gold button into my saddlebag and headed for Vulture City and a much-needed drink to cure my growing headache.

The phrase "It never rains but it pours" was almost certainly coined by some poor fool trying to make a go of things in the mining business. I had not gone to inspect either the Hattie's Hope or that blasted mill I'd bought for four days. Drinking beer in Sam Cobb's saloon was a lot cheaper.

God was stoking the desert's furnace and the temperature was likely a hundred degrees in the shade when Farley Fairweather came wheezing into the Beachcomber late one afternoon. I noticed his wide eyes and immediately suspected something was seriously wrong.

"Kelly Herman's got himself kilt over at that mill of yours," Farley sputtered loudly.

Sam Cobb spoke before I had the opportunity. "What happened to him? Was it an accident?"

"Yep an' a terrible one at that," Farley bellied up next to me at the bar. "Gimme a beer an' a shot, Sam, I surely need one after the way Kelly got kilt."

"Tell us about it," I said.

Farley had a whitewashed look about him, so I waited until he finished his shot to begin.

"We had a rock that wouldn't smash up in the crusher," Farley said hoarsely. "Kelly took an iron pry bar an' tried to jam it between the rock an' the jaw. Of course the crusher was runnin' at the time. There ain't nothin' wrong with doin' this. Hell, I've done it plenty of times. Only somehow the bar got caught just right an' flew right up ol' Kelly's middle. Gutted 'im like a hog. Damnedest bloody thing I ever saw, an' it all happened quicker than a snake can strike."

"This is awful," I said. "I don't know what to do or say."

"Ain't nothin' you or anyone can do now. The boys are fetchin' back a buryin' box to lay him away in. Reckon we'll ship 'em back to Prescott. Kelly's got a wife an' kids there."

Sam Cobb cocked his head. "This Kelly was the mill expert you hired, weren't he?"

"Yep," Farley said. "He was a durn good one, too. I'd have never thought some crazy thing like this would have kilt a man like him."

"You've had a passel of grief with that mine," Sam Cobb said to me.

Farley spoke up. "Two men got shot over that hole right in the beginnin'. That kind of thing puts a curse on a mine fer certain. Not only won't the gold catch on the plates, the vein's petered out."

It was my turn to sputter. "What do you mean the vein's petered out?"

"You ain't been there for a spell, Swartze. We lost that vein two days ago. I've had the crew keep diggin', but there ain't a speck of gold in sight. Hell, there ain't even a trace of where that vein oughtta be."

I was dumbstruck. "What are you pulling? Everyone knows that gold veins get wider with depth."

"Reckon the good Lord didn't see fit to follow your line of thinkin'," Farley said angrily. "The vein petered out an' that's that. Poor ol' Kelly figgered out the gold's got too much copper mixed in with it to ever amalgamate. Reckon it don't matter now. There ain't no gold in that mine anyways."

I laid a silver dollar on the bar. "Sam," I said, "I believe I'd like a beer *and* a shot."

"Comin' right up, John." Sam Cobb filled my glass and slid it over. "Sure sorry to see you get all this bad news at once. Sounds like your vulture mine turned out to be a turkey."

Before I could answer, some kid poked his pimply face through the batwings. "Mister Swartze, I come to tell you the stage is in an' there's a mighty purty woman at the station askin' for you."

I tossed the urchin a quarter, then slugged down my drink while wishing I had time for a few more. I'd rather have gone to face Wild Bill Hickok than tell a sweet little lady that the gold mine she had traveled all this way to help operate had gone bust and her partner in the venture was nearly broke. Aside from getting snakebit, I couldn't fathom much else that could go wrong today. This was one of those few times in life I was mistaken about something.

When I trudged inside the stage office I beheld the loveliest, most angelic vision of a woman I ever dared imagine existed. My throat suddenly became dry as the desert and my feet were leaden.

The lady who I knew from the faded photogravure to be Hattie Jane sat patiently on a wooden bench, a large portmanteau on the floor beside her. I was quite taken aback that her cascading curly hair turned out to be fawn-colored rather than auburn; a spray of freckles dotted her cheeks and lithe neck and wonderfully accented her full, ruby lips. Hattie Jane's happy green eyes sparkled in the light like precious emeralds.

I swallowed hard to assure my mouth would work, then stepped over to make my introductions. I was forming in my mind what I would say to this most beautiful lady when a rotund, old gray-haired idiot jumped out of a chair he was lounging in and poked out his hand in greeting.

"Well, hello there, Reverend Swartze," the fool boomed. "That was mighty fine send-off you gave that feller they hung up in Colorado, the man whose head got popped off. What brings you to a place like Vulture City?"

Thirty-nine

Hattie Jane fixed those green eyes of hers on me. "Reverend Swartze," she said, "would you happen to be any relation to John Swartze? He is a local mining man I am here to meet."

When a person is caught by a past untruth such as I had been, there is no alternative except to expand upon it.

"I am John Swartze, Missus Jordan," I replied, pumping the dunderhead's hand. "After the terrible affair this gentleman mentioned, I became disenchanted with my religious calling and laid the Good Book aside for a pick and shovel."

The old man spoke up. "Sorry to hear that, sir. My name's Parnell Watterson, an' since you were such a fine preacher I figgered for sure you were bringin' the Word to this heathen town."

Hattie Jane said to Watterson, "My husband found a rich gold mine near here and was murdered for his claim. Mister Swartze comforted him during his final hours. He then rescued the mine from the hands of villains and began working the mine at his expense while giving me half of everything."

Half of nothing doesn't total up to much, I thought, but this sure wasn't a great time to bring up the subject.

Parnell Watterson's lower lip began quivering. "The

Lord works in wonderful an' mysterious ways, ma'am. I'd say the reverend is still movin' the Good Word even though his faith *is* bein' tried."

"Thank you, brother," I said.

To shorten this rather thorny conversation, I grabbed up Hattie's portmanteau and nearly added to my woes of the day by getting a rupture. I had forgotten that all women travel with an anvil in their luggage.

"If you will excuse us, sir, I'm certain the young lady is tuckered out from her long journey," I said with a groan.

The old man dabbed at a leaky eye when he said to Hattie, "There's a true man of God for you, ma'am, always thinkin' of the welfare of others first."

"Have a safe and pleasant journey, Mister Watterson," Hattie said. "And I wish you much success in Yuma."

Parnell said to me, "I sell supplies for prisons and jails. The sturdiest of steel bars for doors and windows, strong locks, leg shackles, and handcuffs. I even sold the prison in Colorado the rope they used to hang that poor fellow with. I'm sure sorry the affair upset you so, but at least my rope held firm. I'm heading for Yuma where they're buildin' a new territorial prison for Arizona." He chuckled. "If there were more good folks like you about, I'd be forced to find another occupation."

"Thank you, sir, for those kind words," I gasped as I struggled through the open door with Hattie's luggage. That portmanteau was so darn heavy I couldn't have mustered enough wind to say any more even if I had wanted to. At least I managed to haul the thing over to Hattie's quarters without pulling my innards loose.

"You'll be staying here in my house where it's quiet and private," I said once I'd recovered. "I've taken a room over at the hotel."

Hattie Jane looked at me, aghast. "Why, Mister Swartze, this is simply too kind of you."

"No, ma'am, it's fine. The hotel's no place for a lady. I have already taken my things over there. It would be a comfort for me to have you stay here. And one more thing."

"Yes?"

"Please call me John, and what that fellow at the stage office said about my being a preacher, well, I hope you understand that is in my past. No one hereabouts knows of this, and I would prefer to have them continue to think of me as a simple mining man."

"Of course—John, I shall honor your wishes. I must tell you, however, that I very deeply appreciate your many courtesies and shall endeavor to repay you."

"Could you give me a smile?" I asked.

Hattie beamed at me.

"Thank you, ma'am," I said. "I consider myself paid in full."

"You are too kind, John, and please call me Hattie. I am very much looking forward to getting to know you better and learn more about our gold mine you have in operation."

I swallowed hard. "I'm certain you're tired out. Make yourself at home. I believe you'll find everything you need. I hope you will consent to join me for dinner tomorrow. Then we'll rent a buggy and I'll fill you in on the way things are going at the Hattie's Hope Mine."

"Hattie's Hope!" she exclaimed. "I didn't know the mine was named after me."

"It was Dillon's dying request. I thought it was a wonderful gesture. Now you get some rest and I'll pick you up tomorrow around noontime."

My toes curled when she stepped close and pecked a kiss on my cheeks.

"I will be counting the hours," she said sweetly.

The lingering aroma of lilacs followed me into Sam Cobb's saloon. I ordered a beer with a double shot of whiskey, and spent the entire evening pondering on how I could soften the sad news I had to give the beautiful lady on the morrow.

There was no choice but to tell Hattie the truth of the matter. In a small town such as Vulture City some half-wit would blurt out the facts to her anyway. Once again I was caught between the devil and the deep blue sea and my heart was breaking.

Hattie Jordan stared glumly into the back depths of the mine shaft. The wind whipped her long tresses when she turned to Farley Fairweather, who had joined me in explaining our plight. "So you are certain there is no more gold?"

Farley seemed genuinely sad. "Yes, ma'am. There weren't much to begin with, just a rich seam that had so blasted much copper mixed in, the mill couldn't recover but a little of the gold. Now, even the vein itself is gone. If'n we keep workin' there's a chance of findin' more ore, but when it won't mill out, I really don't know how it would make money even if we did hit pay dirt."

Tears were welling in Hattie's emerald eyes when she looked at me. "Oh, John, I feel so sorry for you. I know you must have spent a fortune trying to make Dillon's dreams come true, and all you have to show for it is a worthless hole."

"Don't you worry your pretty head over the way things turned out. The claim was a good bet. I'm only sorry that you came all the way out here just to find bad news."

A burning lump formed in my throat when she said, "I'm glad I came, because I found a friend and a truly good man in you, John Swartze. Most men would simply have taken the claim for themselves, but you are honest to a fault and now I fear you have spent far more money in an attempt to help me than you could afford."

"You are an astute observer," I said. "The inheritance I received from my parents' estate after they were killed when a buggy overturned is nearly gone. I was an only child and am alone in this world, so no one else need suffer from my misjudgments in the mining business."

I felt terrible about having to tell Hattie an untruth, but I really had no choice in the matter. I was smitten by her sweetness and beauty and wished with all of my heart to someday be able to cradle her in my arms. Should anyone, even lovely Hattie, suspect I was the wanted man-eater Al Packer, who was still being vilified in newspapers and magazines, my future would be quite bleak indeed.

Hattie's lithe form slumped in despair. She choked back a sob and embraced my hand. "John, no one has ever sacrificed so dearly in my behalf. Perhaps it might be possible to sell off the machinery to cut your losses. Please come over and let me fix you supper tonight. Then we'll visit and see if there is anything I can do to help."

Farley butted in. "Swartze, if'n you're of a mind to sell out, an I can't figger out why you wouldn't be, I'll personally pay a thousand dollars for the mine an' mill. Now this claim ain't worth nothin', but if'n I was to own it I could leave the machinery here until I have need for it elsewhere."

Hattie Jane batted her green eyes. "Why, a thousand dollars is an awful lot of money."

I sputtered, "It surely ought to be worth more than that. Just a few short weeks ago I paid three thousand dollars for the mill and equipment."

Farley cut off Hattie's reply by saying, "That was when

you had a gold vein an' everyone thought the mill would work. I'm takin' a chance buyin' the thing myself."

"We'll talk on the matter tonight and I'll let you know later on," I said. "This is a big decision for me and the little lady. After all, her late husband lost his life over this claim. I reckon she should have a say as to what we do with it."

Hattie squeezed my hand. "John, you are simply the nicest man. Please take me back to town now." She rolled moist emerald eyes toward me. "Tonight, I want to fix you a really good supper. How does fried chicken, mashed potatoes with cream gravy, and a peach cobbler sound?"

"Just like heaven," I replied as I escorted her toward the waiting surrey. "Just like a little taste of heaven."

Spending time with Hattie Jane was akin to being in the abode of the blessed. The sweet little lady's good cooking only added to her image as a goddess. She glided cheerfully about the house with all of the grace and beauty of evening sunbeams dancing through crystal glass.

We talked of many things, and I was somewhat taken aback by her candor when she told me that her marriage to Dillon Jordan had not been a happy one. Many times her late husband had, without notice, taken off for months on end, leaving only Hattie and her ailing father, Jonas, to work their six-hundred-acre ranch. During Dillon's excursions he never wrote her or sent any money to help out. Upon his return he would simply say that he had been "off prospecting," and sullenly return to ranch life until again being struck with wanderlust.

I also learned that Hattie Jane had married Jordan

seven years ago, when she was only sixteen years of age. This meant she was now a delightfully young twenty-three-year-old lady. She added sadly that her troubled marriage to Dillon had produced no offspring.

I began to understand that Hattie's wellspring of inner strength had been born of necessity. I was no longer mystified as to how well she had accepted the fact that our gold mine was a total failure; this sweet and stalwart young woman was well acquainted with disappointments in her life. My sorrow that the failed Hattie's Hope Mine had only added to her problems caused my heart to burn in my chest like a raw sore.

A dying scarlet sunset was fast giving way to the shadows of night when I lit a coal-oil lamp and placed it in the center of the dining room table. Hattie poured us both a steaming cup of coffee, then set out two bowls of peach cobbler that were swimming in a sea of sweet cream. She scooted out a chair across from me and sat down.

After a long moment she demurely began spooning her cobbler and asked, "Are you planning to accept Mister Fairweather's offer to purchase the mine and your machinery?"

"I hate to do that, Hattie," I said solemnly. "It would be admitting the mining claim is a failure. I have nearly eight hundred dollars of my inheritance money left. Perhaps if I kept the crew on for a few more days—the cost of this is about a hundred dollars a day—we might yet unearth a bonanza."

Hattie's shoulders slumped in despair. "Or if the gold is gone you will be broke. John, I cannot allow you to do this for my sake. And, if I understood Mister Fairweather correctly, even if we did uncover some ore, there is no way to recover the gold with the machinery you have."

"I know it's taking a big chance, Hattie. A will-o'-the-wisp at the end of the rainbow at best, but I feel that I owe it to you to continue on."

Hattie laid down her spoon, reached across the oak table, and softly intertwined my hand in hers. "John, I was married to a man who chased chimeras. His lust for riches ended only when he died pursuing one. I don't want you to wind up like Dillon. Please don't spend any more money on the elusive dream, at least until we take some time to think on the matter. Perhaps I could hire a mining engineer to give us a professional opinion. I have over a hundred dollars. Surely, this is a decision that does not need to be hastily made."

"No," I said. "You are right. There is no reason to make a fast judgment. I will look up Farley Fairweather yet tonight and have him lay off the crew. Tomorrow, we shall investigate your excellent suggestion of having an expert come and check out the mine."

I really had no great hopes for the gold mine ever amounting to anything. I did, however, know for certain that I wanted to spend more time with Hattie Jane. A lot more time. I loved her cheerful demeanor and happy, musical voice. I was taken by the way her emerald eyes sparkled in the flickering lantern light, and delighted in being enveloped by the wonderful aroma of lilac perfume.

Most of all, I was fast falling in love with Hattie Jordan. A shining jewel such as she was would surely be pursued as a sweet flower is by bees. Beautiful and available ladies were far more scarce on the frontier than gold-mining claims.

"I appreciate your patience and thoughtfulness," Hattie said.

"It is your future at stake here. I agree that we shall do everything possible to assure we are not making a mistake before accepting Fairweather's offer. From what he said, he's only interested in buying the machinery anyway. I don't believe us taking time to examine the mine thoroughly will upset the deal."

Hattie tightened her embrace on my hand. "John, you are so wonderful."

Reluctantly, I retrieved my hand and scooted back my chair and stood. "I must be going if I am to visit with Fairweather. Also, I am sure you are tired after such a long and trying day."

Hattie glided to my side. She stood on tiptoes and planted a quick kiss near my lips. "Let's have breakfast together in the morning, then if it's not too much trouble, could we climb down into the mine and look it over ourselves? I would like to see it myself, even though I've never been in a gold mine before. I was quite surprised when Mister Fairweather refused to let me enter the shaft."

I knew it was considered bad luck for a woman to enter a mine. That hole had already been plagued with so much trouble I couldn't fathom where there could be any more damage done. "We'll take the buggy and spend as much time there as your heart desires."

This time her kiss found my lips. When I got the Beachcomber Saloon and bellied up to the bar, my heart was still pounding like a drum.

Forty

The Hattie's Hope gold mine turned out to be a total failure. The sweet lady and I spent most of the next day inspecting every foot of the workings by candlelight and found none of the white quartz that indicated gold.

We sent a telegraph to Max Reed, a mining engineer in Prescott. He replied with a request for five hundred dollars, in advance, to make an evaluation of the property. Hattie and I agreed that this would likely be a complete waste of money.

Through Sam Cobb, I made the acquaintance of James McLaughlin, the mine foreman for the Vulture Company. He offered to check out the mine and give us his opinion for twenty dollars, provided we wait until Sunday, which was his only day off. McLaughlin was a young fellow and from the hungry stares he kept giving Hattie, I knew he was far more interested in her than any mine, but I paid him anyway. We needed an expert opinion before selling, and I knew McLaughlin would most likely look after the young lady's interests better than any high-paid engineer ever would.

The next five days passed quickly as a lightning flash. While awaiting James McLaughlin's investigation, I took the opportunity to spend every possible moment with Hattie. We took the rented buggy and drove into the hills for evening picnics. On soft sand beneath towering saguaro cacti we would spread a quilt. Then, while a brilliant red sunset painted a panorama on the western horizon, we sipped wine and talked until the moon was hanging golden in the night. Never before had I experienced such utter happiness.

"You couldn't dig enough gold out of that mine to fill a bad tooth," was McLaughlin's not too surprising assessment of our situation. "I'd reckon the whole affair was just a little pocket. There sure ain't no vein like it takes to make a payin' mine."

I thanked him, then pointed the idiot toward the saloon and told him to go have a drink on me. The manner in which he kept leering at Hattie Jane was becoming quite upsetting to me.

Later that same day I signed over all of the machinery at the mine and mill along with a quit-claim deed to the Hattie's Hope to Farley Fairweather in exchange for one thousand dollars in cash money. I was somewhat taken aback when the grouch couldn't find something to complain about; for some reason I could not fathom, he actually seemed to be in a good humor and never once so much as gave out a cough.

I was simply glad to be out of the mining business. When I got around to filing a claim on my Colorado property, I would take the money and run before anybody had a chance to build a blasted mill or dig a lot of holes. I was not in need of any more education as to how to make money from a gold mine.

I stuffed the money into the pocket of my Levi's and retreated to the Beachcomber Saloon, where I ordered a dime glass of beer and mulled my future.

Alferd Packer, the wanted Colorado man-eater who had been unjustly tried and condemned by a biased and bloodthirsty press, was dead. He had ceased to exist here in the vast expanse of the Mohave Desert. John Swartze had been reborn by the same love that had killed Packer. I could never have allowed myself to follow the urgings of my heartstrings should this have not been the absolute truth.

"You're lookin' plenty chipper for a man that just went bust," Sam Cobb said with a wry grin. "I'd reckon that purty li'l lady you've been keepin' company with is enough to keep most any man's mind off'n his troubles. She's cuter than a speckled pup."

"That she is, Sam," I said. "And if things go my way tonight, I'll be leaving this fair city. I intend to go ask Hattie to marry me."

Sam reached across the plank bar and took away my half-full glass. "I generally hate to lose a payin' customer, but there's times when good sense comes to bein' a necessity. If'n you don't get over an' propose to that sweet thing, I'm gonna spread the word that she's available an' lookin'."

I nodded. "You're a wise man, Sam Cobb. I'm on my way."

"Don't go an' let her throw the hook," Sam hollered as I stepped onto the boardwalk. "That lady's a keeper."

I have never understood why women take to crying whenever they're happy as well as sad. This behavior can really throw a man for a loop until he figures out which way the wind is actually blowing.

After I popped the question to Hattie Jane, she grabbed a lace handkerchief from her handbag and wept into it for what seemed like forever.

"You have made me the happiest person in the world, John Swartze," she finally sobbed. "I never dared dream a wonderful man like you would ever have someone like me." She daubed at her teary green eyes. "But I fear there is something terrible that you must know about me."

I stepped close and wrapped her in a sheltering embrace. "Whatever the problem is, we'll work it out—together."

Hattie pushed me away, then spun to face the wall. "John—I don't believe I am able to—ever bear children."

I placed my hands on her shoulders and gently turned her to face me. "Hattie, it's all right. The will of the Lord is often hard to understand, but I love *you* and all I ask is your love in return."

She buried her face into my chest. "Oh, yes, John, I shall be your wife. Could we please be married in a church? I know you must wish the same and there is no church here in Vulture City. I am certain, however, we can find a minister in Prescott."

"Yes, my darling, I agree that a church wedding is the only way to start our new life together. I only have this house and a mule to sell. Then we will take the stage to Prescott and find a preacher. We can enjoy a few days in a good hotel there, then be off to your ranch in Wyoming."

Hattie rolled her beautiful freckled face to mine. "You mean *our* ranch," she said before giving me a kiss that curled my toes.

Three long days later Hattie Jane changed her last name to Swartze in a small white-frame Presbyterian church in Prescott, Arizona. The minister was a kindly silver-haired fellow by the name of Kinsey Wolcott. His wife, Minnie, played on a pump organ while he held the Good Book open and said the words over us.

Hattie looked exactly like an angel wearing her frilly white dress. Lilac bushes were still in bloom and I had cut a spray of lavender flowers for her to carry. Even the sky was crystal blue, and the day windless and delightfully warm. It was as if God himself was smiling upon our union.

When we got back to the hotel, I scooped her into my arms and carried her, giggling, across the threshold. Earlier on, I had made adequate arrangements with the clerk to provide room service to us for the next few days. This was sound thinking, for we never left that room for four blissful days and nights.

On occasion, I wonder what Heaven must be like. But back then, during those halcyon days when my soul soared high on gossamer wings, I knew the place well. To this day, it could not be called Heaven if there wasn't a Hattie Jane there to share eternity with.

It was on a warm and sunny July morning when my new wife and I departed Prescott on a swaying stagecoach bound for the town of Santa Fe in the New Mexico Territory. From there we would travel on a succession of trains and stages before eventually arriving at the military outpost of Fort Fetterman in Wyoming.

I did not relish having to pass through Colorado, and sincerely hoped Wild Bill Hickok had left Cheyenne for greener pastures. Of all the people I wished to avoid, Hickok was at the head of the list. While my red hair had done an excellent job of hoodwinking idiot lawmen, it would become a beacon for a bullet should I again cross paths with that arrogant, humorless gunslinger.

I decided that wrapping my arm around Hattie Jane and quickly ushering her to the nearest hotel room whenever we had a layover would not only be pleasurable, it could also be of salubrious benefit for my general welfare.

We had not gone ten miles from Prescott when a slovenly idiot who had plopped himself in the seat across from us began flapping his gums about everything he knew. This didn't seem to amount to much until he starting rattling on about the mining business.

"My name's Fred Hammersmith," the man said, which got my full attention. "I've never felt so good about leavin' a place before. I went plumb broke on a gold mine down in Vulture City. Had a mill, too, but the thing wouldn't work."

"I'm sorry to hear of your misfortunes," I said. "But there seems to be a lot of that going around."

"Yep," Hammersmith said with a sigh. "I've gone an' learned my lesson. I'm headin' for Texas an' gonna buy me a ranch. I was lucky enough to have a sucker by the name of Farley Fairweather buy me out. He was fool enough to pay two thousand dollars for the mill and mine. Shucks, I'd been trying to sell that stuff for months an' no takers. I was relieved as a politician in Heaven to get as much as I did for everything, considerin' the mill was junk."

Should Alferd Packer have been about, I'm certain he would have returned to Vulture City and had a rather heated and smoky discussion about ethics with a low-down swindler named Farley Fairweather. That flim-flam artist had bought my mine and mill from me with my own money, and I had been none the wiser.

John Swartze simply hugged his sweet wife and decided to let bygones be bygones. I had a new and wonderful life to look forward to. Of course, if the opportunity ever presented itself, I would shoot Fairweather in a heartbeat.

For the present, I was more concerned about reaching Wyoming alive.

Forty-one

It turned out that I need not have fretted the journey to Wyoming. I never saw hide nor hair of Wild Bill, and any lawmen we ran across paid far more attention to lovely Hattie than to me. Having a pretty wife certainly has its advantages.

Hattie's father met us at Fort Fetterman with a dray wagon hitched to a pair of dapple horses onto which I quickly loaded our luggage, including my wife's leaden portmanteau. During a layover in Denver, Hattie had sent him a telegraph message telling him when we would arrive.

I immediately took a liking to my new father-in-law, Jonas Baragree. Only a pallor to his face, which he kept shaded by a big slouch hat, betrayed his ill health. Jonas was forty-two years old with salt-and-pepper hair, slender as a beanpole, and clean shaven, with a wry sense of humor which I came to admire greatly. I had learned that Jonas suffered from Bright's disease, a debilitating kidney ailment that caused his lean body to puff up when it struck him with a bout of sickness.

"Sure hope you're better at stickin' around an' doin' a day's work than the last man Hattie come up with," Jonas said when he eyed me for the first time. "She said you used to be a preacher. They only strain themselves one day a week, an' then don't work up a sweat less'n there's a revival goin' on."

"Now, Papa," Hattie scolded. "John's industrious and we have no other plans except to build up the Windy Hills into a paying ranch."

Jonas flicked the reins and started the old wagon to creaking westward. "If'n that ranch was to make money"—he eyed me straight on—"reckon a preacher might be what it takes, for we'll sure in hell need a miracle for that to happen."

"Don't curse, Papa," Hattie said.

Jonas pulled his hat low and returned his gaze to the dusty, rutted road. "Can't see no damn reason not to. My back's ailin' an' your new husband's got plenty of time to cure my soul afore I have to get it measured by Saint Peter."

As I have said, Jonas Baragree was a very singular man.

The Windy Hills Ranch house sat on a tree-studded bank of the North Platte River. What I noticed most of all was everything about the place had an air of permanence. The main house, barn, and two smaller cabins, that were obviously meant to house hired help, were all built of huge well-chinked logs. On one end of the main house a massive stone chimney jutted skyward. I noticed a wisp of smoke drifting from it and caught the delightful aroma of cooking food.

"Looks like someone's expecting us," I commented.

Jonas nodded. "That'll be Placida, Bartolo's wife. He's turned out to be a right fair hand. I've got him out cuttin' fence posts today. Placida's a durn good cook, too, so long as a person likes peppers hot enough to burn the lint outta their belly button in everything they eat. She's fixin' us a pot of chili an' some tortillas for supper."

"Sounds good," I said. "Hattie and I are both getting plenty tired of taking our meals in hotels and way stations."

Jonas reined the wagon to a stop in front of the house. "Restaurant cookin' would choke a goat. I'll put the team away an' come over after I've rested a spell. I've gone an' moved my things into the second cabin to give you lovebirds some privacy. This way I don't have to fix them squeaky bedsprings."

Hattie's face flushed red. "Papa, how could you talk like that?"

Jonas grinned at her. "You wouldn't be a sittin' there if'n your ma and me hadn't rattled the bed on occasion." He spat a wad of tobacco on the ground. "Ain't nothin' to be shamed of once a preacher says the words. Enjoy it while you can. The opportunity don't last forever."

Women have curiosity that would cause a cat disgrace. Hattie and I had finished proving her father correct about the bedsprings being squeaky when she rolled over and fixed her green eyes on me.

"John," she cooed. "I've been wanting to ask you a question."

Since she was staring at the top of my head, I quickly figured out what had attracted her attention. "Yes, my dear, what is it you wish to know?"

"Your hair, I keep wondering why you dye it?"

I smiled and stroked her cheek. "A few years ago, when I was preaching the Gospel in Florida, I told my flock that I was on fire for the Lord. I colored my hair flame-red, which got my point across nicely. I liked the look and have kept dying it ever since."

"You're so sweet and caring. I know someday you'll want to resume your mission to save souls. When you do I'll understand and be by your side."

"Someday," I said softly, "that may come to be, but for as long as I can see into the future, I only want to work here on the ranch and spend time with you."

Hattie kissed me. "Whatever makes you happy is all I desire."

I told her truthfully, "For the first time in my life I am content being right here and I have no yearning to leave this fine ranch."

"I love you," she said tenderly as she melded her naked body against mine.

"That's good, because you're stuck with me for life."

When I said those words I had no idea how fleeting our time together would be.

Spending those hard months early in my life working for Old Man Hapsburg back in Pennsylvania was excellent training for living on a ranch. I had learned to plow straight furrows and till the ground for crops and run herd on cattle. All of this placed me in good stead with Jonas, who in spite of being quite ill on occasion, kept the ranch in operation.

I quickly learned how the ranch came to have the name of Windy Hills. In Cheyenne the wind blew a lot more than I cared for. Here, along the rolling sage-brush-covered hills of the North Platte, the zephyrs rarely ceased. If the wind had ever stopped howling across that country, the locals would likely have taken it as a sign the world was coming to an end and sacrificed a goat to start it blowing again.

Jonas quipped the only reason we ever had fresh eggs to eat was that he mixed lead buckshot in with the chicken feed, which caused the hens to not get blown away.

Hattie loved to take the wagon and go to Fort Casper for shopping. Fort Fetterman was actually closer to the ranch, but Casper had a bigger trading post, which explained why she had the mail sent there. Women don't think a thing of driving another ten miles to visit a store if they might have a larger selection of hair ribbons; getting the mail was just a grand excuse.

I always made an excuse to stay on the ranch when Hattie got struck with the urge to shop. There was plenty of work to do, so she never surmised my real inclination sprung from not wishing to run across any lawmen.

My luck turned for the better on a Sunday, the Twenty-fifth of June, Eighteen Seventy-Six, when Colonel George Armstrong Custer found more Indians than he was looking for up north on the Little Big Horn.

Then in August, my nemesis, Wild Bill Hickok, added to my good fortune by allowing cross-eyed Jack McCall to sneak up from behind and blow his brains out.

These events had the wonderful effect of removing any mention of Alferd Packer from newspapers and magazines. While I never left the Windy Hills ranch for several years, I always asked Hattie or Jonas to bring me back many newspapers and books to read. It was always quite gratifying to find other, more deserving folks were receiving all of the attention. Alferd Packer had never done anything wrong in the first place. It tore my heart to have read what those vile writers had said about me. It was a blessing for them to have others to pick on for a change.

Here, I must speed forward through the years. My editor, Layton Laird, has counseled me that happy times hold no interest for readers. And my years I spent with Hattie and Jonas were the most idyllic I could ever have imagined. Most joyous of all occurred on a pleasantly warm though windy day, the Sixth of May, Eighteen Seventy-Nine, when my sweet Hattie presented me with a healthy son. We named the boy Jonas, after her father, which pleased the increasingly infirm old fellow a great deal.

You can understand by now the depth of my sorrow and rage when, on the blustery and rainy evening of March Tenth in the year Eighteen Eighty-Three, I returned home from a day of repairing fence to find the ranch houses had been burned to the ground.

Jonas was the first body I noticed. He lay sprawled facedown in the mud, arrows bristling from his back. Bartolo and his wife Placida had been savagely hacked to pieces with what I knew must have been tomahawks. I could only recognize them by the clothes they wore, so terribly were their heads smashed in.

My feet were leaden and my heart numb beyond the point of feeling pain when I began the search for Hattie Jane and our cherished son. I knew from what I had found that a band of renegade Indians, bent on nothing except killing, had struck while I was gone and not here to defend my family.

I remember screaming like a panther when I stumbled across my wife's naked and violated body in the growing dusk. I plucked her from the mud and held her limp form close and cried aloud, my tears mixing with the cold rain that was falling from a bitter sky.

My son had been kidnapped! The savages had taken my only child to be raised as an Indian or traded to another tribe as a slave. The brutes could not have gone far. I picked up my sweet Hattie Jane and carried her to the wagon that I had been using. Gently I laid her in the bed of it and carefully covered her nakedness with a canvas. I could not see a mark on her and remember wondering if, when the raping was over, they had allowed her an easy death.

I felt only a strange dullness when I climbed into the driver's seat and whipped the horses to take us to Fort Fetterman. Everything I had ever dreamed of or loved was gone, destroyed. Only my son was left. With each muddy cold mile that I came closer to Fort Fetterman my numbness turned more into a seething red rage.

I would seek out the post commander and with the help of the military my little Jonas could at least be spared.

Forty-two

The trek to Fort Fetterman took me the entire night, and I did not arrive there until midmorning of the next day. The bitterly cold rain turned to snow, which caused the dray wagon to slide off the road and become stuck. It was nearly impossible to even see the road, let alone how to dig the wagon free.

I climbed into the bed alongside Hattie's lifeless form and covered myself with the big canvas. Exhaustion and terrible distress caused me to drift instantly to sleep.

I awoke to a gray dawn and was greeted by the return of a slow and frigid rain. It took me an hour of cutting sagebrush, which I wedged under the wheels with a shovel, before I was able to whip the horses into pulling the wagon back onto the muddy road.

When I arrived at Fort Fetterman I quickly ran inside the first building I encountered to escape the cold rain and ask the location of the post commander. Instead I confronted a lone sheriff by the name of Carson Rudin. The lawman set his steely eyes upon me, and before I could even take the time to explain my presence, I found myself facing into the barrels of a cocked sawed-off shotgun.

"I reckon this was my lucky mornin' to be goin' through old wanted posters," he gloated. "I was burnin' 'em in the stove an' look here what I spied just when you come in."

With his free hand Sheriff Rudin proudly held up a flyer announcing in huge print a twenty-five-thousand-dollar reward for the arrest of Alferd Packer. The likeness of the sketch was eerily accurate, for a man with long black hair and a goatee.

"I don't know what you're talking about," I cried. "Indians attacked our ranch, killed my wife and father-in-law along with our hired hands, and kidnapped my son. My name's John Swartze. We own the Windy Hills Ranch between here and Fort Casper."

Rudin chuckled gruffly, then tossed the poster aside and came up with a set of handcuffs, which he tossed to me without wavering that shotgun an iota from my middle. "Snap those on good an' tight. Then you can warm yerself in a cell while I send off a telegraph to Denver."

"But my son has been kidnapped by Indians. There is no time for this. Every minute we delay the less likely we can find those renegades and rescue him."

"Indians is the Army's problem, Packer. If what you say is true, most likely your boy's either already dead or so far outta this country we'd never catch up with 'em anyway. Savages move like the wind."

"Why do you insist I'm this man Packer?" I pleaded. "I told you my name is Swartze. I demand to speak with the post commander."

"Snap those cuffs on or I'll blow one of yer feet off. The reward ain't worth nothing' if'n you're dead, but it don't say nothin' about bein' crippled."

I did as he said, and felt the steel rings click tight against my wrists. I remembered how Alonzo Wall's handcuffs had done the same back in Saguache so long ago.

"That's right smart of you," Rudin said coldly. "Now

you can stand on the trapdoor when they hang you without havin' to lean on a crutch."

The sheriff uncocked the hammers and laid the shotgun aside. He opened a drawer of his desk and extracted a hand mirror and shoved the thing in my face. This was when I noticed the rain had washed nearly all of my hair dye away, leaving only a few scarlet streaks on my stubble-bearded face. I had been too heartbroken to even conceive of such a thing happening to betray my identity.

"Ain't no normal man would dye his hair unless he was on the dodge," Rudin said firmly. "Now you git your man-eatin' self into a cell. I gotta go find out when a fellow by the name of Sawyer Noon can send for you an' pay me my money. He's been lookin' for you for quite a spell. Hell, I'd have burned that flyer an' wouldn't have thought a thing more about it if'n you hadn't come in when you did leakin' hair color."

"I've never even heard of a man by the name of Sawyer Noon," I fairly screamed. "My wife's dead in the back of the wagon. My God, man, please let me see to burying her."

"If'n she's dead, there ain't no rush. I'll send the undertaker to fetch her. This Noon feller had a brother by the name of George that you killed an' ate along with four other innocent folks back in Seventy-Four. Catchin' a famous wanted man like you'll get my name writ up as quite a lawman." His mustache wiggled when he grinned evilly. "An' that big reward will set the missus an' me up for life."

Dear God, there was nothing I could do but allow this calloused sheriff with a heart of stone to lock me away like some wild beast while my son's captors made their escape.

My time of happiness had been but a brief span of nearly eight years. I knew for certain that I would be caged and transported in chains back to Colorado. I could only hope my end would come quickly and I would not be vilified and gloated over by lawmen and a heartless press.

It really did not matter. My soul had departed along with dear sweet Hattie's. I had no future to look forward to. I was, after all, the wanted cannibal Alferd Giles Packer. At least little Hattie would never learn of my past or that terrible incident on Slumgullion Pass when I had done nothing more than survive as any reasonable man would have, should he have been in my place.

Forty-three

I found it hard to comprehend the progress that had been wrought since I was last in the high country of Colorado. Even though I was manacled hand and foot with heavy chains, there were windows through which I could observe the trappings of civilization and freedom.

At this time Chief Ouray had been in the ground for three years. I remembered well how wild and remote this country was when I first met the kindly Ute. His giving up the sacred mountains had killed first his spirit, then the man himself.

The city of Gunnison did not exist when my foredoomed party and I had gone seeking our fortunes. A mere nine years later, I rode into the booming metropolis on a chugging steam train. From the depot I was ushered by a small army of armed guards through a milling crowd of angry, jeering onlookers into a stagecoach that immediately departed for what I was told would be Lake City.

A bustling town of over two thousand souls now sprawled along the rushing clear waters of the Lake Fork of the Gunnison River just below the serenely beautiful Lake San Cristobal where Gidd Trevor had met his untimely demise.

I could not help but idly wonder if the rich vein of gold that was the mainspring for my misfortunes with the law had been discovered by others and opened into a paying mine. Not that it mattered to me any longer. Money had no value in the netherworld where I would quite likely, in short order, become a resident unless my luck took a drastic change for the better.

I was taken aback when, through the window of the rattling stagecoach, I saw a red brick building with a huge tiger's head painted across the top part along with a sign advertising it to be The Tiger Spit Saloon.

The jail where I was lodged unfortunately turned out to be quite sturdily constructed of heavy granite stones, with thick iron bars riveted securely in place over the doors and windows. This time there would be no sweet Letty to come to my rescue with a smuggled key. With my being rather famous, a plethora of unsmiling armed guards kept an eagle eye on me, which marred any plans I entertained for making a quick escape.

In back of the neat-looking two-story white-frame courthouse, plainly visible from my cell window, I watched industrious carpenters building a scaffold that I assumed was being erected for my benefit.

My mind was awash with plans to leave this place at the first possible opportunity. Failing this possibility, I needed to rely on the services of a good attorney. I had certainly done nothing to deserve the treatment I was receiving. The biggest problem I faced was the fact that I was broke. Lawyers are a species motivated only by money. As you can easily discern, I found myself facing a bleak future.

After seeing a saloon called The Tiger Spit, I was not surprised by my first visitor.

"Glad to see you again, Packer," Larry Dolan said through the bars with a wide smile. "Business has been boomin' since word got out you was comin'. I'd reckon the streak will last until after the hangin'."

"Wish I could say it's good to set eyes on you," I

said. "And I hope it won't come as a terrible disappointment that I plan to get out of this fix." I craned to see around him. "Where's Ol' Ed Whitmore? I figured he'd be along to visit."

"Oh, Ed's busy talkin' to folks, but he'll be around. He's the sheriff here these days. Saguache has dried up like a winter weed fixin' to blow away. That's why I come an' moved my business over here where all the money's at."

"Ed Whitmore's the sheriff!"

"Yep, the pay's better than tendin' bar for me or stretchin' necks. He told me there's a professional hangman that works over at the prison in Cañon City comin' to do the honors for you."

Suddenly I felt rather weak in the knees. "I haven't even been tried yet."

"Most folks can't see where a passel of lawyers gummin' away will change anything. It's a well-known fact that you went an' dined on your five partners. If'n that ain't a hangin' offense, I sure don't know what is." Dolan cocked his head. "You feelin' all right, Packer? You're lookin' mighty peaked."

I managed a wry smile. "It was likely something I ate."

Two days later Ed Whitmore came to see me. The job of sheriff had obviously been good to him for he'd gained a solid fifty pounds and had all of it stuck right out front where he could keep an eye on it. He rolled the ever-present stub of a cigar around in his mouth, then turned to one of his deputies. "Open up the cell. I need to let our prisoner get acquainted with his lawyer."

The iron door creaked open and my heart fell when I beheld the eastern dandy who was supposed to be my salvation. Dressed in a cream-colored suit with a red silk cravat and black derby, my hoped-for savior didn't appear to be even old enough to shave.

'Alferd Packer,'' the colorful idiot packing a brown leather valise piped while sticking out his lily-white hand. "I am Aloysius Thorndyke Poindexter. The State of Colorado has appointed me to act as your defense counsel."

I sighed deeply and returned his handshake. It was like grabbing on to a wet bar towel. "Tell me honestly, does your mother know where you are?"

The lawyer snorted haughtily, "I will have you know that I graduated with honors from the Cambridge School of Law. I am here to save your life, Mister Packer. I do not believe insulting me to be in your best interests."

"No offense intended. It's just that your youthful appearance took me aback. I'm sure you've successfully represented many men accused of something that's liable to get them hung."

"Actually, sir, you are my first client. Now, if you don't mind, I wish to take an hour or so and review your case with you."

Ed Whitmore's cigar bobbed as he choked down a snicker. "You just let out a holler, Mister Poindexter, when you're ready to leave. An' Deputy Kincaid here will let you out." The portly sheriff commenced to waddle off when he turned to me. "Al, there's a bevy of newspaper reporters an' writers pesterin' me for a visit with you. I'll leave it up to you if you want to see 'em."

Aloysius Poindexter squeaked, "My client and I shall prepare a statement for the Fourth Estate. Under no circumstances is he to make any statement without my being present."

The sheriff said with a shrug, "I don't know nothin' about any estate, but I did give 'em a look at ol' Al's confession that he made. Reckon with that they won't need to bedevil him any."

"What!" the lawyer spat. "My client gave you a confession? This is the first I've heard of the matter. This is outrageous."

I shook my head. "I only told the truth. I couldn't see where that would do any damage."

Poindexter sighed. "We are dealing with the law here. In a court trial the truth can often be disastrous." He nodded toward a table in my cell. "Sit down, Mister Packer. I believe that I have my work cut out for me."

The sun had dipped below the rugged mountains and a chill was building in the air when the young dandy returned his notes to the huge leather valise that never left his reach.

"Packer," the lawyer said, "I shall do whatever is possible to win you an acquittal. I must warn you that the confession you so unwisely gave may very well have driven the nails into your coffin."

"I don't reckon that was very smart of me."

"What you must know is that I do not believe you killed anyone except the man Bell. And that was in self-defense. The act of cannibalism, while detestable, was a matter of self-preservation, such as happened with the tragic Donner Party some years back. I shall attempt to draw upon this as a parallel."

I said, "My conscience is clear on the matter. If I hadn't done what I did to survive, there would have been six bodies found on the mountainside instead of five."

"I understand that. What I must tell you is one of the victims' brother, a man by the name of Sawyer Noon, is a very wealthy man. He paid the reward for your capture, and I have learned that he is responsible for Hamilton Beesley being appointed as the prosecuting attorney. Beesley is a very capable lawyer and has many friends amongst the legal community, including Judge Gerry, who will preside over the trial."

"Hamilton Beesley!" I yelled. "I hired him to get me out of jail in Saguache."

"Unfortunately, you did not pay his fee. If money had changed hands, I could get him removed from the case, but this did not occur."

"No, I found it wiser to leave before the shyster showed up. Tell me, did this Sawyer Noon fellow cause you to be my lawyer?"

Poindexter grinned for the first time. "Yes, sir, he did. That was a huge mistake on his part."

I stared past the lawyer through the barred window at the now completed gallows. "I surely hope you're right about that. I hope to God you're as good as you think you are."

My trial was held on the second floor of the courthouse and went on for seven long days. Hamilton Beesley gave a turgid performance that would have done justice to a stage show. The prosecutor played to the jury with all the enthusiasm of a stump preacher at a revival.

Poindexter, on the other hand, got tongue-tied to the point of stuttering every time he made an effort to speak in my behalf. The young lawyer gave me great cause to consider any means of escape. There were three huge windows behind the judge's bench that gave everyone, especially the jury, a grand view of the waiting gallows.

I would likely have made a dash and crashed through one of those windows, stolen a horse, and headed for parts unknown if it hadn't been for the heavy ball and chain Ed Whitmore had fastened around my left ankle.

The rotund sheriff had earlier caught on to my efforts to chisel away mortar from the bars on the cell window using a metal letter opener I'd pilfered from my lawyer's valise.

"You're drawin' too big a crowd to up an' leave us,"

Whitmore had said when he shackled me. "Business this good has to be looked after."

It was disgustingly obvious the bald, cigar-chomping, ex-bartender and hangman had evolved into a surprisingly competent sheriff. I only wish I could have said the same for my lawyer, who never once objected to any of the vile things the flamboyant Beesley said about me. When it came time for my educated lawyer to speak, he spent more time stuttering than defending my actions on Slumgullion Pass.

Larry Dolan's version of Judge Gerry's verdict and sentence came as no surprise to me or anyone and was written up and published in the *Silver Record* as follows:

"Alferd Packer, stand up," the judge boomed
mightily, and pointed his finger at the
defendant. "There were seven good Democrats
in Hinsdale County and you, you man-eating
son-of-a-bitch, went and ate five of them.
I hereby sentence you to hang by the neck
until you're dead, dead, dead as a warning
against reducing the Democratic population
of the fair State of Colorado."

In actuality, Judge Gerry was a professional and educated man. His verbiage was much more refined and eloquent, but the facts remained the same. I had been found guilty of murder and on the Nineteenth day of May, a mere six weeks hence, my soul would be sent to join Sweet Hattie on that faraway shore where the trials and tribulations of this world are but a foggy memory.

Forty-four

"Packer," Ed Whitmore said, mouthing his cigar, "that lawyer of yours is so darn good he's gonna get you hung before we're ready for the event."

Larry Dolan, who stood alongside the sheriff outside my cell door, said, "I reckon we oughtta ship you over to Gunnison straightaway. The jail there's sturdier and has more guards."

It was nigh onto midnight and a half moon hung high and orange over the scaffold outside my window. The revelry from the saloons downtown had been growing in intensity since late that afternoon. Ever since word had gotten out that Aloysius Poindexter had filed an appeal on my sentence that might work, folks had begun to fear I would not be available to give them a holiday and the rumblings of a lynch mob were building like a spring thunderstorm.

I rattled the heavy chain that was attached to my ankle. "Boys, if you'd take this thing off me, I'd be able to move a lot quicker."

The sheriff shook his head firmly. "Nope, I ain't a-gonna do that. Alonzo, over in Saguache, ain't never been able to live down lettin' you get away from his jail like you done. I can't have you goin' an' makin' a fool outta me, too."

"But I can't ride a horse wearing this iron ball," I pleaded.

Larry Dolan smiled evilly. "That ain't a problem, Al. Ed an' I've got a plan." He then stepped aside to allow four men who were packing a wooden coffin inside the cell block.

My heart began pounding when Ed stuck a key in the lock and the sheriff swung the door open and nodded to me. "Get in the box."

"But I'm not dead yet," I shouted.

"We know that, Packer," Dolan said with a shrug of impatience. "And we'd prefer to wait until you was to do this, gol darn it. I ain't done such good saloon business for a coon's age. The problem is that drunken mob's gonna lynch you in a bit."

"They'll likely bust up my jail," the sheriff interjected. "I can't have that. An' it won't look good if I let this sort of thing keep happening to me."

I asked, "What do you mean *keep* happening?"

Dolan spoke up. "A couple of months ago three miners got on a tear and shot a bartender dead. Before ol' Ed could do a thing about it, a bunch of concerned citizens had ropes around those men's necks an' then went and hung 'em from off a bridge. The next mornin' school was let out so the kids could see what happens to lawbreakers."

The sheriff pointed a pudgy finger at the open coffin. "If you know what's good for you, you'll climb in there an' let us nail the lid shut. We've gone an' put in some air holes. Digger White, the undertaker, will put your coffin in his hearse under the bodies of some men that got themselves bad blown up with dynamite. No one will want to rummage through a mess like that an' nobody'll suspect a thing. Digger's always haulin' bodies over to Gunnison to get shipped off on the train."

The sound of a distant gunshot made up my mind.

I grabbed up that heavy iron ball, shuffled over, and settled into the coffin. "If I don't live through this, I'll never forgive you."

Larry Dolan snorted, "Don't go blamin' Ed Whitmore an' me. It's the fault of that dandy lawyer of yours. All of us had rather you hung on schedule."

"I'm sorry to be such a disappointment," I said as the lid was being fit over the coffin.

It was the next afternoon and inside the jail in Gunnison when the nails were finally pulled out. I blinked my eyes into focus and saw I was surrounded by lawmen.

"Welcome to Gunnison, Al Packer," a thin man with a big shiny star pinned on his shirt said coldly. "Glad you made it here without gettin' yourself lynched. I ain't never had a famous cannibal to lock up before. Reckon come election time, I'll get some benefit outta the likes of you."

I had been inside the cramped confines of that coffin so long a pair of beefy deputies had to help me stand. I admit to not being in a good mood when I stared at him and said in a matter-of-fact tone, "I agree with you, Sheriff. I also strive to get all the good that I can from my fellowman."

I was lodged in a small stone cell that always felt cold. A massive iron door furnished my only light, there being no windows where I could view the outside world. My cage was but one of many that faced onto a dreary hallway that had only one exit, this being barred by another strong steel door.

Any guard who came into the cell bock never had a key to the main doorway, only access to individual cells. Should a prisoner be lucky enough to overpower the man, he could not leave the hallway. This made escape quite out of the question.

I had never thought of the legal process as moving with the speed of a glacier on its way to the sea, but it surely did so in my case. The law is quick to convict and take a life, but interminably slow when it comes to admitting that a mistake might have been made.

I languished in that terrible dungeon for two and one half years while Aloysius Poindexter argued for my appeal. Each time he came to visit I could not help but feel a chill and wonder if he had lost. Should this have occurred I would have quickly been chained and returned to Lake City to provide the illustrious citizens with the entertainment of a hanging.

Not that Larry Dolan or the rotund hangman turned sheriff, Ed Whitmore, would have benefited from this happening. Only a few short weeks after my departing Lake City so ignominiously, both men had been shot and killed attempting to thwart a late-night burglary of The Tiger Spit Saloon. The last I heard of the matter, neither the outlaws' names nor their whereabouts were known.

My lawyer, however, did not lose. Poindexter may have dressed colorfully enough to put a hummingbird to shame, and generally had the appearance of a considerable dandy, but he was tenacious as a bulldog. It took him until the Thirtieth of October in the year Eighteen Eighty-Five to get my unjust conviction reversed.

Nevertheless, I was not freed. Following the usual compassion of a system run by lawyers, I was ordered to remain imprisoned until I could be given a new trial. Poindexter told me, without any emotion or surprise on his part, that this would occur the first week of August, *next year.*

When a solitary man is at the mercy of a heartless, self-serving system of so-called justice, he has no rights or privileges. I could do nothing but await the outcome. The only salve for my tortured soul was the fact that

Hattie did not have to suffer through this along with me.

Books, magazines, and newspapers became my window to the outside world. Some women's league kept a steady supply of the latest periodicals and novels available to inmates. This was a most commendable act of compassion. Many of my cellmates were illiterate, and I often read aloud to them for hours on end. Such are the things that make the passage of the days of a prisoner tolerable.

While literature conditioned and improved my mind, my body required that I devise a plan of exercise. I would grab on to the top of my cell door and raise myself up with my arms. After the passage of several months, I needed only use one arm to accomplish this. I ran in place and spent many hours bending over, twisting and thrusting outward with my arms and legs. My usual good health remained unimpaired by captivity. Only a pallor to my skin disclosed the fact that I had been locked away from God's glorious sun for many years.

My second trial for murder and cannibalism (yes, those *were* the charges so unfairly brought against me) was held during the first week of August in the year Eighteen Eighty-Six. The event was conducted in the courthouse which was alongside the jail. This thrifty arrangement seems to be standard for the legal system, and I did not know beforehand the courthouse was within walking distance. I had been brought into the jail nailed inside a coffin back in May of Eighteen Eighty-Three. I had not been allowed outside of its confines until my second trial began.

The judge's name was Harrison, an aristocratic-appearing man sporting muttonchop whiskers and a silver head of hair. Hamilton Beesley's job of prosecuting attorney had been turned over to a local shyster with the unlikely name of Herschel Hogg, a shifty-eyed, clean-shaven man with a rock where his heart should have been.

Aloysius Thorndyke Poindexter remained as my counsel. After the passage of so much time, I had begun to feel as if we were related. The colorful Englishman was certainly determined to garner all of the attention possible from defending such a widely known and famous case as mine. I could not fault the lawyer for this. He had, after all, saved me from the hangman's noose. So far, anyway.

The trial, which began on the Second day of August, was well attended by the press. There was standing room only for onlookers, so many curiosity-seekers wished to view the cannibal who now was popularly accused of eating only Democrats. It is amazing how a well-told lie can come to be believed more so than the truth.

My sole crime was that of surviving a terrible situation. Members of the Donner Party had done no worse than I had, yet sympathy abounded for them. This was not to be the case for Alferd Giles Packer.

Forty-five

My second trial opened with the prosecutor, Herschel Hogg, launching a scathing attack upon my character. He harped on the fact that I had taken money from my deceased companions and spent it freely in saloons and upon women of ill repute. This tirade was so unfair of him. What was I supposed to do, leave all of that cash lying about where some thief could steal it?

Aloysius Poindexter had reached the stage in his career where he could conduct himself in a courtroom without stuttering too badly. The lawyer did a much better job of presenting my side of the affair here in Gunnison than he had done in Lake City.

He hammered away on the fact that there were no witnesses to refute my killing only Wilson Bell and then only as an act of self-defense. There was no use in refuting the fact that I had survived for many weeks by cooking and eating the flesh of my companions. The evidence there was plain, and I also had unwisely signed a confession to doing this.

Poindexter's earlier admonition about my telling the truth turned out to be disastrously accurate. Suffer me to say that my lawyer's valiant efforts served to save me only from a decidedly unpleasant session on the gallows with that incompetent hangman from Cañon City.

Judge Harrison pronounced me guilty of cannibalism,

which he worded as manslaughter. Then he viciously sentenced me to forty years in the state prison. I was ordered to be locked away eight years in a steel cage for each of my five fellow companions' deaths.

I trembled like an aspen leaf. I was devastated by this terrible turn of events more than mere words can describe. Three long and miserable years I had already languished in a cold dungeon awaiting my emancipation. Now all of my hopes and aspirations had been dashed by some curt words and a simple stroke of the pen from a heartless judge.

At the age of thirty-eight I had only a lifetime of imprisonment to look forward to. And my only crime was that of survival.

"Don't give up, Alferd," Poindexter said, placing a comforting hand on my shoulder. "There are other avenues we have yet to pursue. I shall immediately petition the governor for a pardon. I also believe there is reasonable cause to appeal the verdict to a higher court."

I turned to him and found my voice. "Do as you wish. I have lost my family and now my freedom for absolutely no wrongdoing on my part. My only regret is that I did not hang in Lake City. At least then I could have rejoined my loved ones. Being in prison is a far worse fate than death."

The lawyer sighed. I noticed a wetness in his eyes. "My friend, I am solidly convinced of your truthfulness and innocence. You must keep alive the flame of hope within your heart. I give you my solemn word that I shall not rest, nor leave any stone unturned, until you are once again a free man. Promise me that you shall never, ever, give up."

A pair of deputies came and manacled my wrists with handcuffs. Before I was led away I looked Poindexter square in the face. "Keep fighting for me. I have only you to give me hope, but I believe God's good justice will prevail."

Poindexter dabbed at his eyes with an handkerchief. "I'll come to visit you in Cañon City shortly. There are papers I will need you to sign."

I said, "Reckon I won't be hard to find."

Jack Goode greeted me upon my arrival at the prison. It came as no great surprise he was still the warden there. When a person settles into a soft government job they have a tendency to stick.

"I liked you a lot better as a preacher," the warden said, cold as blue ice. "Now you'll just be a number. We do not use names here in prison. From here on you will be known only as prisoner thirteen eighty-nine. I'm locking you away in cell-bock three. That's where we keep all of the hard cases. If any of them act up and cause trouble, I'll tell 'em that I'll put you in the cell with them and give you a knife and fork. That oughtta settle them down mighty quick."

I will never forget the warden's disgusting laughter as I was escorted from his presence to my cage. People who work in prisons develop a very queer sense of humor.

I must once again slide through years as a knife through soft butter. There is very little to say about time spent behind thick granite walls and steel bars that would be of interest.

While words may speed through time effortlessly as an eagle glides among the clouds, I assure you this was not the case for me or any person deprived of their freedom. The poet Oscar Wilde wrote in *The Ballad of Reading Gaol* that a single day in prison is like a year, a year whose days are long. This is a far better description of how time passes behind stone walls than any I could pen.

As promised, Aloysius Poindexter visited me often. Each time he told me of encouraging progress he was making in my case. Letters were being written, appeals filed. All or any of these actions by my lawyer would possibly bear fruit . . . someday.

I slowly slipped into the routine of being a prisoner. Seasons melted into years while I observed Poindexter's dark hair turn silver as he grew quite fleshy. Only his eternal optimism and promises of my eventual freedom and vindication kept my hopes alive.

No matter how badly they abused me, I caused no problems for any of the guards. Due to my exemplary behavior I was eventually given yard privileges and the status of a trustee.

I found that I had a natural talent for gardening. The planting and tending of colorful flowers such as pansies, tulips, mums, and the delicate columbine along with peonies and majestic roses became the mainstay of my lamentable existence.

Reading novels in my cell at night before the coal-oil lamps and candles were ordered extinguished and tending my wonderful growing plants during the days became passions that enabled me to endure.

It was not until the year Eighteen Ninety-Eight, shortly after the USS *Maine* was blown up in Havana Harbor and the United States went to war with Spain, that my luck took a turn for the better. The source of this assistance came as a complete amazement to both me and Aloysius Poindexter.

Forty-six

An idiot writer by the name of John Randolph started my troubles when he got himself lost and stumbled across my deceased companions before I had the opportunity to clean up the mess. Now, in the strangest of ironies, a star reporter for the *Denver Post* came forth to champion my cause.

Polly Pry was this wonderful lady's name. She was, and still is, a most respected and widely read writer. While I never have had the opportunity to meet with her personally, we did correspond quite often through the mails and, on occasion, by a telephone the new warden consented to let me use.

In a short while I once again became front-page news. Only this time the absolute truth was printed about the incident that had happened on Slumgullion Pass so many years ago. Before, I had been vilified by lies bandied about by biased lawmen and men who wished to cause me ill for their own gain. I will venture the saloons and hotels in Lake City were deprived of thousands of dollars in revenue when I denied them the spectacle of my public hanging.

As I had learned all too well, the legal system moved with all the speed of a crippled snail. Having such a powerful ally as the *Denver Post* along with a skilled and truthful writer such as Polly Pry gave great impetus in the rightful drive to free me from prison.

I continued to tend my flower gardens, but now I also dared to begin contemplating what I would do with the rest of my life once justice prevailed.

I realize I have failed to mention that Aloysius Poindexter had been successful in restoring my military pension. He was even able to convince the government to pay me for the time I was shanghaied and became forced to endure the horrible ordeal that befell the *Mary Celeste*. The lawyer made the case that I had received none of the money sent to the bank in Denver that had gotten washed away. To my utter amazement I actually got paid a great deal of money. To further stun and bewilder me, Poindexter refused to accept any compensation.

"You've been terribly wronged," Aloysius said. "I will not add to the insults you have suffered by taking any payment."

Occasionally, a lawyer can come dangerously close to acting like a decent human being.

I spent but little of my pension money. Most of what I did use up was to purchase novels to read and decent cigars to smoke. These are wonderful treats for a man condemned to live in a cage. My funds in Eighteen Ninety-Eight totaled slightly over eight thousand dollars. I had maintained my good health through vigorous exercise and was a hale and hearty fifty years of age. And at long last there was good reason to plan for the future.

There were many things I dreamed of doing. I could not help but wonder if my rich gold vein above Lake San Cristobal had been found. The attraction of prospecting shall always stir my blood. I suspect this to be a longing for the freedom and solitude of the majestic mountains rather than a desire for riches.

Foremost in my thoughts were those of my lost son who had been kidnapped by Indians. I owed it to sweet Hattie's memory to pursue this quest above all others, even though after the passage of many years, I had no idea where to begin.

I had yet to gain my freedom. Little did I realize how much longer this would take, nor could I at this time have conceived of the invisible chains that can shackle a man once he is outside of prison walls.

Lightning bolts danced among dark thunderheads building over the mountains to the west on the afternoon of July Eighteenth, Ninety-Nine, when I was escorted to the warden's office to take a telephone call.

I was not surprised when I heard the voice of Polly Pry. Then my heart fell.

"Mister Packer, I hate to be the bearer of terrible news," she said solemnly. "But I need to let you know that Aloysius Poindexter has died."

After a long moment I asked, "What happened to him?"

"The doctors tell me he had a stroke in his office. He went quickly."

"Oh, my God. I wish I could at least attend his funeral. Poindexter was the only man who has stood by my side all these years."

"He is being shipped back to England for burial as requested in his will. I was surprised that he never married and has no family here in the country. I agree with you, he was a good man."

"Yes," I said, thinking back on the fact that Hattie, Poindexter, and everyone who had ever cared for me were gone. "A lot of good people die well before they should."

* * *

The *Denver Post* hired a lawyer by the name of William Anderson, who everyone called "Plug Hat," to represent me. The bombastic attorney came to visit me in prison. Plug Hat was a slender man, bald on top with white hair around the edges that reminded me of patches of snow clinging to a round hill.

The lawyer brought along a sack of peanuts which he shared with me while spelling out the *real* reason the *Post* was trying to gain my release from prison. No one in this cold, cruel world ever does something to help another fellow human being without expecting some form of payment. I suppose a preacher is an exception to this rule, but they *do* expect to get paid in the next world.

I must say one thing for Plug Hat, he did not mince words. The owners of the *Post*, Frederick Bonfils and Harry Tammen, wanted me to become a sideshow freak for their Sells-Floto Circus.

The owners' goal was for me to tour the country while being displayed in a curtained booth among the reconstructed skeletal remains of five men scattered about a campfire and pretend to eat human flesh. He told me droves of people would part with a dime to observe a famous, real-life cannibal at work.

I was shocked and revolted at the prospect of doing such a despicable thing. I also felt terribly betrayed by Polly Pry and hurt by the fact that I had perceived her efforts in my behalf as altruistic.

"It's your choice, Packer," Plug Hat said in a matter-of-fact tone. He shelled a peanut, plopped it into his mouth, then shoved some legal paperwork across the desk to me. "This is a contract that's binding for a period of six years. The Sells-Floto will pay you one-fourth of all gate receipts to your exhibit. As added compensation they also agree to cover my fee and have Polly Pry continue her writings in your behalf. Should you not sign, I fear the lady may have a change of heart toward you. I must also add that the *Denver Post* has a great deal of political pressure it can bring to bear. It is all up to you which direction this influence will take."

I forced down a nearly overpowering urge to reach across that oak desk and choke the life from a certain peanut-munching lawyer. While this act would have greatly improved the quality of civilization in general, I certainly would have been hung for my noble effort, and most assuredly law schools would have kept right on spitting out other idiots to replace him with anyway.

I was painfully aware of the fact that I had been left with no choice if I wished my freedom. I could not help but wonder if Sawyer Noon was behind this affair. Aloysius Poindexter had warned of this man's skullduggery and hatred toward me. Now that my one true friend in the legal business had passed away, there was no way I could find out.

Through clenched teeth I said, "If I may borrow your pen, my friend, I will sign the contracts." I thoroughly enjoyed watching the lawyer's eyes widen with fear when I added, "They do not trust me with anything that could be used as a weapon."

Charles S. Thomas held the office of governor of the State of Colorado at the time. With Larry Dolan's fictional account of my eating only Democrats becoming popularly accepted as fact, I should not have been shocked at Thomas's actions toward me; the governor was a staunch Democrat.

As I was to find, while the *Denver Post's* political machine was a powerful one, there were other influential factions battling them for supremacy. It was to my misfortune to become caught in the cross fire.

Even with the efforts of a talented writer, a well-known attorney, and the *Denver Post* on my side, the legal sys-

tem dragged out my case for a long while. It took until
the tenth day of January, 1901, nine days after my fifty-
third birthday, before I received a signed *parole* from
Governor Thomas and received a freedom of sorts.

I was released from prison, but not from the shackles
of law. Even Plug Hat Anderson was taken aback by the
governor's dastardly actions.

All along I had been led to believe that I would be
granted a full pardon for what occurred on Slumgullion
Pass. I surely deserved no less for being so terribly
wronged by the law and tormented by the press, but
this was not to be.

By granting me a parole instead of my deserved pardon, the governor was able to use me as a slap to the
face of Bonfils and Tammen, who I found out later on
were his bitter political enemies.

Governor Thomas's tersely written conditional parole
stated that I was, upon my release from prison, "To
proceed at once to Denver and there remain, if practi-
cable, for a period of at least six years and nine months
from this date. Under no circumstances or reason is the
parolee, Alferd Giles Packer, to venture past the confines of Denver in any direction for more than a distance of fifty miles and only then for the purposes of
gainful employment."

With this order I could not become a freak and tour
the Sells-Floto Circus. I also could not travel to Wyoming and search for my long-lost son nor visit my sweet
Hattie's grave. I had even been forbidden to return to
the area of Lake San Cristobal to find out if my gold
mine had been claimed by others.

As I have said earlier, not all chains are forged of
steel.

Forty-seven

A person who has been locked away in a cold and dreary cage for nearly eighteen years for doing absolutely nothing wrong will embrace any latitude of freedom like a long-lost lover.

When the heavy iron gates of the state prison crashed closed behind me, I never once turned to look back. Time had not dulled the public's interest in my case. Literally hundreds of curiosity-seekers and reporters turned out to witness Colorado's famous cannibal being released from prison.

I tarried briefly to visit with some newsmen. Then I made the short walk to the depot, where I boarded a train for Denver. One young idiot with a notepad kept hammering away at me with pointed questions that I did not care to have posed. I received great satisfaction from his shocked expression followed by his rapid retreat when I placed my hand on his shoulder, looked him square in the eye, and asked in all seriousness if he was a Democrat.

As was the case with Wild Bill Hickok, legends born and built up by writers exceed the truth to the point where fiction becomes gospel and facts are buried for not being interesting enough to publish.

Since I had a fair amount of money saved up, and knew I would most likely be forced to reside in Denver until the requirements of my parole had been fulfilled, I purchased a home. It was a rather humble, yet comfortable white-frame abode on the west side of the city near the towering mountains that I love so dearly. There were over five acres of land upon which the house sat. The simple act of walking my property any time I wished without having to beg permission from a guard was indescribably refreshing.

At night I could read my books by the wonderful Edison incandescent electric light. These were a vast improvement over smoking, flickering coal-oil lamps. Best of all, I did not have to endure some lout in a uniform banging the bars on my cell with a nightstick and growling, "Lights out." I could enjoy my novels until I chose to sleep. And sleep soundly I did. For the first time in many years, yelling, screaming, and cries of my fellow inmates that echoed through the cell blocks incessantly were pleasantly absent.

My love of gardening continued. I planted multitudes of rosebushes and pink peonies, which are my favorite flowers. Along with a huge vegetable garden. I seldom care to eat meat anymore.

I had hoped that with the truth finally being printed about me, I might be able to cultivate some friendships. To my heartbreak and dismay everyone, even my neighbors, treated me as a pariah.

I sincerely hoped the passage of time would heal the unreasonable bias against me. Even innocent children, whose presence I desired above all, were warned away from my welcoming home where I always kept candy and assorted sweets should I ever receive a visitor. Alas, I was left severely alone.

As I mentioned when I began penning these memoirs, a considerable fray arose between Plug Hat Anderson and the owners of the *Denver Post* over payment of fees incurred to secure my release from prison. This culminated with the irate lawyer pulling out a pistol and shooting both Frederick Bonfils and Harry Tammen in their office. The reporter, Polly Pry, was present for the occasion, but remained unscathed.

While Plug Hat's motives might have been laudable, his aim was quite lousy. The owners of the *Post* took two bullets each and took them quite well. The duo recovered after only a few days in the hospital. Plug Hat was of course promptly arrested and tried for assault and attempted murder. Once the usual legal balderdash had run its course, he was found not guilty.

This came as no surprise to me. Plug Hat was both a lawyer and a prominent Mason. That combination would have gotten John Wilkes Booth off with only a severe warning against shooting any more presidents.

Strangely enough, this scrape with flying lead turned to my favor. When Bonfils and Tammen were released from the hospital and returned to work, I was summoned to their office.

"Alferd Packer," Frederick Bonfils wheezed, sitting in a chair behind his massive walnut desk. One of the lawyer's bullets had nicked his windpipe. "Harry and I cannot afford to have deranged and angry folks coming around and shooting us."

Harry Tammen, who stood beside Bonfils with his arm in a sling, said, "We have talked this over and believe that a man of your—ah—*special* reputation would serve us well as a bodyguard. To mollify what our rivals in the press may say about the matter, your official title will be that of a doorman."

"You'll be paid fifty dollars a week," Bonfils gasped. "We'll furnish you with all the guns and knives you want and even pay for your transportation to and from work. All you'll have to do is look mean and, if you have to, shoot anyone who pulls a gun. Neither of us can stand being shot anymore."

I saw an opportunity to rid myself of a distressing situation. There was always a chance I might receive a pardon should the governor's office become inhabited by a just politician.

"Gentlemen," I said after taking a few moments to ponder the matter, "I very much appreciate your help in the past and your kind offer of employment. However, I do not wish to ever degrade myself by becoming a sideshow freak. If we can agree to modify our contract in this regard, I will be glad to tour with your Sells-Floto Circus whenever I am legally able to do so."

Harry Tammen spoke up, "What do you want, Packer?"

I said, "Simply to maintain my dignity. I wish to be able to tell the audience what really happened that terrible winter on Slumgullion Pass. I do not and shall not deny being a cannibal, for this is the terrible truth of how I alone survived. I just do not want to play the part of a monster devouring human flesh and frighten women and children out of their wits."

Tammen looked at Bonfils, who nodded. "Your point is well taken, Mister Packer. I have always thought the idea of having you sitting behind a campfire munching on a leg was in bad taste anyway. I suppose just being able to meet you and listen to your side of the story will likely draw as large a crowd."

Harry Tammen added, "If you agree to come to work for us, we will direct our attorneys to modify the contract to meet your request."

"Thank you for considering my feelings," I said. "With this small matter resolved, I shall be happy to work for the *Denver Post*. I also give you my assurance that I will use the utmost discretion and due diligence to prevent any more harm from coming to your persons."

Bonfils coughed, then sputtered, "That, Alferd Packer, is what we're both counting on."

I came to thoroughly enjoying working at the *Denver Post*. Aside from Plug Hat's ill-humored actions, no one else ever dared make a hostile move toward either Bonfils or Tammen.

Much to my gratification, the duo credited my constant and omnipresent residence outside their plush offices for their safety. I added to my image, as had Wild Bill Hickok, by dressing the part of a hardened gunman. No matter the weather or how hot the radiators were set, I always sported an ankle-length long coat, well-polished boots, and a stiff felt bowler hat, all of solid, somber black.

Whenever any visitors I did not know personally came around, I kept a hand thrust inside the coat and fixed the newcomers with a steely gaze. During my term of employment as a doorman, the owners of the *Post* were seldom pestered with an abundance of callers.

Occasionally, my employers would be absent for many weeks. They maintained a summer mansion high in the Rocky Mountains near Estes Park, a scenic area where many of the elite go to escape the oppressive heat of Denver. This area was well beyond the distance where I could legally travel, which gave me much time to tend my gardens or do some prospecting along Deer Creek.

I never found any valuable minerals. The region there was barren as a lawman's thinking. Cripple Creek, however, had been scoffed at as worthless for decades. I kept my usual optimism and kept looking over any promising outcrop. At the very least it gave me opportunity for solitude. When a man is able to raise his head and gaze upon majestic, towering peaks, it's hard to remember just how cold and cruel this world can be.

Always, I had to eventually return to civilization. My respites into the mountains, however brief, gave me focus and restored my soul.

Seldom did much time pass without some idiot pestering me to have their picture taken with me or for an interview for a magazine or newspaper story. I asked a dollar for my autograph or photo session. I thought the high price would discourage people, but it worked just the opposite. Many days I made more money allowing people to take my picture than a laboring man earns in a week.

Then, in the late summer of Nineteen-Six, slightly more than a year before I received my complete freedom, I was most unexpectedly given the wonderful opportunity to finally clear my name by telling what actually occurred on Slumgullion Pass. Hundreds of thousands of people would then know the absolute truth and I could again walk among men as an equal instead of a pariah.

This good fortune that had come my way would also pay me quite handsomely and enable me to do things I have longed to pursue for many long years. The task would require considerable effort and my complete concentration.

Without a regret I immediately resigned my position at the *Denver Post* and began the moral quest to set right the atrocious wrongs that had been inflicted upon me by a biased press and a host of dishonorable writers.

Forty-eight

I had been engaged by none other than the great Slayton Publishing Corporation of New York City to write down my memoirs for worldwide publication. Slayton Publishing is one of the largest and most respected of the major houses. Any book published by them receives the utmost regard and readership. They are among the giants of the literary world.

I have long dreamed of such a wonderful opportunity. For much too long I have suffered the slings and arrows of the press. Now, thanks to Slayton and a kindly and helpful editor by the name of Leyton Laird, the world will, at long last, know what truly happened on that icy cold and snowy mountainside so many years past.

When first approached by Mister Laird I was at my home, working in the garden pruning some unruly sprouts from my rosebushes. I quickly sized up the slender, sliver-haired man who wore a threadbare gray pinstripe suit, and assumed that he was simply another hack writer wishing to pay me the ten-dollar fee I charged for an interview.

You may well imagine my shocked astonishment when he presented me with his business card and quickly set forth the reason for his visit. Leyton Laird, acting on behalf of Slayton Publishing, offered me one thousand dollars on the spot to begin penning my memoirs. My knees grew weak and my heart throbbed in my chest when he offered me a contract stating I would be paid fifty thousand dollars as an advance once the manuscript was completed and ready to go to press.

I immediately accepted the offer, signed the proffered contracts, banked the thousand dollars, and cloistered myself inside my home and began to pen my memoirs.

It was in October of 1906, one year distant from my complete freedom from the curse of the law, when I began my writings. I was quite naive as to such matters and assumed the task would consume a few weeks, at most.

The final words of my memoirs that you now peruse were not penned until the month of April, Nineteen-Seven.

Leyton Laird visited me often offering criticism and asking for many revisions.

"Your words will be read by millions of people," he advised. "We must strive for utmost accuracy in every detail, no matter how minute it may seem."

Laird made many corrections to my manuscript, mostly in grammar. Occasionally he demanded much more detail in some areas than I cared for, but I acquiesced to his desires.

My life's story is now set in ink. I cannot restrain my desire to hold the finished book in my hands.

No longer shall I be a pariah, an object of fear and loathing. My memoirs are scheduled to be published in October, the same month in which the requirements of my parole will become completed.

The dreams of many sad years shall soon be mine to enjoy. I intend to embark on a lecture tour whereby I can sign books and proclaim my true innocence. In spite of the many wrongs done me, I still possess a zest for life and a desire to live. Were it not for the flame of hope that burns forever within the human heart, life would certainly be beyond endurance.

I shall soon have my freedom and the means to fulfill many of my longings.

I have a long-lost son, who I know in my heart is alive and will welcome his father's embrace.

Most of all, I wish to visit my sweet Hattie's grave and erect a proper headstone. Throughout my lifetime, the only season when I was truly happy was when we were married and lived together on that small ranch alongside the clear cold waters of the North Plate River.

I have crystal memories of those halcyon days. These are sufficient to sustain me until I too cross to that distant Great Beyond where hatred and death do not exist and love endures for all eternity.

Wait for me, my love.

Afterword

Alferd Giles Packer was found dead on the floor of his home the Twenty-Third day of April, Nineteen-Seven. His demise, which coincided with the completion of his memoirs, was written up by the press as due to "Natural Causes, Worry, and Heart Failure."

Yet, as we are to discover, there is more to this story. Much more.

Tucked safely inside Packer's memoirs I found a faded letter that was obviously penned in the same delicate handwriting that formed the editorial corrections on the manuscript. By my reproducing the message in its entirety, dear reader, you will learn the true ending to the tragic saga of Alferd Packer.

My Darling Daughter, Isabella,

I have entrusted my lawyer, Hamilton Beesley, with the task of delivering this letter, along with a copy of my will and one sealed package to you upon my death. My heart was saddened that I could only bequeath to you the humble home in Cañon City that we shared those many years.

Alas, it is all that remains of a fortune reduced to ashes by a burning desire to revenge the unspeakably horrible death of my dear brother and your uncle, George.

The law failed us miserably, my dear. The cannibal fiend, Alferd Packer, could not be allowed to continue his blighted existence upon the earth. It was God's will that he die. Surely, you know this.

I tried so hard to avenge George's murder by every legal means at my disposal. And when I was a wealthy man, I had many means.

The famous Marshal Wyatt Earp and the Pinkerton Detective Agency were both paid huge sums by me to track down the fiend, Packer, to no avail. In the end, it was a twenty-five-thousand-dollar reward that led to the cannibal's capture, but not his well-deserved hanging.

Unfortunately, I became so distraught by this failure of justice that I neglected to tend to business affairs. Had I not been distracted by a ghoul, I would surely have foreseen the collapse of the price of silver and withdrawn my investments with Horace Tabor before it was too late.

Due to Alferd Packer, I did not do so. All that was left after the debacle was a small trust that I had set aside for your future. It was from this that I purchased our home. Horace Tabor fell from being the richest mining magnate of his time to work as a postmaster. I was reduced to teaching school to earn a living. I am grateful that your mother and you did not have to share in my degradation.

Rage and anger wracked my soul when the monster who had caused so much pain and grief was released from prison on parole. When I learned that after a period of six years and nine months from then, Packer's freedom would be complete and he planned to tour with a circus, demeaning poor George's memory on a daily basis, you can see I had no choice but to act.

It was a great advantage that Packer had never set his evil eyes upon me earlier. I had spent a fortune to avenge my brother. It only cost me an additional thousand along with a few dollars to have some business cards printed announcing me as an editor with Slayton Publishing Corporation, a man by the name of Leyton Laird. This is how I accomplished my long quest for justice.

No one will ever suspect that it was by my own hand that the Lord's wrath prevailed. In the end, Packer's own vanity and greed accomplished what the law could not.

It was to my great sorrow that the ghoul died so easily, but cyanide is a most effective poison. My surreptitiously adding an ounce to the fiend's coffee seemed far too easily accomplished.

When he drank a single swallow, the cyanide stilled the beating of his foul heart and he collapsed to the floor of his squalid home. After a long while, I picked up the cannibal's memoirs and tucked them into my valise. I now leave them to you so that you may know more of the fiend who ruined both our lives.

My sweet angel, I should have left you with a mansion and millions of dollars. Instead I reach out to your heart from the grave and beg absolution. I was but a mortal man, thrust upon a trail of tears to find his way. My final hope is that your path shall be straight and sunny.

My darling Isabella, may God's infinite mercy shine upon your soul and temper it with forgiveness. This is all I ask of you, and with it I shall rest in peace for eternity.

Your loving father,
Sawyer Noon

Yes, the stooped, white-haired old lady I delivered newspapers to in my youth, was Sawyer Noon's daughter. For many years the terrible legacy of her father lay hidden in her home, only now to surface.

One can only surmise the secret anguish the poor woman must have endured all of those long and lonely years.

The story is told. And may the God who judges the living and the dead have mercy on their souls, and yours, and mine.

Ken Hodgson
San Angelo, Texas

William W. Johnstone
The *Mountain Man* Series

The Wingman Series
By Mack Maloney